Behold Things Beautiful

Behold Things
Beautiful

Cora Siré

Signature
EDITIONS

Cover design by Doowah Design.

This book was printed on Ancient Forest Friendly paper.
Printed and bound in Canada by Hignell Printing Inc.

We acknowledge the support of the Canada Council for the Arts and the Manitoba Arts Council for our publishing program.

Library and Archives Canada Cataloguing in Publication

Siré, Cora, author
        Behold things beautiful / Cora Siré.

Issued in print and electronic formats.
ISBN 978-1-927426-89-0 (paperback).--ISBN 978-1-927426-90-6 (epub)

        I. Title.

PS8637.I726B44 2016   C813'.6   C2016-904952-3
                                      C2016-904953-1

Signature Editions
P.O. Box 206, RPO Corydon, Winnipeg, Manitoba, R3M 3S7
www.signature-editions.com

For Doris Fahle Siré & Harald E. Siré

Part I

Sometimes, when my beloved one and I dream in silence — a sharp and deep silence like an unusual and mysterious sound lying in ambush — I feel as if his soul and my soul were running far away, through I know not what lands never seen, in a powerful and roaring torrent.

"Torrent" by Delmira Agustini,
Cantos de la mañana (1910)

1

Delmira Agustini leaves her parents' house at dusk. She walks down her street to the Plaza Internacional, where the drenched tips of cypress trees loom above the buildings, then turns onto Calle Andes, catching the singsong cries, ¡Diario! Diario!, of boys peddling El Día's evening edition. The street is congested with buggies and motor cars. As she steps over gutters and murky streams to avoid the jostling horses, her umbrella tips scrape the stone facades of houses.

Delmira walks on, wishing she could sink into a trance, the very word, un trance, she evoked during the interview yesterday with the journalist so typically, profoundly ignorant of the cost to one's soul of writing poetry. She sold him that lie about her poems emerging in a dreamlike state, complete works magically produced by sleight of hand. The journalist, narrow and hesitant as a young fox, took down her words while sitting on her mother's sofa, the requisite cup of tea cooling. He was too nervous to trust his hand to lift the cup to his lips and when she asked, "What is your age?" he swallowed hard and said, "The same as yours, Poeta, twenty-seven." She felt for him then, bent over his notebook, blushing at her gaze, unaware she'd never read his forthcoming article full of her lies. She could have encouraged him or reached for his hand but there was between them such an abyss, and she was already receding in the torrent of her making.

A light shines over the entrance to 1206 Calle Andes. When Delmira knocks, Enrique Job is there immediately. She shakes out her umbrella and follows him into his rented room off the main hallway. He locks the door and hovers, an unlit cigar in his hand. The wall behind him is covered with photos of the poet, her paintings and sketches. Delmira stands by the mirror and removes her velvet hat, leaving it on a table along with her purse, which contains a hand mirror and a letter addressed to an Argentine publisher, a man who later claims never to have met her.

Enrique Job shows her the tickets he purchased yesterday, two passages to Buenos Aires by boat. "Please, Nena, think about it. We could —"

"Put them away." She stands by the mirror and unbuttons her dress, letting it glide down her silk slip. Delmira steps out of the dress and sits on the sofa bed to remove her shoes.

Enrique Job lights the cigar. Perhaps he tries one last time to dissuade her. If so, the argument is short. "Where is it?" she might ask with the poet's urge to see, to concretize. He removes the nine-millimetre-calibre Smith revolver from a drawer in the nightstand. If she has masterminded this scene, she must have compromised on the modus. Her verses foreshadow a beheading, smothering and, most often, poisoning, *a spider's poison, pill of delirium* or *divine poison,* but the macho horse-trader must have drawn the line. She loosens her hair and lies down on the sofa bed.

Less than half an hour after Delmira Agustini entered her ex-husband's room, two shots are heard, a pause and two more.

2

Vertigo overcame Alma as she looked down at the sea and the jet's reflection, a black swallow winging across the Atlantic. Flaco's grandmother once told her you could predict Luscano's weather by the flight of the *golondrinas*. If they were flying high, the forecast was good, but beware when the swallows skimmed low.

The androgynous voice on the intercom reminded passengers that Luscano was the first stop, five minutes only, and then it was on to Montevideo. Alma closed her laptop and gathered her belongings. At this point, her brain zinging from the strong Brazilian coffee she had consumed during the stopover in São Paulo, Alma wondered who would stop her if she went on to Montevideo. But after the jet touched down smoothly and taxied to the terminal, Alma made for the door along with two couples, retirees perhaps, dressed in sensible khaki and sturdy sandals. The other passengers, mainly Brazilians, remained seated. Lucky them, she thought.

After the staircase was rolled to the side of the jet, the attendant opened the door and the passengers in front of her made their way down the stairs. Alma stepped out and grasped the railing, steadying herself against the pull of her briefcase and bag. She had an immediate sense of being observed. She scanned the two-storey bunker, stucco still peeling off the concrete, the same tattered blue-red flags whipping westward. There. On the airport roof was a man with binoculars, brazenly surveying the passengers descending from the plane. She couldn't tell from this distance if he was wearing a uniform.

Alma hurried to catch up to the blur of khaki ahead of her, walked with the couples across the tarmac and entered the low-ceilinged hall. A conveyer belt curved in and out of openings in the concrete and soon her luggage appeared. She managed to heave the suitcases, weighted with books, onto a cart, which she pushed towards the booth for customs and immigration. A uniformed PFL officer studied her Canadian passport. She scanned his face against memory. An *ex-militar* might have found work in the Policía Federal de Luscano and he was the right age. He stamped the passport, slid it across the counter along with a card she'd have to submit when leaving the country. It was valid until July 6th, 2004, precisely one year, and more than enough time. "Welcome back," he said.

Alma pushed the cart through automatic doors. Before she could fully process the gleam of chrome and glass in the arrivals lounge, the blur of children in motion, the newspaper kiosk plastered with lottery tickets, the colourful Discover Luscano posters on the walls, Flaco appeared. He wrapped his arms around her and she felt the roughness of his tweed jacket through her shirt. "We survived, *chica!*"

The words surprised. His survival, she was certain, had never been in question. Then Roma was embracing her, lifting her off the tiled flooring. "Alma, you're still so light." A strange observation but that was Roma. Flaco took over the cart and they led her outside, ignoring the PFL guards with machine guns who slouched by the entrance and the bilingual sign, *No Carts Beyond This Point*, the English surprisingly accurate.

Flaco unlocked the same brick-red Fiat he'd always had, wedged one suitcase into the trunk and the other on the back seat. Roma scrambled to perch on top of the suitcase. It took three tries before the car started, the radio blaring a *milonga*, strumming guitars to the beats of a *bombo*. "She never lets me down." Flaco smacked the dashboard. "La Vieja's my only loyal girl," he said with a sideways glance at Alma. In one of his emails, he'd confessed to two ex-wives and three children, none of whom lived with him. As for Roma, Alma didn't know what her situation was. They had not stayed in touch and Alma assumed some guilt about this. But Roma, reaching over the seat to squeeze Alma's shoulder, seemed free of rancour. Flaco steered out of the car park, past a grove of wind-worn palmettos, and turned onto the two-lane highway that sloped towards the seaside capital.

A new billboard beckoned, *Bienvenido a Luscano, Capital federal de Luscano, Población 1 350 000*. So the country had grown despite everything.

Roma and Flaco talked simultaneously, grilling Alma about the trip and how she was, how it felt to come back. She described the trajectory of her flights across the continents and the incredible daybreak over the Amazon, a brown ribbon shimmering through the green vastness scarred by clear-cutting, bald spots visible from the air, while struggling to align these versions of her friends with the ones she'd stored in memory. Roma was stockier, almost owl-like with her black hair cut very short. She wore glasses with round wire frames that enlarged her dark eyes. Flaco had become appropriately professorial, right down to the paunch protruding from his jacket. The two were older of course, Flaco close to forty now, but both bent on resurrecting their student selves, jokey and careless, as if to prove that the twelve years hadn't changed them, that all was well in Luscano and Alma needn't fear.

The Fiat jolted over the ruts and potholes of Ruta 6 — the north-south artery from Brazil through Luscano and down into Uruguay — notorious for head-on collisions and overturned trucks. Alma remembered her morbid fascination with the improvised roadside cemeteries, the makeshift crosses, statues of saints and the Virgin among plastic daisies and offerings of cigarettes and oranges. The stretch of fence separating the field from the road was so dilapidated, it didn't look as if it could keep the group of skittering goats from bursting through. Distant shacks squatted on the fields and there were the tents and trailers of a gypsy encampment. Suddenly the highway branched into four newly paved lanes with tulip-shaped lights springing from a concrete median. Flaco explained that the money for the new *autopista* had dried up before its completion all the way to the airport.

"You'd think," Alma said, "they'd have started from the airport to create a good first impression," and immediately regretted her words. She'd resolved not to criticize or compare.

Flaco glanced at her. "Ready for tomorrow?"

Alma shifted in her seat. "I hope so." A truck roared past the Fiat. Then she asked, "How's Hannelore?"

"Your mother called three times to make sure I'd pick you up. She's waiting for you with the Bolivian."

The spire of the cathedral appeared in the distance. Then, before she knew it, they were in the city, Flaco tearing down the exit ramp. He drove onto Avenida Reconquista and Alma rolled down her window to smell the saltiness of the sea breeze, humid but cool. They entered a residential suburb of homes with shrubs sagging through iron fencing, acacias and palm trees coated with dust, yellowing grass lying tamped within gated gardens. It had been dry, Flaco explained, and the winter harvest of crops in his family's *finca* would be late this year.

They passed a cart pulled by an arthritic horse, the driver stopping to collect empty bottles set out on the curb. Alma turned to look at his creased face under the baseball cap, remembered him well, the man who'd allowed neighbourhood kids to hitch a ride to the beach in his cart. The size of the lots and houses expanded as they approached the sea. Even so, signs of neglect and deterioration were evident in the mildew creeping over the stucco, the rusted fences and cratered sidewalks. There were jalopies of the same vintage as Flaco's Fiat and sun-bleached bicycles leaning against trees.

On the limit of Barrio Norte, the trees had grown. Their branches formed an archway that filtered the sunlight. And there was the jacaranda, its thick clusters of leaves fluttering high above the roof of her mother's home on Calle Buenos Aires.

Flaco stopped at the curb and carried her suitcases to the door. When Alma tried to express gratitude that they'd come to pick her up, Roma whacked her on the arm. "What else are we going to do on a Sunday morning? Come to the bookstore and we'll have a proper talk." As she walked through the gate, Alma glimpsed the faces through the window, her mother and Xenia waiting in the living room. Vertigo of a different kind.

The front door opened and there was Xenia in her woven skirt and white blouse. "*M'hija!*" Alma went to embrace the entirety of her, the compact sturdiness and the scent of sweet grasses Xenia burned in her room to fend off mosquitoes and evil spirits.

In the living room, her mother sat bundled in a shawl, hands grasping the armrests of her chair. Alma stooped and Hannelore touched her cheek, appraising her with eyes still green and canny. Then Alma went back outside for her suitcases and dragged them to her room, returning to drop onto the sofa under the window. Her mother's hair, short as Roma's, but completely white, rose in tufts over her gaunt face.

"You're shocked, aren't you? I'm reduced and it's awful. But you cannot imagine my joy right now. I've always adored Flaco. Now I love him for convincing you to come back. If I were up to it, I'd have Xenia open a bottle of champagne."

"No, it's fine. I'm too exhausted myself."

Xenia returned from the kitchen with two glasses of pomelo juice. Alma drank quickly. Hannelore waved her glass away. "Xenia, stop fussing and sit down. Alma, tell us everything."

Alma attempted a coherent summary of the last weeks in Montréal, marking term papers and exams, subletting her apartment, arranging for a replacement during her sabbatical. Her tongue felt thick, her thoughts disordered. The living room seemed emptier, the wallpaper replaced by white paint, fewer paintings on the wall. "Where's the piano?"

"I sold it after your father died, along with his violin."

Contemplating this house without music, Alma was struck by the force of her father's absence. At times she'd mourned Luscano as if grieving for someone she'd never see again and that grief had included the living. Her father's death two years after she'd left had almost seemed predestined.

"It wasn't easy," Hannelore was saying, "to sell your father's violin but his pension from the orchestra was worse than paltry." Then she spoke of her students, mentioning some names Alma might remember. "I did well enough the last few years with the tutoring and the translation work. Always paid Xenia on time, didn't I?"

Xenia smoothed her skirt. "*Sí, Señora.*" She glanced at Alma with her perceptive eyes, a dark willing away of that old tension. Alma had always loathed her mother's impulse to pointedly delineate Xenia's position in the household as a paid *muchacha*.

Hannelore went on about her students, how often they and her friends came to visit. "No, I'm never lonely, not at all." Eventually her chin dipped and Xenia whispered, "She needs to rest." Alma expected her mother to argue, but Hannelore had closed her eyes.

In the kitchen, Xenia prepared some toast and opened a fresh jar of *dulce de leche*. Then she sat down with Alma at the table. "We have to prepare ourselves. The doctor comes often now." Hannelore's breathing had become difficult. She refused to take steroids anymore. They cranked her up and she couldn't sleep.

"Why didn't she tell me? Why didn't you —"

"She forbade me to mention it."

The two women had conspired to shield her from the details of Hannelore's condition during the weekly phone calls. And Alma had willingly participated. Hard truths were inescapable, lying in wait like traps; Alma knew that, although she didn't know how to prepare herself for her mother's death. Instead, she asked after Xenia's family in Todos Santos.

A sense of homecoming then, as she sat at the table eating toast smeared with *dulce*, the refrigerator whirring in the background and Xenia's voice, the music of her Andean inflections as she described the struggles of Bolivia's coca growers and told of her nephews and nieces, their children and grandchildren.

Later, Alma showered, changed and lay down on the narrow bed beneath the window. She felt heavy and stiff. Flying always made her hands and feet swell. She tried to let herself be lulled by the sounds of Xenia moving around in Hannelore's bedroom next door, hoping to fall into that trance she'd been thinking about on the plane, but her thoughts were on overdrive. The Luscano she'd left behind, with her loved ones — her parents and Xenia, Flaco and Roma — and the landmarks she permitted herself to remember had existed in a time warp. She'd tried to adapt the memory of them to allow for time and fate, sculpting their faces, bodies and countenances, but absence had proven her imagination inadequate. Negating the effects of illness, she'd preserved her mother's physical markers, the posture and elegant legs, the black hair twisted into a chignon. Flaco's invitation to lecture had brought her back and, sadly, Hannelore knew it.

Her lecture was tomorrow. Tomorrow! She should have allowed herself more time to recover from the trip, had assumed the one-hour time difference between Luscano and Montréal would limit the jet lag. Instead of reviewing her notes, the in-flight movies had seduced her with the last chance to wallow in North American culture. *Adaptation,* then *The Hours,* and coincidentally, both had featured Meryl Streep. Watching her perform, Alma had hoped to absorb some of that steely self-awareness and puritanical bearing, qualities her mother had come closer to mastering than Alma ever had, her last lucid thought before falling asleep.

3

Several blocks northeast of the house on Calle Buenos Aires, a man in white trousers and a tennis sweater observed the sea through a telescope by the window. Patrón Pindalo began most Sundays in the third-floor turret of his house, convinced he learned more of the comings and goings in Luscano's port from his telescope than from reading *El Día*'s column on the shipping news. The slow scan of the horizon, the wonder of seeing an enhanced reality in which hidden details were exposed and amplified, focussed him for the morning tennis game he demanded of the pro at the club.

Patrón Pindalo leaned into the high-powered lens. A regatta of sailboats was dispersing from the yacht club's piers, and further east three fishermen hoisted nets of shellfish onto their boat. A ship trolled in direct line with the sun and the glare prevented him from discerning its name or flag. He looked up from the telescope but could not locate the ship, impressed once again by the power of the lens, one of those gringo gadgets he'd purchased on a trip to the north.

The door opened behind him. The *muchacha* stood in the doorway holding the tray with his glass of juice, a concoction of orange, carrot and ginger, an anti-aging strategy to counter the effects of seventy-two years of hard work for his family, for Luscano. Patrón Pindalo approached the *muchacha* and took the glass, swallowing the juice in one long gulp while eyeing the young woman. She was new to the household, quite appealing today, he decided. Other days she struck him as awkward, half asleep, and he had to repeat his orders three times to make sure she understood. Patrón Pindalo returned the glass to the tray. "Did you wake the children?" She nodded. "Get them ready for church. I'll have Damian drop them off on our way to the club." He'd noticed that his grandchildren were often late for church, school, their music lessons. It was time to teach them manners and discipline. He might have failed as a father but now that Ernesto had abandoned the children, he had a chance to redeem himself as a grandfather.

He returned to his post by the window, noticing dust on the sill. Next time he saw the *muchacha* he'd tell her to give the room a proper cleaning. Things were going downhill, including his reputation. It was a national embarrassment how badly his children had turned out. At least Celeste was in Miami, beyond the reach of Luscano's rumour mill, but Ernesto, what had come over him, leaving this house, his wife and children? He should have known enough not to humiliate all of them, his father included, for Luscano to gossip and titter over. Perhaps he'd fallen for the new *muchacha*. That would be understandable if not acceptable. Discretion, he'd drilled it into Ernesto all of his thirty-nine years, was essential to the Pindalo work ethic. His son refused to learn, hanging on his father's back, a lifelong burden of guilt.

Patrón Pindalo eyed the lens again and made out the faint silhouette of a cargo ship. Perhaps it was the one he was waiting for. He'd readied the stevedores on his payroll to receive the goods. Engrossed in his ocean spying, he didn't hear the trunk slam shut in the driveway down below or see the car glide through the front gates. What Patrón Pindalo did see, the Liberian flag and the name, *Belleza*, on the cargo ship, confirmed the arrival of the shipment of olive oil, figs and cashews in which the rifles and munitions were supposed to be buried.

4

The taxi careened around the Plaza Federal. Alma hung onto the strap above the back-seat window. Outside, the capital unravelled in damp bolts, grainy through the downpour, and much of it familiar. Distributed among the old colonial architecture, the *galerías* and coffee counters were a few new buildings, not skyscrapers but high for this low-rise city, their facades streaked with rain. Some bore the signage of banks, their entrances guarded by men in khaki uniforms with holsters. At the campus a damp banner hung from columns supporting the stone archway — *¡No a los sindicatos!* — the *no* crossed off, replaced with a handwritten *sí*. The taxi stopped. Heaving her bag onto her shoulder, Alma opened the door and lunged to the curb. She fumbled with Hannelore's umbrella as the back wheels of the taxi receded.

Alma cut through the quadrant, past the fountain and empty benches, and made for the oldest structure battened with vines. Ivy curled around the cornerstone set by the founding Franciscans: *Anno Domino 1825 Facultad de Filosofía & Humanidades*. Inside, a papery odour blended with stale cigarette smoke. She turned down the hallway. Two young men glanced at her as they conversed in low tones, mindful of the lectures underway inside the classrooms.

The double doors to the lecture hall were shut, a sheet of paper taped to the wood. *Alma, ven a mi oficina, F.*, the handwriting, like her own, representative of a generation drilled by teachers adhering to state-sanctioned rules of script. Flaco's *come to my office* as imperative as his emails, rightly assuming she'd remember the dean's office on the second floor overlooking the river. Alma lingered outside the hall. Carvings on the length of each door depicted trees of learning, books substituting for leaves, the ersatz foliage thick and plentiful. Borges came to mind, perhaps because of his long career at the *Biblioteca Nacional* in Buenos Aires or his poem that celebrated books, *secret and visible like the stars,* from "The Guardian of the Books."

She pushed on one of the doors and it opened to the hall, larger than she'd remembered. Two aisles led through rows of benches towards a raised stage. Alma took the steps to the stage and dropped her bag alongside a tray of bottled water and glasses on a table by the podium. She removed her jacket, draped the pale blue linen over the back of the chair. It was damp and wrinkled, as was her skirt. She tried to smooth the fabric with her hands.

The panelled walls gave off a brittle smell, the incense of prayers, she imagined, intoned by centuries of students fearing failure. Overhead six antiquarian carriage wheels hung from the ceiling, each a spoked circle of light bulbs. She'd once prayed for one of those fixtures to crash onto a mumbling professor's head. Alma would not drone her audience to sleep. But how many would come?

The door opened and Flaco bounded up the aisle. He kissed her cheek and asked after Hannelore. Alma shook her head. He understood it was not the time and helped her set up, lowering a screen behind the stage. Alma plugged an adapter into the socket and connected her laptop to the projector.

Flaco dimmed the lights and ambled to a corner of the stage. "If you stand here you can see the river."

Alma sat down and listened to the rain pummelling the windowpanes bordered by roseate stained glass. Flaco came to sit down beside her. "*Chica,* we agreed, I'm going to tell them in my introduction."

What could she say? He'd probably already told his students. A few were now straggling into the hall.

Alma poured a glass of water and distracted herself with the label on the bottle — *Agua mineral del manantial gitano* — printed in the red and blue of Luscano's flag. For blood and the sky, they'd learned in school, for sacrifice and possibility. She noticed the fine print on the label, *embotellado por Pepsi Cola SA* and showed Flaco. He filled her in on the water wars that had ended with corporate giants controlling the country's bottlers and supply of the precious resource. Today's rain was an aberration, welcome but insufficient. Next door, Uruguay had actually entrenched the human right of access to water in its constitution. "But in Luscano, money always wins," Flaco said, transformed into the dean he'd become in her absence, Dr. Molino conveying the nuances of the water problem. Despite the strands of grey intruding on his dark curls and the bitterness in his voice, he was still the old Flaco, eyes flashing with conviction. Alma drew on his energy, reserving it for her lecture.

The hall was filling up. Students slid along the benches, dropping knapsacks and umbrellas onto the floor. In their jeans and windbreakers, the devices and cell phones they carried, they reminded Alma of her students in Montréal. They had that same looseness in their carriage and aura of resignation. The dean had obliged them to attend the lectures on Latin American poets; this was the last one in the series and Alma could imagine their relief. Older students and faculty members occupied the front rows. Alma scanned their faces as they greeted one another with *holas* and kisses, hands dancing to conversation, a few curious glances tossed her way. Soon all the benches were taken and the last students had to lean against the wood panelling on the back wall. The crowd numbered at least one hundred. Quite the turnout for a dead poet, albeit one with a cultish following.

"Ready?"

Alma resisted telling him, no, you do it.

Flaco winked at her and rose. "We are honoured," he bellowed into the microphone, "to have Alma Álvarez here from Canada. She is our final guest in the series on twentieth-century poets of the Americas. Her lecture, "Evasion and the Sublime," will cover the work of a great Uruguayan poet.

"Professor Álvarez completed her undergraduate studies at this university. In 1991, while finalizing her thesis on the writer she'll be discussing today, she was brought there." Flaco pointed towards the rain-drizzled windowpanes.

It seemed to Alma that everyone turned to look outside. All but one woman, a red scarf draped over her jacket, who kept her eyes on Alma, insinuating herself. Slowly, the scene clarified: the bonfire, this woman shouting through the chaos. It must have been spring 1990, the day a team of thugs in uniform had raided the university library, ordering banned books to be removed from the shelves and tossed into a pile on the quadrant. Alma struggled to resurrect fear from memory with the same accuracy as concrete sensations, the terrible smell of burning books, the sizzling sounds of water dousing the flames and in the smoke, the outraged face of this woman with the red scarf. Alma remembered her now, the librarian cursing the soldiers setting fire to the books. Professors and students, Alma, Flaco and their friends, stood frozen until she incited them into action and they ran to find buckets, teapots, jugs, filling them with water from the fountain. "Save the books!" the woman shouted even after the guns were drawn and all the others had stepped back in fear. Alma submerged Flaco's voice with the words she'd later discovered quite by accident in a library in Montréal. *Where books are burned, they will, in the end, burn people, too.* Heinrich Heine from a play he wrote in 1862, the truth of his words lost and lost again. We should have known, I should have known, she'd thought then and often since.

"After her release, Professor Álvarez left for Canada, where she now teaches. You know her work if you've taken my class on Luscanan poetry. The poem she wrote that so angered the military is included in the anthology *Voces acalladas*..." Alma had never even seen the anthology, *Silenced Voices*, named after the university magazine Flaco had kept going during the junta. Its existence, mentioned here so publicly, meant little compared to the brave woman with the red scarf gazing up at her from the bench.

Applause as Flaco took his seat. Alma reached for the remote, stood up and walked to the podium. She thanked him for the introduction, her voice tinny, the Spanish tremulous. For years she'd delivered a shorter version of this lecture to students who'd never heard of the poet. Most in this audience had studied her in high school but Alma doubted they appreciated her significance. The first slide, a photograph of the poet, appeared on the screen behind her. She wanted her listeners to experience the burning gaze, the tightness of the three strands of pearls around the poet's neck and the hair curled precisely by her temples. It captured the duality of victim and aggressor, obedient daughter and sexual explorer.

"*I die strangely....*

"So begins 'The Ineffable,' published in her second volume of poetry when she was twenty-four. Delmira Agustini foreshadowing her unusual death." Twenty-four, the age of many students in this hall, Alma's age when she left Luscano. "The ineffable: that which must not be uttered. And yet the poet is obliged to speak and the price is costly.

"*...It is not life that kills me / It is not death that kills me, nor is it love.*"

Alma drew into herself to express all that this poet represented. Evasion, Agustini's will to refute fate, and the sublime, a silent, ferocious despair cursing thought.

"*I die of a thought, mute as a wound....*

"Then, in the lines that follow, the incantation of questions addressing the reader so that we participate in the enactment of plot.

"'The Ineffable' is one of her celebrated sonnets and to understand it fully, we have to understand the times. Montevideo in the early twentieth century was a lonely place for the first woman to write erotic poetry in Spanish. Delmira Agustini dared to provoke and transgress, refusing to permit the Uruguay of her time to constrict her words." Perhaps these students would find the strength to prevent their country's charms and limitations from defining them.

Alma's voice warmed as she moved on to the poet's legacy. Gabriela Mistral and Alfonsina Storni later drew on Agustini's work to express their suffocation and despair from finding themselves ahead of the world in which they were born. Papers rustled, heads bent over notebooks, hands propelled pens. Alma too had sat hunched here to absorb the knowledge offered her. But back then, she hadn't understood the nature of the gift, writers who'd delivered her elsewhere, to another country, another life or state of mind. It was the root of her obsession with Delmira Agustini's words, their transcendent powers.

"By the age of twenty-seven, Delmira Agustini had completed a sufficiently large body of work, largely misunderstood by her contemporaries, to conclude that her only hope of true liberation was in death." Alma continued with that. The chilly rain in Montevideo on the evening of July 6th, 1914 as the poet walks to meet her ex-husband in his rented room. Their last minutes together, Enrique Job Reyes's cigar and the Smith revolver he draws from the nightstand. "Enrique Job holds the gun to her ear and fires. He aims at her temple and fires again. Then he turns the revolver on himself, shoots but misses, and fires again."

"*Have you never carried inside a dormant star / That was burning you wholly without shining?*" Alma recited the sonnet projected on the screen behind her. In Montréal, at this point in the lecture, she'd tell her students, memorize the poems you love, you may need them one day and they could save you.

Light played in the stained glass. Through the window, strands of wild moss dangled from the willow tree and beyond, across the river, the abandoned building, the iron bars of its windows covered with graffitied plywood.

Flaco stared at her, chin on his hand, eyes intent on conveying encouragement. She became aware of a generalized squirming, some coughing, as the sea of faces came into focus, among them the librarian with the red scarf, who nodded at her to go on, finish, as if she understood that it's so much easier to tell of someone else's fate, no matter how tragic, than your own.

Alma returned to the poet's writing life, describing how Agustini took her place among the *modernistas*, along with Rubén Darío, whom she met and corresponded with, and José Martí, writers who moved the region's poetry from its Iberian, colonial influences towards a fresh complexity of language. Before opening the floor to questions, she closed with the poet's words. For the students who'd sat through her lecture, for the brave librarian and most fittingly for Flaco, "*In only one kiss we became old.*"

The legs of the table teetered on the cobblestones as Flaco removed his jacket, tossed it onto an empty chair and rolled back the sleeves of his shirt. "You were superb, *chica*. The students loved you!" His loud declarations had passersby glancing back and a man sitting at the only other occupied table outside La Loca peered over his newspaper. "It was brilliant to close the lecture series with you," Flaco said, as if it had been her idea. "Last week after Chico Fulano's droning, self-adulating discourse, my students complained. But with you they were spellbound!"

Alma laughed at the absurdity of being compared to the Mexican octogenarian with scores of novels and literary prizes under his belt. Residual giddiness from the long flight and the effort of the lecture, the students with their questions on how they could get to Canada, and the faculty and staff who'd come to greet her, some familiar, most forgotten or perhaps she'd never met them before, their genuine interest and pride that she'd returned. "Didn't you find it a bit cheap to begin with the murder-suicide?"

"The film noir opening got their attention and that's what a lecturer has to do. Plus you managed to cover the full range of Agustini's works. I'd never seen those prose poems. I tend to think of her in terms of the sonnets." Flaco summoned the waiter from inside La Loca.

A wedge of sea glittered in the sunlight beyond the old city's rooftops. Alma had purposely taken this seat under the coral tree, the cathedral behind her at a far end of the Plaza Federal and the restaurant to her left. La Loca had not changed from the days when they'd come here after classes. Through the windows, she could make out the boxing posters on the restaurant's walls and the framed blue-red soccer jersey, number 42, worn by Luscano's infamous forward, the one who'd become so rich he'd bought a Ferrari for the last president elected before the junta as a payoff for having the tax evasion charges against him dismissed. The outrage at that time, documented in *El Día*, seemed naive, almost quaint now, considering all that had happened since.

The waiter arrived with wine and water, set the bottles on the tablecloth and proceeded to fill the glasses. Alma downed a full glass of water while Flaco deliberated with the waiter on the day's specials. They settled on *milanesas* and salads, and after the waiter had left, Flaco raised his glass. "Now this is a good wine." And he was right, the Uruguayan wine tasted of summer, flowery and pungent.

Among the deprivations of exile, she'd missed the tastes and smells most. Walking with Flaco from the campus through the downtown traffic, Alma had breathed the city's essence in all its layers. Coffee, exhaust fumes, puddles sizzling in the afternoon sun, savoury wafts of empanadas, the leathery pungency of shoe polish, the roses and lilies offered by vendors along the plaza, and the hawkers' cries. A short walk, not more than ten minutes, and an immersion, her footsteps affirming, I'm back, I'm back.

Flaco lit a cigarette from his pack of Parliaments. Alma picked up the gold lighter and ran her thumb over the engraving, *MM,* the initials belonging to Flaco's father, a gambler who'd almost ruined the family. She asked if Mateo Molino was still alive. "He died in his flat ten years ago, beaten by some toughs sent by a money lender, an ugly ending to an ugly life. And that should be the end of it except... when my children ask about their grandfather, I've no idea what to say. I always swore I'd tell them the truth. They'll find out anyway. You know what Luscano's like.

"I don't spend enough time with the children and when I do, well, who wants to launch into heavy conversations about dead relatives bringing shame on the Molino clan? Sorry, *chica.*" He shook his head and the dark curls rearranged themselves. Then he spoke of his grandmother, the family matriarch who'd bound them together, his three brothers and four sisters. "Despite our differences, political and otherwise, we're close and loyal because of her. She died after my first divorce."

The waiter brought the food and Flaco served up mounds of tossed greens and beet salad to accompany the thin filets of beef coated in spices that Alma had never been able to emulate in Montréal. They ate quickly, in the manner of friends accustomed to sharing meals. Flaco entertained her with stories of the university, the gossip among faculty members, careful not to mention mutual friends or any topic that might veer into the past. But she wanted to know about Roma. "I can't believe she still works at the bookstore." All through the junta, Roma had sold banned books from a box hidden in the basement of the store. And she'd never been caught. "She's still one of the bravest souls in Luscano," Flaco said. "Openly gay now. Some people want nothing to do with her. You know how cruel this place can be."

Flaco emptied his wineglass and signalled the waiter to bring a second bottle. "So what are your plans now? This book you're working on, will you translate it into Spanish eventually?" He mentioned a small press at the university that might be able to help.

"I'm going to Uruguay to research the archives for Agustini's unpublished poems and letters." Alma conveyed her plans with exaggerated certainty. She hadn't really worked out a precise structure for the book, which so far consisted of a few pages of biographical prose and the outline she'd written to justify her sabbatical from the college.

And then there was her mother. Alma described her shock at seeing Hannelore. "I'm worried about Xenia, too. Taking care of the household and my mother is quite a handful."

Flaco laughed. "Succinctly put. Your mother, what a character, charming of course but incredibly determined. Now who comes to mind? Ah yes, the lecture, a certain poet's mother. How was she characterized…overbearing and neurotic?"

"You're bad. Hannelore told me yesterday she loves you."

"Your mother tutored my eldest in French until just a few months ago. Fredo adored going to your house, having his lessons outside in the courtyard where your mother used to stage our plays, remember?"

He refilled his wineglass and looked past her at the structure she'd been ignoring. Alma could picture the monolith, the spotlights lighting the spire that narrowed to a point in the dusky sky, a finger accusing the gods. Flaco turned his gaze to her. "Do you regret writing that poem?"

The waiter arrived with a candle flickering inside a red globe and placed it on their table. Alma weighed her reply. "In Montréal, nobody knew of it. Anonymity heals." She wanted to ask, "Do you regret publishing it?" and was just about to when he spoke again.

"I noticed you in the lecture, looking out the window. How hard, no, terrifying, it must be."

Alma touched the globe, felt the burning heat from the candle and kept her hand there until it became intolerable, testing her threshold for pain. But she was in control, nobody else.

Flaco continued. "My friends were being abducted and I was hiding out at my grandmother's *finca*, ostensibly working on my thesis. Most of my time was spent riding horses and getting drunk with the gauchos at night." He lit another cigarette, snapped the lighter shut. "*Chica*, things have changed." Flaco looked up at the night sky towards the first handful of stars.

The man at the next table stared. He was about Flaco's age but leaner, with a white crescent-shaped scar between his eyebrows. He lowered his gaze, folded some pesos next to his plate and rose with his newspaper under his arm. Alma whispered, "He was listening to us. You think he's a military type?"

"The hair's too long. He was just checking out a woman, like any ordinary guy." Flaco regarded her with his lopsided grin. "I don't blame him." He leaned forward and for a moment Alma worried he'd try for a kiss but the table teetered precariously and he drew back. There'd been a night in his room, just before the crackdown. Flaco had kissed well.

"Next week," he said, "I'm throwing myself a birthday party. You've got to come." Flaco raised his glass. "To you, your eyes, the colour of Luscano's sky, sapphires and bright as...let me quote your poet, *un manojo de estrellas*, am I right?"

"You're drunk, Flaco!" What had possessed his family to give him that nickname? Surely he'd been born robust and bowlegged as a gaucho, nothing feeble about him, but the nom de guerre that meant the very opposite of all that he was had stuck for forty years.

Leaving Alma at the front gate of her house, Flaco doubled back towards the university. On Avenida Reconquista, the flow of pedestrians thickened with the day's last shoppers. He caught sight of himself in the reflection of a pharmacy window, a plodding figure with messy hair. *¡Qué pelotudo!* Is that what she's been looking at all evening? Alma hadn't changed much, her hair shorter than the blond curtain behind which she'd hidden herself when they were students, the same watchful blue eyes. Flaco had checked, discreetly, he hoped, for scars on her hands, face and legs. Detecting nothing, he hoped she'd been spared. But he knew he was deluding himself, that restraints, electric cattle prods, near drownings rarely leave visible marks. The most excruciating scars were invisible. Too many in exile had never returned and there were all those who had hanged themselves, walked into the sea or shot a gun at their heads for relief.

He entered the campus and felt for the plastic vial of pills in the pocket of his jacket, considered taking one. The doctor had warned against mixing the sedative with alcohol and he was still feeling the effect of the wine. No wonder the walk back seemed arduous, worsened by imagining Alma's reaction when she discovered why he'd instigated her return. Flaco gritted his teeth. Somehow he'd have to speak to her before the party or else tell all the others not to mention his project. How does one ensure the discretion of what, at least twenty other people? He'd lost track of how many friends he'd invited to his fiesta. By the time Flaco entered the building he concluded it had been a mistake to invite her. *Hijo de puta*, that's what I am. Self-disgust gripped him as he stamped up the stairs, unlocked the office door and turned on the lights.

The secretary had left a stack of phone messages on his desk. From his students, some guy called Ernesto, and the sculptor, whom he called immediately. The answering machine kicked into Luis Corva's distinctive voice, high pitched and quick with an accent, Slavic or Nordic, exacerbated on tape. Flaco left a message, trying not to sound concerned.

He lit a cigarette and stood up from the desk, walked towards the windows to look down at the site where the sculpture would be erected. It was too dark, the riverbank invisible beyond some strands of light rippling on the surface. The phone rang. Flaco returned to his desk, picked it up, hoping it was Corva. "*¿Hola?*"

"Is this Doctor Molino?"

"Who is this?"

"Ernesto Pindalo."

His heartbeat surged and he wished he'd taken the sedative. "Hello?"

What in hell would a Pindalo want? "I'm here."

"I've got some information." There was hesitation in the man's smooth diction. "Files, actually...I think you should have them."

"Why?"

"I've heard of your work. The files could help."

Flaco stared through the windows. It was black out there, just a handful of stars scattered across the sky. He'd wanted to confess to Alma what he saw most nights when the stars flickered on. Hundreds of eyes imploring him until dawn. Then they disappeared. "What's in the files?"

"You'll find out when I bring them."

Flaco flipped open the agenda on his desk. His gut told him to see the guy, but as a precaution it had to be daylight, during the week with students and professors milling in the halls. They agreed on Thursday morning and the stranger hung up.

He'd probably met this Ernesto at some point but couldn't remember his face. They were a tight family, those Pindalos in their Barrio Norte fortress. It lay next door to the beach house where Flaco had spent summer weekends with his grandparents and siblings until he was about ten. That year his father had lost the property to some general in a card game. Flaco remembered the mansion hulking behind the trees that separated the properties, how he'd aimed his slingshot at that turret, envious of the splashing and shrieking from the swimming pool to which he'd never been invited, the Pindalos' ascendancy coinciding with the Molinos' decline.

The phone rang and it was the sculptor. "I've ordered a sheet of titanium large enough to shape over the bodies in my piece. I need your help in transporting it to my studio." Luis Corva described the progress of his work, how the metallic sheet would be blinding when the sun was out.

Flaco could picture it perfectly, a glaring indictment by the river.

5

The sun crossed the Atlantic over the shores of Cape Town, Luscano's latitudinal twin, the two equidistant from the Tropic of Capricorn, that imaginary marker encircling the globe. A faint bleaching on the horizon and the country stirred, beginning with the airborne, *horneros* and swallows and pigeons, and above them, the first airplane of the day sliding south through Luscanan airspace.

Inside the droning vessel, sleepless passengers peered down at the country shaped like a discarded cape some bullfighter might have dropped onto the sand. A man-made creation, Luscano's outline delineated by the sea and inland frontiers fought for in bloody incursions and still subject to sporadic disputes. Within these arbitrary borders, an oceanside grid of streetlights marked out the avenues of the capital. A beacon flashed from the spire of a cathedral hunkering in the city's heart, a plaza out of which arteries became highways, then dirt roads snaking through fields. From the lush tangle bordering Paraguay, the river emerged as a glint of silver opening into the sea. A brief montage of a country few, if any, could identify as Luscano, with its capital of the same name, before the plane crossed the Uruguay border and began its descent to Buenos Aires.

The southern constellation faded, handfuls of stars snuffed out by the first rays of sunlight. Earthly residents began to twitch. Roosters scratched, goats bleated and horses flicked their tails.

The fishermen set out, loading nets and gear onto wooden skiffs moored on weathered docks jutting out of the coastline. The more prosperous shoved off wharves in the port. These larger vessels, with their supply of fuel and radios that sputtered warnings of coast guard inspections and armed pirates, were taking a calculated risk. Despite fishing within the limits allowed them by well-equipped Brazilian fleets, they were subject to sabotage. Shots fired in the air or, worse, at the boats themselves. At least once a month the bloated body of a fisherman washed ashore, discovered by early risers.

Rubén was spared a gruesome discovery on his morning walk from the seminary. White egrets skittered among the shadows of debris and driftwood. The Franciscan always scanned this stretch of sand on his way to the cathedral, squinting into the dawn hues for the evidence he'd heard of but never witnessed, the fishermen of late and longer ago, the living thrown out of military planes. Innocents whose bodies had refused to disappear. Rubén considered their memory a daily reminder to his conscience.

He trudged uphill and crossed the Plaza Federal, where pigeons pecked at the windowsills of the Ministry of Justice. Rubén trailed behind the flower vendors, who'd left their shanties in the *villa miseria*, stopping at the market, where they'd haggled with farmers and wholesalers selling flowers from stalls and pickup trucks. Carrying their wares in plastic buckets, they'd chatted and complained until they crossed the river, falling silent for a moment as they passed the abandoned prison. By the time the vendors reached the cathedral, the ball of sun balancing on the horizon brought to life the roses, lilies and carnations they stooped to arrange in white pails beneath the eaves of the cathedral. The aroma of coffee from La Loca drifted across the plaza. Rubén could smell it commingling with the flowery sweetness as he greeted the vendors, "*Buen día*," and they answered, "*Que le vaya bien*, Padre," silent envy in their eyes as they turned to watch office workers, government employees and security guards line the counter inside La Loca for *medialunas* baked in the wood-burning oven. As the first city bus heaved out of the nearby station, the bells of the cathedral began to toll and the rest of the capital struggled to consciousness.

Rubén unlocked the cathedral door, genuflecting into the darkness, then flicked on the light switches. Candelabras above the altar cast a golden light. He completed the preparations for mass, then as he waited for the devout, paced the marble floor in and out of the blue reflections from the stained-glass window above the chancel where the Virgin stood with outstretched arms, her palms turned heavenwards, a gesture that Rubén wished would inform his own attitude, an open-mindedness that he had to struggle to maintain, especially in this parish. The cathedral's lavish interior dome and elaborate fixtures struck him as painfully ostentatious, more representative of Luscano's oligarchy than of the congregants who occupied the pews on weekday mornings.

Rubén delivered his mass alone. He did not see the necessity of altar boys and assistants. Older priests performed the well-attended masses and the bishop presided on Sundays, allowing Rubén to focus on his true vocation, the music and choirs. He kept the ceremony tight, as free of dogma as he could get away with. Two widows stopped to shake his hand after the mass. Then he waited inside the confessional for the requisite fifteen minutes. Just as he was about to leave, someone entered the booth. A man his age, definitely not one of the shoeshine crew coming to confess a wallet lifted or a scam perpetrated on a tourist. No, this man spoke an educated language, something about betraying his father and courage and theft and where to hide *los archivos*, for he was in deep trouble. Through the grille, Rubén made out the glint of a gold watch, a white shirt and blond hair. He recommended coming clean, facing the victim, talking it out. "Impossible." He told the fellow to think about it, then prescribed some Hail Marys and Our Fathers. And that should have been the end of it, but the man lingered in the confessional. Rubén asked, "Should we pray together?" But the fellow said nothing. Finally, he left and one of the widows took his place. "Forgive me, Padre, for I have sinned," to which he would have liked to reply, "Who hasn't?"

Ernesto did not feel cleansed as he got into his car but at least he'd figured out what to do next. The morbid chill inside the cathedral, the lingering incense and the grave authority of the priest's voice all prompted ritual, death and then, eureka! The cemetery.

He drove away from the plaza, up Avenida Primero de Abríl into the anonymity of dense morning traffic. The cemetery was a gamble. He didn't know whether Gabriel Seil still ran the place and tried to recall how many years had passed since he last saw the guy. An *asado* at the house, he decided. Gabriel had arrived seeking information on his brother and they'd smoked cigars in the old man's study. Ernesto had endured Gabriel's angry staring through the smoke of the *cohibas*. Months later, after he'd heard about forensic teams digging up remains from mass graves, he'd thought of phoning Gabriel but never did. Their meeting had opened his mind, a process of awakening that had led to this. Grand theft, conspiracy, treason. Betraying his father was like betraying the country. No, it was quite the opposite. He was no longer a traitor. It was over. For the first time in his thirty-nine years, he'd done something that made sense to himself. Removing the files just as the *muchacha* made for the stairs with the glass of juice, an unfailing Sunday ritual. The old man, out of some twisted loyalty to his first wife, had never bothered to change the combination on the safe.

Since stealing the box of files, his plans had unfurled smoothly enough. Dr. Molino had agreed to meet him in two days. All Ernesto had to do was leave the files in a safe place until then, keep a low profile and hope his father wouldn't notice the missing files. If he found out, it was game over. But it was game over anyway. He had nothing to lose. With a sense of euphoria, Ernesto turned into the Cementerio Real and waited for someone to unlock the gates.

The bus rolled past his stop, obliging Gabriel to jump to the curb, an arabesque from the bottom step of the moving bus that went off beautifully. He didn't catch his briefcase on the railing, didn't stumble into pedestrians on the sidewalk in the plume of black exhaust. He took the success of his personal leap of faith as an omen, the only disappointment being the absence of witnesses. On the days he stumbled or tripped, there was always an audience.

Gabriel zigzagged through traffic on the avenue and hurried towards the cemetery gates. Breakfast at La Loca had made him late. He was trying not to eat there every day but his mornings still began with a list of promises-to-self: eat breakfast at home, arrive at the cemetery on time, go to kick-boxing classes at the gym twice a week.

And if he could only quit smoking, cut back on the drinking and find a woman to make him forget about Aude...the list went on and on.

As he rounded the gravel road, he spotted Castillo carrying something into the office. Outside the building was a fair-haired guy in a white shirt, tie flipped over his shoulder. Someone about a burial, he assumed, but then he noticed the black convertible, a dead giveaway. Gabriel's first impulse was to turn back and hide among the pine trees flanking the gravel road. But Ernesto spotted him and came running.

Gabriel forced himself to trudge up the hill. It was the worst possible way to start a day. He'd much prefer a burial.

"Gabi!" The guy lunged in for a rib-crunching *abrazo*. "How long's it been?"

Gabriel stepped back and pretended to contemplate the question. He knew precisely the last time he'd seen Ernesto. November 1998. Gabriel had gone to the Pindalo house for help and this idiot had shrugged him off. "A while, I guess."

"You look well, in shape, a little less weight. How's your mother?"

"Surviving." The false politeness prompted vicious fantasies. Gabriel imagined delivering two deft blows, a jab on the nose, uppercut to the chin, the crunching sound of the neck as the guy's head jerked back on impact.

Castillo started up the tractor for his morning rounds of the cemetery grounds. Ernesto waited for the tractor to pull away. "I've brought you some documents. For safe-keeping until Thursday." He smoothed his tie down.

"There's no way —"

"You won't believe it, Gabi. I've done something right. You can trust me, I swear. Keep the box locked in your office and don't tell anyone." Then he jumped into the car and drove off, the tires churning up pebbles and dust.

There was something off-kilter about Ernesto but Gabriel couldn't pinpoint what it was. He entered the building, made for his office down the hall. The morning sun slid sideways through the windows onto the mahogany desk. In making room for the box on the corner,

Castillo had carefully pushed aside papers Gabriel had neglected to put away yesterday. More importantly, Castillo knew enough not to let Ernesto into the office. Never trust a Pindalo, a rule that ought to be entrenched in Luscano's constitution. No hope of that.

Gabriel opened the box. Inside, a jumble of folders, yellowed papers sliding out, the letterheads glaring at him. *Policía federal. Ejército de Luscano. Servicio militar.* A memo stamped "secret" from the office of General Galtí. He dragged one of the visitor's chairs to the door and jammed it under the knob. Then he dumped the files onto his desk.

The cathedral bells chimed for noonday mass. Hannelore covered her ears. "Infernal." Her green eyes blinked until the ringing stopped then she grasped Alma's forearm. "Tell the truth, daughter, will it be heaven or hell for me?"

Alma pondered the question, if only to ease that grip on her arm. Outside the bedroom window, the sky lured bright and clear. "*El Cielo es nada más que el cielo,*" came to her in the crisp cadence of her mother's former voice. "Didn't you always say heaven is nothing but the sky?"

"I never cared about what happens after death." Hannelore wheezed. "But it matters now."

"Maybe it's just a long sleep. The lights go out and —"

"The curtain falls, the drama ceases. I used to believe in Sartre. '*L'enfer, c'est les autres.*' Hell isn't other people, it's oneself. And I'm receding from that, all my certainties called into question, the circle of my life getting smaller and whatever's waiting for me looming larger."

"A peaceful calm? Nothingness?" Alma dug deep. "'*Je veux choisir mon enfer.*'"

"Inès in '*Huis Clos.*' Well done. But Alma, we choose how we live, not how we die and what happens after. It makes me nervous, the prospect of dying...will anyone else be there, or will it just be me? That's the worst scenario. Like going to a party and you don't know who else, if anyone, is invited. And you know how I used to love parties..."

The alarm clock on the night table ticked off the seconds in loud lurches. Before leaving for the market, Xenia had said, "Be patient, *m'hija*. Time goes very slowly with the very young and the infirm." The clock stood among pill bottles, a water glass, photographs in tarnished silver frames; the absence of books most telling of Hannelore's condition. Deprived of books, what else was there? Music. "What about Papa? Don't you think he'll be waiting for you if heaven exists?"

"Really, Alma. You think your father's gained access to paradise? That he bides his time playing his violin for the dead in his parents' Russian village like some figure in a Chagall?"

Alma picked up a silver frame with the wedding photograph taken outside a church in Buenos Aires. "Look at this! His face, that's how he always looked at you." Her father's expression almost delirious, his hair on end and that look of surprise as if he'd never imagined marrying a woman as beautiful as the one in his arms.

But Hannelore was off on another track. "What are the criteria for entry to heaven? As lapsed Catholics, we'd all fail. Yes, we were baptized, showed up for mass at Christmas, weddings, the odd funeral. But the dogma never made any sense to me and the priests, a bunch of hypocrites cowing the faithful with fear! Except for a few exceptions who adhere to liberation theology, the rest are co-conspirators delivering superstitious nonsense. Your father, in his quieter way, claimed music as his faith and was rewarded by an easy death, while my life progressed into agnosticism and I'm paying for it now with this slow disintegration. On theological grounds, the only person in this household who'd pass the test is Xenia."

"She's always been religious. I remember when —"

"During that terrible time, Xenia went to the cathedral every day. Irony of ironies, she went to that place to light a candle and pray for you. At night she burned those weird herbs in her room while chanting some Bolivian mumbo-jumbo. Your father and I, our nerves were shot, and there was Xenia, carrying on with her prayers and incantations."

"It's her way of coping. She —"

"You think her rituals saved you? Please."

"I meant that her hardships —"

"I knew you'd defend her."

"— strengthened Xenia's faith."

"To live is to suffer, Alma. You know that. And suffering has a way of sorting people into those who say I survived, there must be a god, some greater good that looked out for me. But I say no God would allow such suffering: there's no mercy in imagining what they did to you. God did not save you and neither did Xenia." Hannelore coughed. "Still, if a passport to heaven...requires a life of goodness, I agree that Xenia qualifies. The criteria...being honest, charitable, not hurting others, respecting nature and human beings...loyalty, that's a big one. Your father, was he faithful to me at all times during our thirty-three years together? He was so easily charmed, there was an innocence to him. I forgave him. He always returned home, and he —"

"What about you? You flirted with all my friends."

"Like Flaco? Who could resist him? I never understood why you two didn't...well, maybe you did and I never noticed. The point is, yes, I loved men but I never acted on my impulses. I couldn't have looked you in the eye. Such an observant child. But you didn't see that when your father returned from his concert tours with gifts, jewellery for me, books for you, he was atoning.

"Alma, you're old enough to see things clearly now. I told you this many times on the phone: don't be blind, learn to see your past with clarity. I told you to see a therapist and you promised me you did. But I see you now and it's obvious you have put a wall up around yourself. Alma, don't gloss over things. You'll waste your life in a fog like your father did...music saved him and there's beauty in that. But dead, he's just a granite etching at the Cementerio Real."

"Are you saying he's not in heaven?"

"I'm saying that if he's in heaven, I'm going there too." Hannelore closed her eyes. "Let me sleep."

Alma left the bedroom and went down the hallway to the courtyard. The door slid open with rusty resistance. She dragged a wicker chair from the corner, whacked dust and dry leaves off the cushion and sat down, her sneakers resting on a low table.

Overhead a bird cawed, *acá, acá,* as if intent on marking the house with its ample wingspan, 'here, here' is the next destination. She watched the circling bird and tried to make sense of Hannelore. The taking stock was new, but her mother had always railed. An article on longevity Alma had once read maintained that feistiness was the one common feature of people who'd lived for more than a century. Her conclusion, that Hannelore would live another twenty-five years, was negated by the sight of her. It struck Alma that her mother wanted to hear that she'd been good as a mother, a wife, a human being. Like Flaco yesterday at La Loca, she was seeking absolution.

Alma tried to escape into the practical, mentally listing all that she needed to do in Luscano. Visit Roma at the bookstore, register at the Canadian consulate, check out the university library for her Agustini research. She kept circling back to her mother's revelations. What difference did her father's philandering make at this point? She suspected a malicious intent, Hannelore's misguided revenge for Alma's long absence and jealousy over Xenia. It was true that Alma worried for Xenia. She was old, too, and here in this courtyard there were signs of neglect. Hibiscus plants wilted in their clay pots, the long table was coated with dust, the chairs stacked in the corner were covered in leaves and dirt. It had been years since her parents had thrown one of their parties lit by shimmering lamps on the stucco walls, Eugen playing his violin, Hannelore swirling among the musicians and guests. Even more years had passed since the scandal erupted over one of the plays staged in this courtyard.

During her summer holidays, when she was ten, Alma had written "Todos Santos," distilled from Xenia's bedtime stories about her pueblo. Act One: the wedding and fiesta in which Alma's character, more than loosely based on Xenia, marries Mauricio, played by a giggly neighbourhood kid. Act Two: the action moves from the town square to a house, Alma depicting Xenia's dead babies by burying dolls in a clay pot, a humble cemetery of stick crosses. In her deepest misery, the outlaws arrive. Doctor Reveres Guevara and his guerrillas, including Roma, deliver hope to Cochabamba province, hiding by day, teaching the poor at night. Flaco in a red beret, fourteen years old and taller than the rest of the cast, wearing a real holster and gun, plays Che brilliantly until his execution by Bolivian *federales*, two kids with American flags sewn onto their shirts. Act Three: inspired by Che's teachings, Mauricio and his co-workers stage a strike to denounce conditions in the tin mine but Mauricio dies in an accident attributable to the indifference of corporate owners, chortling as stage hands toss fistfuls of dirt and stones onto his writhing back. The grand finale, Alma's solo scene as she packs her bag to escape further tragedy in Todos Santos for salvation in Luscano. Applause to Flaco shouting, "*¡Hasta la victoria siempre!*" into the sky above the courtyard.

A few neighbours in the audience took issue with the glorification of a communist. So the true drama testing Hannelore's courage lay in the repercussions that October 1977, ten years after the real Che was killed in Bolivia. Hannelore was accused of corrupting Barrio Norte youth, and Eugen faced threats of being blackballed from Luscano's symphony. Hannelore took on the oligarchy and triumphed because she was beautiful, articulate and feared, because she spoke seven languages and without her tutoring, too many Barrio Norte students would have failed their baccalaureate. Flaco's grandmother was the first to capitulate, with a precedent-setting invitation to a Sunday *asado*, and the others followed suit, caving like sandcastles in a rising tide.

I should have learned from all that, Alma thought, but at ten, what she'd taken from the experience was that casting Flaco in a play guaranteed he'd steal the spotlight and that the Barrio Norte oligarchy could be taken on with impunity. Both absolutes, the first a truth, the second, a fallacy with one exception: Hannelore could take on anyone.

When Xenia returned from the market, Alma helped her prepare the promised lunch of *humitas*. They shucked corn, chopped spicy peppers and onions. Xenia hummed a Bolivian folk song to the rhythm of her knife scraping kernels from the cobs. Then she stirred grated cheese and milk to make a paste with the vegetables. She laid out the husks, filling them with handfuls of the paste, and showed Alma how to fold them like envelopes and tie a twisted strand of husk around each *humita*. "In Todos Santos, we baked them over a wood fire. *M'hija*, when God takes your mother, I'm going back to where the *humitas* taste right, made from the corn raised by my nephews, grown men I've never met."

"You can stay here, where you've lived for…" Alma wanted to say, "as long as I've been alive" but this was untrue. After a revolving door of *muchachas*, Hannelore had settled on Xenia when Alma was almost two.

"This has been a good home, but I want to die where I was born and be buried with my children." Then she instructed Alma to set the table in the dining room and open a bottle of wine. "Your mother wants a fiesta."

The three women occupied one end of the dining room table. Hannelore, listing in her chair, jabbed at the *humitas,* then pushed her plate away. "Really, Xenia, what were you thinking? They're far too spicy." She drank her wine greedily. When Alma suggested the alcohol would interfere with her medication, Hannelore laughed her off. "You think wine will kill me? Put some music on." Alma found a 1974 recording of the Luscano Symphony Orchestra and placed it on the turntable. Paganini's *Cantabile* filled the dining room and there was consolation in the scratchy strains of her father's violin accompanied by guitars.

After the meal, Hannelore returned to her armchair in the living room. Alma sat cross-legged on the sofa, leafing through *El Día*. She recited the headlines to her mother. Local stories on traffic deaths, flooding from Monday's heavy rains, the shipping news, and the season's bullfighting schedule. Alma stopped at an article on Iraq. "Luscano's finest stationed in Basra."

"They can stay there as far as I'm concerned," Hannelore huffed.

The article described Luscano's contribution to the "coalition of the willing," strangely translated as *El club de los voluntarios*, and the platoon of soldiers, tanks and a frigate dispatched to the region. A photo depicted the soldiers waving the blue and red flag atop a tank. "Our boys are used to the heat," some commander was quoted as boasting.

He did not mention their lack of familiarity with actual combat, Alma was about to point out, when brakes squealed on the street outside. A vehicle door slammed shut. Heavy footsteps approached through the front gate, up the lane and stairs. The doorbell chimed.

"*Me voy,*" Xenia called from the kitchen.

Alma stopped herself from shouting "Don't go!" and turned to peer out the window. A white van, obscured by iron fencing, idled on the street. She went to the front door, where a man handed Xenia a bouquet of flowers and left.

Xenia unwrapped the cellophane and brought the white roses to the living room. "Your mother has a secret admirer."

Hannelore sniffed the buds. "Divine! Quickly, Xenia, put them in a vase. Who knows how long they've been in sitting in the delivery truck."

"You don't know who sent them?" Alma asked.

"I have my suspicions. You were afraid just now, weren't —"

"Who do you think he is?"

"Are you surprised, a woman my age and in this condition? Well, let me tell you, daughter, love is possible anytime, anyplace and usually happens when you least expect it. So never give up. On men, I mean."

Alma forced a laugh. She sat down and picked up the newspaper.

"But seriously, are you still fearful? Your father used to jump every time the doorbell rang. 'Eugen, don't do that,' I'd tell him, 'it scares me to hell and back.' They don't bother with a doorbell. Xenia said they banged on the door that night. You can still see the dents in the wood!"

The newspaper slid to the floor as Alma rose. She went to the entrance and opened the front door. The wood was scratched and weathered. How could a fist dent this door? They didn't have a crowbar, guns surely, although they never brandished them. Xenia had opened the door to the persistent pounding, then tried to block their entry, the tiny woman no match for the two thugs. She returned to the living room. "No dents, Hannelore."

"I meant it figuratively."

"You were embellishing. Don't you think it was bad enough?"

"Worse than bad, a nightmare. We shouldn't have been out that night, Alma. We thought we'd lost you. Whenever I see Patrón Pindalo, I never fail to thank him."

"Who?"

"That night when we came home, I contacted everyone I knew, called in all my favours. I begged. Patrón Pindalo, when I finally got hold of him, promised to help."

The facts of her release rearranged themselves. Alma had always assumed bribery but the question remained, with what? Her parents' savings had never amounted to much. "Isn't he a banker?"

"With the right contacts." Hannelore shrugged, "You know Luscano. He helped me because years before I'd tutored his daughter. It was all very sad. The mother, Pindalo's first wife, was killed in a helicopter accident. Little Celeste Pindalo was a mess, couldn't study, wouldn't eat. I helped her through that school year, Xenia fed her and somehow she pulled through."

Alma tried to single her out from the mental parade of children tutored by Hannelore. "Why did you wait so long to tell me?"

"Why did you wait so long to come back?"

The questions hung between them in a noxious silence until Xenia bustled into the living room. "It's time, *Señora*, for your pills."

Hannelore fixed her green eyes on Alma. "I want you to go visit your father's grave and, while you're at it, check out my spot right next to his."

Alma walked to her bedroom, shut the door and sat on the bed. Through the wall she detected Xenia's murmuring, the sound of drapes being pulled. She felt adrift and depleted. For all her fragility, Hannelore retained the power to wound. Alma could not lash back; it was unfair. But searching her memory, through all the adolescent spats and scenes that had been necessary to establish her identity as distinct from her mother's, Alma knew she'd never really taken on Hannelore directly. And now, at thirty-six, how could she spew venom at her dying mother?

Before leaving the house, Alma checked her laptop, as if by miracle she'd discover messages from Montréal. She'd have to find out from Flaco how to go about getting an Internet connection at the very least. She needed to talk to someone, a friend, outside of this world of illness and old age. Her friends in Montréal wouldn't understand. But Roma would. Alma toyed with the idea of going to the bookstore instead of the cemetery.

Outside, the street was quiet. It was siesta time and the shutters on neighbouring houses were drawn. Once she left the shade of the jacaranda, she noticed the sky, a colour that could only be described as Luscano blue. What made it so incredibly vivid, the thinner air, the salt breeze?

When she reached Avenida Reconquista, she considered walking downtown for a visit with Roma. Cursing her sense of duty, Alma turned northwards, proceeding past the shuttered shops. Xenia had told her to take the bus, but she needed the exercise, needed to walk off the frustration Hannelore managed to inflame.

The stationery store where she used to buy her notebooks and pens still existed, as well as the newspaper vendor and wine store. The shoe repair shop had been replaced by a cell phone supplier, the fruit store by a supermarket.

The cinema was open for the afternoon's first showing of *Las Horas*, the movie she'd seen on the plane. Before she'd left, it had taken months for foreign films to open in Luscano. On the next block, in an abandoned shop entrance, a group of kids were break-dancing beside a boom box blaring hip hop, the fast rhythm as catchy as a *merengue*. A few bystanders watched, tapping their feet, moving to the music as the kids practiced their moves and back flips. At first Alma thought the lyrics were in English until the chorus's third repetition, "*¡No puedo, no puedo, no puedo más!*" Angry resistance in the drumbeats and words, "I can't, I can't, I can't anymore!" and the type of music that had once been banned from Radio Luscano. "Best group in Luscano," a girl next to her said, "they call themselves *Los Desaparecidos*."

Alma tried to fathom how a band could pick such a loaded name, The Disappeared. Either they were deeply cynical or nihilistic. Nonetheless she found herself moving to the rhythms.

It was already late in the afternoon by the time Alma made her way up the gravel road to Cementerio Real. Facing the gates was

a snack bar advertising empanadas and Coca Cola Lite. Xenia had
told her to enquire in the stone cottage at the top of the hill for the
location of her father's grave. She climbed the hill until it crested to
a view of fields with tombs and graves and came to a stop under the
immense jacaranda that shaded the cottage. From somewhere inside
the building there was a faint rummaging sound. She clapped her
hands but there was no response so she opened the screen door and
stepped inside the narrow hallway. Beyond the kitchen to her left
was a closed door. There were whiffs of coffee, cigarette smoke and
something indefinable, the smell of grief perhaps.

Alma knocked on the closed door. Footsteps approached, then
the knob turned and a man peered out. After she explained she was
looking for a grave, he invited her into his office, introducing himself
as Gabriel Seil. He was her age, perhaps a little older, and there was
something familiar about his face, the scar on the bridge of his nose,
the eyes, intense and grey. The fearful lineup of faces reeled past but
she could not find a match. Perhaps he'd attended her lecture. She
stated her name and he extracted a file from the cabinet.

"Álvarez. Right. Hannelore. Your mother? She came by a few
months ago. I remember her." He coughed. "This is a difficult time. We
at the cemetery are entirely at your service. Please accept our sincere —"

"She's still alive. It's my father's grave I'm looking for."

He blushed and laughed quickly. "I'm so sorry." He looked
through papers in the file. "Here we are...Eugen Álvarez, buried in
1993. Before my time." Gabriel fumbled with a ring of keys, locking
the filing cabinet, his office door, the front door to the cottage. "State
secrets in there." That distressed laugh again.

They crossed through a *glorieta* and entered an alley of
mausoleums adorned with carvings of angels and assorted saints.
Here lay the families of Barrio Norte, the plantation owners like
Flaco's ancestors, the Molinos, their names etched on the exterior.
Nearby, the Pindalos, a slew of them buried inside a white marble
vault. Alma stopped short.

"Do you know them?" Gabriel asked.

She shook her head. "Do you?"

"Not the dead ones."

"Patrón Pindalo?"

"Vaguely. His son, Ernesto…a friend of my brother's." Gabriel looked down and kicked a pebble into the shrubs. The keys jangled in his pocket. "There's a joke in Luscano, '*el hombre propone, Pindalo dispone.*' Sad but true." He laughed at his wordplay on 'man proposes, God disposes.'

"They're that important?" Alma asked, reverting to the code used during the junta.

His grey eyes looked at her intensely. "Caution, always."

So. Hannelore was likely telling the plain truth for once.

They left the alley, walked through another arbour and towards an open field of gravestones standing inert like guardians of death in the afternoon sun. Gabriel broke the silence first. "I think I saw you on the Plaza Federal, a few days ago."

Of course! The man behind the newspaper, the one Flaco had said was checking her out. "What a relief. I thought I was going —"

"— *loca*," he finished her sentence. "This place does that to you." Alma couldn't tell if he meant the cemetery or Luscano. The gentleness of his self-deprecation felt like a salve after spending the day with Hannelore. He pointed towards a granite tombstone in the shade of a pomegranate tree. "That's it over there. The gates don't close until sundown, so take your time."

Gabriel left her and walked along the path. Once he'd crossed the field, he glanced back. Her shoulders lifted inside the white shirt, the lightest strands of her hair catching the sunlight. If that was her stance in grief, she was containing her sadness admirably. Gabriel had witnessed all the variations, from sobbing and falling to the ground to cold disbelief.

He returned to his office, smoked a cigarette while staring out the window, embarrassed by how inept he'd been assuming Alma's mother had died. All the years working at the cemetery, he still stumbled when obliged to confront harsh realities. She'd caught him off guard. Alma. A good name, spiritual but not overtly religious. There was a soft rhythm to the two syllables, unlike "Aude," a door slamming in his face. He resented that comparisons came to mind every time he met a woman. "You're on the rebound from that Estonian," his sister had said when he'd confessed the habit. "I'm on the rebound from death," he'd answered. "It's an occupational hazard." No wonder its inverse, life, had him jabbing and reeling, a pathetic shadow boxer.

He stubbed out the cigarette and retrieved the box from the filing cabinet. What an idiot, Ernesto, for assuming he'd store the files sight unseen. Gabriel had spent the last days examining the military orders, lists of supplies, most typed and stamped, initialled by the chain of command. Nothing overtly damning until he'd opened a worn black-bound ledger. Pages and pages of columns, names with dates ranging from 1989 to 1991, in various forms of handwriting, some quasi-illiterate. The label on the cover page gave the contents away, 40 Calle Dominicana, the riverside prison known by its address, La Cuarenta. The truth of it chilled.

Gabriel took the ledger to a storage room where the photocopier stood among coffins, brass stands and velvet cordons. Standing at the photocopier, with its clunk and whirr, its erratic flashes of light he copied one page at a time. Some of the entries were in pencil and he had to ensure that every name and date was legible.

The room darkened as the sun dropped west, and through the oval window, Gabriel spotted Alma leaving the cemetery. He watched her back recede downhill until it was no longer visible. The family name common. Alma, less so. The two together in the ledger's entry, "Alma Álvarez," alongside "6/01/1991, 21:16" narrowed the odds.

6

On Thursday morning, Flaco got into the Fiat to clear his mind. He had slept badly, trying to imagine what Ernesto Pindalo wanted from him. Flaco drove from his campus flat down into the old city near the port, weaving in and out of the traffic. He loved the luxury of letting La Vieja deliver him and his chaotic thoughts to spontaneous locations. Swerving past pickup trucks parked along the entrance to the market, he narrowly missed an empanada stand on wheels pushed by a boy his son's age. His brakes squealed like an ornery hog and the crowds turned to look, including a familiar figure on the opposite side of the street.

La Vieja handled the U-turn to perfection and Flaco shouted the lawyer's name through the open window. Lalo Martín walked over and stooped to greet him. In his belted gabardine jacket the lawyer resembled a colonialist railway inspector, but Flaco resisted teasing him, did not want to malign the one person in Luscano who deserved his support. Flaco asked how the work was going, noting the dark rings under Lalo's eyes.

"We're taking testimony today from a lieutenant, one of Galtí's cronies. I'm hoping he'll break. So far, most are pleading Nuremberg: 'We were just following orders.'"

"I got a call from Ernesto Pindalo, claims he's got some documents. I'm seeing him at my office this morning. I can't figure out why he didn't contact you."

"He's probably scared, like all the others."

Flaco could not bear the resignation in the Special Prosecutor's voice. "My friend's back, the one I told you about."

"When's she coming to see me? If I don't produce some hard evidence soon, they'll cut me off."

Flaco promised she'd be at his birthday party. "You'll meet her tomorrow night." He swerved back into traffic and watched in his rearview mirror as Lalo's creased beige figure plodded uphill. He had to admire Lalo Martín, commuting to work alone on foot so the office could direct scant resources to the real work. Any other lawyer — and there had been others named to similar jobs in the Ministry of Justice — would be seated in the back of a bulletproof vehicle with an armed chauffeur for protection.

Flaco drummed the steering wheel. He'd have to speak to Alma, didn't relish the pressure he'd have to apply, especially given her mother's illness. He hadn't factored that in when he'd planned his deceit, luring her back to Luscano on the pretext of the lecture. *Hijo de puta*, why did I even mention her to Lalo? Then he immediately retracted the thought.

Leaving the city limits, Flaco heard the distant clanging of the cathedral bells. Against his will, the memory of his first wedding resurfaced. Such misguided elation he'd felt, emerging from the cathedral alongside the eighteen-year-old Ana, daughter of his grandmother's maid, as they ducked the handfuls of rice tossed by their families. Even his grandmother had joined in, flinging the surprisingly hard grains into his face. She'd come to the wedding despite her threats to disown Flaco. She'd been right for the wrong reasons and sometimes, on her behalf, he regretted that she'd died before the marriage had fractured, robbing her of the satisfaction of throwing failure in his face. That wedding had been nothing but a pent-up act of rebellion fuelled by lust. He dismissed the memory — eleven years ago and what the hell can I do about it now? — as the ringing receded from the carillon in the spire.

Whatever horrors played out in Luscano, he realized, there were always those ringing bells. The country's single consistency. The bells marked Luscano's rituals from its beginnings in 1895. Armed *caudillos* led by his great-grandfather chased the Spaniards back to their ships for good. "Bravery begets brutality," Flaco reminded his students. Invoking Lorca, he'd warn them about the dangers of too much spilled blood, boding badly as in a bullfight. Privately, he conceded that the curse of history was easily overlooked in the theatre of daily life, scraping for pesos, prevailing through breakdowns and deaths, caring for children and ex-wives. So few had the time or inclination to dwell on what future was possible when the gains of the past were won so dishonourably. Lalo Martín, me and a handful of others...maybe Alma.

Flaco picked up speed on the seaside highway leading down to Uruguay. The absence of vehicles on the road this early allowed him to enjoy the views. To his left, the vast expanse of sea glittered in hues of blue and green. To his right, the cliffs of clay so fertile, small trees and shrubs emerged from the crevices. He was tempted to drive on towards the sculptor's studio, but Luis Corva was rarely up before midday. Instead, he soon veered onto a mottled road leading inland towards his grandmother's plantation.

Through the alley of cypresses, La Vieja jostled over the dirt road, past the fields of soya. Everything looked parched, dusty and more than a little rundown. He parked at the back of the house and entered the screen door to the kitchen.

"Papa! I knew you were coming today! Didn't I tell you?" Armonía asked her brother. The children left imprints of jam and hot chocolate on his shirt, but no matter. Flaco poured himself a coffee and sat down at the table. Their joy at seeing him was well worth the risks of exposing himself to his brother's admonitions and his ex-wife's demands.

"Where's the beautiful witch?"

"She's sleeping." Armonía giggled. "That's not what you're supposed to call Mama."

"Better than ugly witch, don't you think?"

Fredo came to his side. "I don't feel like going to school. Let's go riding, eh, Papa? We've got some new polo ponies in the stable."

Eduardo appeared in the doorway. Flaco rose to embrace him, a gesture that required extra effort for this brother in particular. He asked Flaco to drive the children to school. "You have to stop in and talk to Fredo's teacher. He's been getting into fights."

Flaco studied the eleven-year-old. Fredo played football and rode horses but was not the aggressive type.

"Fredo beat the hell out of a boy in his class," Armonía said.

"He insulted my parents. I had no choice."

"You always have a choice and fighting's never the right one. So what did he say?" Flaco was not surprised. For years, Ana had been the subject of whispered derision, a *muchacha*'s daughter taking advantage of the Molinos, her string of lovers coming and going from this house.

"He said you're a troublemaker!"

Flaco laughed. "That's nothing new."

Leaning against the doorway, Eduardo crossed his thick arms over his chest. "It's not funny, Flaco. People are talking about you messing around with the past. This business with the prosecutor's office, he's paying for it," he said, nodding at Fredo.

Flaco grabbed a piece of bread and chewed to compose himself. "I'm sorry, son. I'll talk to the teacher. Go get your books. We leave in two minutes." There was no point in asking how Eduardo knew about his activities. This brother, retired with distinction from the military, now ran a security firm, a lucrative operation that paid the taxes on the estate and kept the plumbing going. All Eduardo's employees, subcontracted to guard the banks, offices, museums and even the port, were ex-military men who gathered over whiskies to play cards and trade gossip. Eduardo knew everything going on in Luscano, above and below board, but loyalty to the family came first. Once the children had left the dining room, Flaco said, "You didn't have to spell it out like that."

"What else do you want me to say? You've told me never to lie to —"

"How about defending me?"

"I do all the time."

True enough. "So you've got some new horses."

"Yeah, we're boarding Patrón Pindalo's polo ponies. It's good money. I've hired another stable hand. Soon we'll be able to repair the stalls."

Flaco considered asking his brother about Ernesto Pindalo but he didn't want more trouble. He helped Fredo with his knapsack, called to Armonía to hurry up in the hope that his shouting would rouse Ana. A proper mother would say good-bye to her kids before they left for school. Then again, he was not much of a father himself. Eduardo took care of them more than Flaco did, let them live in the house, treated Ana with kindness and paid the employees on time.

The village school was a short drive from the plantation. As soon as Flaco stopped the car, Armonía and Fredo scrambled out and hurried to the courtyard to find their friends. Flaco entered the school for a brief conference with the teacher. All his resolve at taking her on fizzled with her opening remark. "Doctor Molino," the prim woman, possibly a nun, began, "I know you abhor violence as much as I do." Of course he had to agree, telling her that Fredo had been duly cautioned. "It shouldn't happen again," he promised.

When he was out of sight of the school, Flaco floored the accelator. He sped back to the capital. The sea was less placid now, with churning waves and whitecaps. A lone windsurfer crossed into the bay. Flaco raced him until the traffic thickened, obliging him to keep his eyes on the curving road, alert to oncoming trucks heading down towards Uruguay. He pushed La Vieja as fast as she would go until he reached the city. The traffic slowed on the bridge over the river. To his left lay La Cuarenta, an abandoned blight in the morning's lemony sun. There on the dusty space that was once the prison yard the sculpture would stand. Luis Corva had promised his installation would shock.

Gabriel paced at the window while keeping an eye on the gravel road. The jacaranda was sparser this time of year, allowing more light into the office and a clearer view outside. In the distance, the tractor was idling by a newly dug grave. Castillo was loading a trailer with the exact amount of soil that would not be needed, displaced by the casket once it was lowered into the narrow trench. It was a calculation that Gabriel deemed miraculous. If only he could anticipate things with such precision. There'd be no shocks or surprises, no Aude in and out of his life. It was the unknown that had him pacing, unable to concentrate on the preparations for this afternoon's burial.

Gabriel had not slept the previous night, trying to guess where Ernesto had found the files and where he was planning to take them. It seemed impossible to hand evidence back to someone so fundamentally untrustworthy. His mother would know what to do. She had never given up on her efforts to have an accounting for the junta's abuses. But calling her now would implicate her and that seemed as cowardly as his past inaction.

Finally, the black convertible swerved over the hill in a cloud of dust. Ernesto parked and hurried into the building. The screen door opened and closed, his footsteps approached the office. Gabriel sat down on the chair behind his desk as if guarding the locked filing cabinet behind him.

"There was an accident, Gabi. The traffic was horrendous." Ernesto hadn't shaved, wore the same shirt, less the tie, he'd been wearing when he brought the box. The blond hair no longer lay neatly blow-dried across his forehead.

"You want a coffee?"

"No time." Ernesto stood by the desk, shifting his feet. "I'll take the box and leave."

"Sit down for a minute." Gabriel took his time lighting a cigarette. "You owe me this. Where are you —"

"The less you know the better."

"You don't trust me?"

"It's for your own good, I swear." Ernesto sat on the edge of the desk and rubbed his hands over his creased pant legs. "If it comes out I stole them from my father's safe…my God, I'll be in the deepest shit."

Gabriel forced himself not to react. "Tell me where you're taking the files."

"The university."

And slowly Gabriel extracted the information, not by throttling the guy's neck as he would have liked, but by wrapping himself in the cloak of his cemetery administrator persona, absorbing the distress of the person across from him and returning an emotionless calm. He learned that Ernesto was meeting one Federico Molino, a professor who'd organized a conference last year on the legacy of the junta's dirty deeds. Gabriel recognized the last name, another old Luscanan family. It was not reassuring. "How do you know you can trust him?"

"He's the only contact I've got."

Gabriel looked through the window at the jacaranda, its halo of leaves lit by the morning sun. The powerful trunk gave him strength, but in tasks usually disassociated from himself, comforting the bereaved or planning a burial. He tried to adopt the same detachment now. The only alternative was to accompany Ernesto to the university. If this professor seemed suspect, he'd make Ernesto bring the files back here. In the meantime, he had the photocopy of the ledger.

Ernesto pushed his hair off his forehead. The Rolex on his wrist caught the sun from the window and the gold gleamed of complacence. Gabriel knew that he and Ernesto were stepping towards the trench they'd long avoided.

Flaco scratched his chin. The pair sat across the desk from him, a box on the floor between them. When they'd entered the office, he'd assumed the intense fellow in the sombre suit had to be Ernesto Pindalo. But it turned out he was Gabriel Seil, manager of the Cementerio Real. Ernesto was the fair-haired one, agitated, his clothes creased as if he'd spent the night sleeping in an alley. Flaco now remembered the blond beauty living next door to his grandmother's house in Barrio Norte. He'd spied on her through the trees while she sunbathed in her bikini by the Pindalo pool. She must have been Ernesto's mother, the one killed in a suspicious helicopter accident in Brazil. The other fellow, a few years older, smoked a cigarette, regarding Flaco with a morose stare.

Ernesto fidgeted, waiting for Flaco to speak, as if this meeting were commonplace and he'd know what to say or do. They couldn't sit here all day, so Flaco asked, "This box, what's in it?"

Ernesto rubbed his hands on the thighs of his wrinkled khakis.

Gabriel spoke. "Tell him."

"Military papers…and documents."

Silence until Gabriel prompted, "What kind of documents?"

"Supplies, orders, a log of some sort with names, dates…I think they might be of help."

"For what?" Flaco asked.

"You know, investigating...the military, the disappeared... all that."

"You've heard of Lalo Martín?"

Ernesto nodded. "We were in law school together."

"Why not bring him the files? He's running the investigation. He's got a mandate from Congress to —"

"That's the problem. He's got judicial powers to issue subpoenas. I'd have to say where I found the files and..." Ernesto clasped and unclasped his hands.

"Then what?" Gabriel asked, exhaling a ring of cigarette smoke.

"I'm as good as... Never mind. Please, I've got two young children."

Flaco's gut told him the fellow's fear was real, something to do with the father perhaps. He felt a tightening around his heart. After the elections, the military had scrupulously destroyed all documents. But he'd always believed that something incriminating somewhere had survived. Running an operation on that scale, terrorizing a population so efficiently, eliminating dissent with such precision required documentation, and the military was, in the end, a bureaucracy. It bothered him, Ernesto's back-door approach, his presumptive arrogance of dumping the evidence on Flaco. "Why are you doing this?"

Gabriel prodded Ernesto's foot with his loafer. "Tell him."

Ernesto shrank into himself.

There was a knock on the door and a young woman peered in. "Doctor Molino, some students want to see you."

"I'm busy, Sara. Ask them to wait." The door closed.

Staring at his hands, Ernesto spoke, his voice so low Flaco had to lean in to catch the words. "When I first found the files...a few months ago...I thought of going to a journalist...but you know...they get harassed or murdered if they publish anything incriminating the military —"

"Or lawyers. Or bankers," Gabriel added. "All Barrio Norte untouchables."

The sarcasm didn't help. Ernesto stood up unsteadily. "This is as far as I go."

"Sit down." Gabriel yanked Ernesto's sleeve. Ernesto stopped but didn't sit.

Flaco couldn't allow a fight in his office. He promised to look at the files and decide whether to pass them on to Lalo Martín. "It depends on what's in them and where you found them. Were they removed from army property? Because the military's lawyers could argue that they were stolen and discredit any —"

"I didn't take them from army property."

"If the Special Prosecutor wants to use them as evidence, he'll have to prove their authenticity. He may ask you to testify."

"Can't you just say you found them in a garbage dump somewhere? Or that an anonymous source provided them?"

The questions eroded Flaco's empathy, the lies of convenience so typical of the oligarchy's thinking. "The whole point of Lalo Martín's assignment is to uncover the truth."

Ernesto backed out of the office. The door opened to the sounds of students milling the hallway and closed again.

"How do you know him?" Flaco asked.

"He was a university friend of Roberto, my brother. Out of nowhere, Ernesto showed up at the cemetery and asked me to store the box in my office."

The whole thing was perplexing, the two types showing up at his office, one half-deranged, the other a professional dealing with death.

"What are you going to do with the files?"

"Exactly what I told Ernesto." Flaco glanced at his watch. There was only so much of the university's time he could devote to his work for the disappeared. Plus he needed to see Alma before his afternoon lecture. This meeting, the box of files, Alma's return, they were like passages in a labyrinth. Which ones were dead ends? Lalo Martín had once described his work as a convoluted process driven by bizarre coincidences and fateful discoveries.

"Keep them locked up in the meantime," Gabriel said.

"You've read them?"

Gabriel stared noncommittally at the bookshelf behind Flaco. "Did you lose someone?"

"Too many friends."

"You don't give up? I mean, it's been years —"

"My students. How can I teach them and ignore what happened?" He'd been asked the question so often the words came out perfunctorily. "I can only influence this generation if my actions support my words."

"So they're like clay?"

"I suppose."

"Then they live their lives until they come to the cemetery where they're transformed back into clay."

"Maybe the soil's a little less toxic with each new batch?" Flaco decided he trusted the fellow and hoped to God his instincts were on track, that he hadn't been scammed.

"Does it work? Do they adopt your zeal?"

"They're engaged in alternate ways. Disrupting free trade negotiations, exposing polluters, abolishing bullfighting, those are the issues they care about. They can't quite fathom what happened here during the junta." Flaco looked around, trying to figure out where to store the box. His cabinets were already jammed. "Do you know where Ernesto got the files?"

Gabriel rose and walked to the window, looking outside as if searching for the answer. "Sometimes blood isn't thicker than water."

Flaco refused to consider the dangers of taking on Patrón Pindalo. "Listen, if you're not doing anything tomorrow night, come to El Barco in the old port around nine." Someone in the crowd might know this Gabriel and vouch for him. Flaco reminded himself to call the restaurant to ensure a room large enough for his party. He couldn't seem to stop inviting people.

"I was grilled in this office once on *Don Quixote*. You still teach Cervantes?"

"Of course."

"Something about you." Gabriel opened the door and addressed the busy hallway, "The errant knight."

A student slipped past him into the dean's office. "Dr. Molino, I have a question about the paper on the *modernistas*?"

Gabriel navigated the crowds and hurried down the stairs. He'd recognized Flaco immediately as the talkative fellow who'd been with Alma at La Loca a few nights ago. But it was the bookshelf behind the desk that made him trust the guy. There, in full view, was a long row of books banned by the junta, a reminder, perhaps a prop Flaco showed his students.

Outside, noonday traffic inched across the bridge. No point in flagging a taxi back to the cemetery, better to bypass the congestion on foot. He had to admire Flaco, the young women lining up to see him, the book-filled office and mostly his apparent fearlessness. With a professor like that, he might have turned out differently, instead of marking his days at the Cementerio Real, receiving widows and arranging burials. But after years of standing behind the counter in the bookstore, he'd been seduced by the mahogany desk and the salary paid in U.S. dollars.

As he waited at a stoplight, Gabriel noticed a blond-haired figure lying in the grass under a willow tree. Ernesto Pindalo. Let him brood or sleep or whatever the hell he's doing, he decided. Ernesto had plenty on his conscience. Gabriel crossed the street. It nagged him, though, seeing Ernesto collapsed on the ground. The compassionate thing to do would be to go over and talk to him. But really, their business was finished. What more was there to say? It had been obvious in Flaco's office that Ernesto didn't want to talk.

On the far side of the river, the bunker crouched in a dusty field. And it struck Gabriel that if a ledger existed recording all those detained by the junta at La Cuarenta, there must be another list naming the prisoners who'd been loaded on trucks at night and brought to fields further up the road. He'd heard they'd been given shovels to dig their own graves. Dodging the traffic, Gabriel couldn't fathom how someone as shallow as Ernesto got to live, while others, like Roberto, in every way his antithesis, had been tortured and killed.

As he drove to Alma's house, Flaco rehearsed his speech. It had to be compelling and quick, his lecture was in an hour. He formed phrases, "it's our last chance" and "we're counting on you" and rejected them immediately. Too pat, clichéd. He smacked the steering wheel. *Hijo de puta,* how can I convince her? Quote Neruda. *Maybe we still have time / to be and to be just.* No, too condescending, she's not a student.

Alma opened the door, barefoot, wearing jeans and a T-shirt, her hair in a pony tail. He stooped to kiss her. She looked younger, distinct from the lecturer in a suit for whom he'd practised his speech, more like the student who'd handed him a poem those years ago, a gesture with terrible consequences. But she seemed pleased to see him and led him to the courtyard. Hannelore, she said, was sleeping, Xenia at her bedside. It had been another bad night.

Alma went to the kitchen to get some coffee while Flaco waited in a wicker chair. He felt at home here in the courtyard where he'd once played Che Guevara. The part had empowered him at a time when his father's gambling was pulling the Molinos into ruin. There were moments with his students, his children and here with Alma when he felt he was acting, playing someone more competent and assured than he really was.

Alma brought him a cup of coffee and sat down, crossing her legs. A rip in her jeans just above the knee flashed a half moon of skin. She mentioned her laptop and it took him some seconds to realize she was asking for advice. Then she spoke of her mother. "Yesterday Hannelore gave me her instructions for the funeral, where to find her will and papers. Our conversations tend to be morbid." Suffering shaded her eyes. Flaco recognized that state, duty conflicting with self-preservation. Alma had never accompanied a loved one on their deathbed as he had. The difference was his ever-present circle of brothers, sisters, aunts and uncles and, although he complained about their interference, it struck him now that he'd never had to endure anything as entirely alone as Alma. At least the Bolivian was around.

Flaco sipped the coffee, wishing it were alcoholic and numbing. At the first opportunity, he leaned forward, the wicker creaking under his weight. "You're still coming to my birthday party?"

Alma nodded.

"You're going to meet some people... I want to prepare you. Things are going on that you should be aware of."

"What things?" Alma studied the sky. "Look, see that bird? Every time I come out here, there's a *carancho* circling overhead. As if it's warning me."

"It's looking for food. Don't read too much into it."

With her head tilted back, her lips parted, her profile was graceful but vulnerable, too. Flaco wished he could deliver some cheer but forced himself to talk and talk, like a salesman closing a deal. Beginning with some hackneyed gibberish about dealing with the past, he talked of the future, how it will always be poisoned if Luscano doesn't face up to what happened. He cringed at his words, the very clichés he'd sought to avoid.

Alma drew her knees to her chest, propping her chin just above the rip in her jeans, staring quizzically at him.

Flaco veered into politics, explaining that Stroppo, nearing the end of his second term as president, wanted to leave things clear for another victory for his party in 2005. With the drought and spill-off from Argentina's collapse in 2001, the mad cow embargo and continuous strikes, the economy was faltering. "Stroppo's scrambling to divert attention and appease. Congress has managed to renew the military's image and get the Americans to reinstate aid by sending a platoon to Iraq, young recruits from the countryside.

"The promise to investigate the disappeared, repeatedly made and broken, has resulted in the appointment of a Special Prosecutor, Lalo Martín, a lawyer with good intentions for once."

Alma tensed. He'd feared silence or, worse, that she'd tell him to leave. He plowed on. "Lalo's mandate is to indict, name names, not only of those responsible but also of the victims. There's no record of the disappeared and abducted. It's his job to lay it all out in a report, what the junta did, based on evidence collected from witnesses."

Alma gave him an icy stare. "I've been less than a week and —"

"Those who survived left." He chose his words carefully. "You're the only person in Luscano...we know of...held in La Cuarenta at the time."

"You can't be serious."

"Consider it. Maybe you remember the guards or the —"

"We were hooded most of the time."

"And the other prisoners? Any piece of information —"

"They're dead!" Alma paused. A look of incredulity came over her face. "Is this why you invited me to lecture on Agustini? Just to get me back?"

Bits of broken wicker dug into his palms as he gripped the chair, waiting for her to get it out, the anger.

"If this investigator's so special, he'll find other witnesses." Alma stood up.

"Lalo's putting together an intricate testimonial. Any detail could be important."

"I've put it behind me and I'm not going back." There was a vehemence to her that he'd never witnessed. Perhaps she had inherited her mother's spirit. Alma would need it if she ever agreed to help.

"The other day Hannelore revealed how she got me out of prison. It was Patrón Pindalo. He intervened, spoke to someone, possibly paid them off. I was upset at first, but really, what's the difference? I got out."

Flaco couldn't describe the scenarios of her release that had come to mind over the years, hearing the others' stories. Of Alma being raped and discarded as worthless. Or some officer falling for her, wanting to protect her. A guard who'd known her and decided to help. Then there were all the families waiting outside La Cuarenta at the time, uselessly holding bundles of cash, jewellery, watches, deeds to properties, prepared to barter their souls to have their loved ones released. Flaco forced himself to continue. "Isn't it important to you to know Pindalo got you out? It can't undo what happened, but facts remove some of the mystery and fear from memory. Anything you share could be important, if only to document what they did to you." Talking and talking as Alma paced the courtyard, kicking at little piles of dried leaves in the corners.

Until finally, she began to tell him of her arrival in Montréal, not knowing another soul and running into them — Latinos from all over the Americas — and discovering what had brought them to leave their countries. How slowly, often coincidentally, through work or at the Hispanic bookstore, in a lineup to a movie or at a music festival, she'd encountered those tortured in Chile, abducted in Argentina, prosecuted in Uruguay, imprisoned in Paraguay. "The language they used to express their suffering was a lot more subtle than the code we used during the junta, Flaco."

Alma mentioned a Chilean teacher she'd met at her college. "Arrested in 1973 during the coup, Tomás was brought to the stadium in Santiago, held there with hundreds of others, until he was sent north. Tomás spent six months in a prison, where he was tortured on a regular basis. Six months! When I met Tomás, it had been eighteen years since his kidnapping but he was still building up defences against memories of the pain."

Flaco sensed she'd loved this man, it was in her eyes, but he couldn't help himself. "Did he tell you how it felt? Seeing Pinochet's return to Chile on TV after his year of house arrest in Britain? After claiming to be too ill to face prosecution? And watching him rise from that wheelchair, a cockroach creeping along the tarmac, oozing scorn as he waved his cane in the air like a weapon in front of all the cameras? While the generals in Chile, Argentina and Luscano were breathing a massive sigh of relief. How'd your Tomás feel about that?" Flaco still wondered how the world had slept that March night three years ago.

"Tomás left Montréal. I don't know how he felt about it."

If she'd had an affair with this Tomás, Flaco guessed it had ended badly for her. "*Chica*, you don't have to decide now. I just wanted you to know what's going on before you come to my party." He had to gamble that in meeting Lalo Martín, she'd sense his commitment and genuine compassion. Just as Flaco had when he'd met the lawyer at a conference last year, the first public discussion of Luscano's disappeared and the consequences for a generation silenced.

Alma stood in front of him and delivered the argument he could not refute. All the investigations in Argentina, Chile, Uruguay and elsewhere, what had they actually accomplished? A few senior officers convicted over the long years. "Governments don't really want to mess with the military, do they?"

True enough. "Even if we don't get a single conviction, at least we've aired the truth and broken the silence."

"What are the risks?" Alma asked the question she should have posed in 1990 when she'd submitted her poem for publication. "It's not the time," she said, "to distress this house."

Flaco was unwilling to admit what had happened to some who'd come forward in the recent past. The journalists Ernesto had alluded to, found dead in their cars after an article condemning a general here, an oligarch there. He conceded that there were those who'd do anything to sabotage the inquiry. "The ones protesting loudest, they've good reason to be alarmed. There is no statute of limitations for what they did."

"Your students, do they care? '*Los desaparecidos,*' they're just a band these days."

The words stung. He couldn't lie and say his students cared, despite his efforts to engage them. Flaco rose. He was already late for his next class. "May I say good-bye to your mother?"

Alma waited by the front door as Flaco entered the bedroom. Hannelore opened her eyes, her face against the pillow as bloodless as the roses on the nightstand. She gestured at the bouquet. "From an admirer. Can you believe it?"

"There must be thousands out there!"

Hannelore reached for his hand. "*Gracias,* Flaco, for getting her back. Did she tell you how long she'll be staying? I don't dare ask."

"Her sabbatical ends in January." He wondered what Hannelore would make of his plea to Alma, could only hope the fighter in her would approve.

"*Adios,* Flaco."

The common farewell, to God, had never sounded so apt.

The absence of sound in the house was disconcerting. A storm had knocked out the electricity and silenced the whirr and clank of the refrigerator, the hissing of the water heater, the sputtering moths scorched by light bulbs, leaving only the alarm clock marking the seconds to midnight and her voice. For hours now, Alma had been sitting by the bed in the flickering light of candles, reading to her mother. Every time she tried to stop, Hannelore ordered her to continue.

Alma began Valéry's "The Seaside Cemetery." *Ce toit tranquille, ou marchent des colombes, / Entre les pins palpite, entre les tombes....* Alma read all twenty-four stanzas until the last one, opening with *Le vent se lève!...Il faut tenter de vivre!*

"I hear it, the wind picking up." Hannelore whispered. "Let the waves...break!"

Alma closed the book. Her eyes were strained. She preferred the railing and taking stock to this, her mother's laboured breathing. The curtains were open to silhouettes of trees bending against the sea wind and through the silence, unwanted sounds, vivid as Valéry's images but violent, dredged up by Flaco's visit. Still, one truth remained that she could hold to: poetry steadied. Whenever the fragility of existence overwhelmed, there were always words.

"What...did Flaco want?"

"He wanted me to...come to his birthday party."

"Go. You must."

"It's tomorrow night."

"I'll be fine. Xenia's here... You know, Alma, I've been thinking...Flaco needs a woman to direct his energies. Not you... he'd smother you. You need someone...to cherish but who'll give you the space you need."

Alma had to agree. But her craving for space was so often misunderstood. After Tomás, she'd given up on Latino men and turned to nationals, Canadians and Québécois, more reserved in the way they loved. Eventually, after a few months, Alma became restless with these men who wouldn't touch her scar, couldn't process the parts of her past she shared with them. They lacked the imagination to understand how it was to come of age in Luscano. Exile became the roadblock to intimacy.

Alma watched the duvet rise and fall. She waited through each exhalation, holding her own breath, fending off panic until she saw the next inhalation. What if the breathing stopped? She'd call Xenia, they'd summon the doctor, an ambulance. It would be awful.

Just after three in the morning, Xenia came to the bedroom to relieve her. Alma pulled the duvet to her mother's chin. Hannelore briefly opened her eyes. "Did you find the envelope...in your wardrobe?"

Alma hadn't bothered arranging her clothes, preferring her suitcases open on the floor and the readiness to flee.

"Your father. A piece he wrote for you."

Alma carried a candle to her room, cupping her hand over the flame. She opened the wardrobe, felt around the top shelf and found an envelope. Perhaps she should wait until morning before opening it. It was dark, she'd not left the house all day, felt exhausted from the immobility of her bedside vigil. The pressure from Flaco weighed on her. How to make him understand the distance she'd come in warding off memory, the hard work of relegating the past to a vault, one holding dangerous goods? As long as she kept it shut, it couldn't contaminate her.

She sat down on her bed and contemplated the manila envelope. Another truth came to mind. Only two people had ever loved her without any expectations, Xenia and her father. She'd always sensed her father's implicit understanding and wordless love. Alma couldn't remember having any of the conflicts she'd had with her mother. Even the night she'd left, distraught and panicked, he'd said very little on their drive to the airport. After purchasing the ticket, he'd handed her a packet of cash and said, "You'll be fine as long as you keep writing." As he waited with her in the departure lounge, he'd spoken of his music and how it had carried him through the worst of his life.

Alma tore open the envelope, removed a single page and held it close to the flame of the candle. The bars of sheet music were pencilled with tiny signs, hand-written notations, crescendos and legatos. She tried to hum the melody, a complicated minor key, but she'd never been good at sight-reading. It took several bars before she understood from the phrasing and tempo that the music had been written with her poem in mind. Sometime before he died, her father, sitting at the piano, had transposed her lines and stanzas to create these sounds. By conveying a refusal to retract, to keep silent, her father had assumed some part in her suffering. There was comfort in this but shame as well.

It was a weekday morning when Hannelore had called her in Montréal to tell her of the sudden heart attack. "An easy death," she'd said. "Eugen didn't suffer." Alma had gone to the college as usual. Only for a moment in the classroom, when a student was reading "Los heraldos negros" by César Vallejo, had she felt an inner hammering. *Hay golpes en la vida, tan fuertes....* Returning home after class, craving solitude, she'd found Tomás at the kitchen table. He was cutting out tiny figures from black and white photographs of his student days in Santiago. The friends, she'd guessed, who'd disappeared. She took the scissors away from him and held his hands to dispel his delusions.

7

Palm fronds and debris scattered across the Rambla del Mar slowed the traffic into Barrio Norte. "This mess from the storm, it's been here for days. Why doesn't someone clean it up?"

"There's a strike," Damian answered without looking back at his boss through the mirror.

"There's always a strike. Who gave them the right to strike anyway?"

"Not me, Patrón, that's for sure."

Damian pulled the car into the driveway and activated the remote to open the gates. Patrón Pindalo grabbed his briefcase and left the idling car, entered the house and hurried into his study. He went to lower the blinds. Outside the window overlooking the garden, his grandchildren were playing games on a table by the pool. He fumbled for the light switch on the wall, dropped his blazer on the sofa and sat down at his desk.

He removed the money-counter from a drawer and switched it on, admiring the sleek design of the gringo gadget he'd purchased in Vegas. Before divorce was legalized in Luscano, he'd gone there to extricate himself from his second wife, an American who'd tired of Luscano in less than a year. He'd bought her off with enough cash to open a gallery in Santa Fe in exchange for the certificate of divorce issued by the State of Nevada. And this prize, purchased the day he'd checked out of the casino hotel, had sweetened the deal. The money-counter impressed him more than the slots and tables where unhealthy gringos sat losing their nest eggs in, of all places, the richest country in the world. On that first visit to Vegas, he'd never considered opening a casino in Luscano. That brainstorm had come later.

He opened his briefcase and stacked the ten envelopes on his desk. Half a million dollars laundered through his bank, one of the smoothest deals ever. As soon as the rifles had been unloaded from the ship, they were on their way south in a truck destined for Buenos Aires, all the evidence — the cargo ship, the arms and ammunition, the monies — dispersed and untraceable. The broker had handled the entire shipment. Patrón Pindalo had assumed that from Argentina, the rifles would be exported elsewhere, to Venezuela or Colombia, but no, he was told supply could hardly keep up with demand in that country. Those crazy *porteños*! Home invasions and express kidnappings had them arming themselves like civil warriors. With Argentina's crisis, the complete default on its bonds and debt, millions of workers had been plunged into poverty. Many resorted to theft and their rich targets became vigilantes, protecting their valuables and their homes. "*Son locos,*" the broker explained. "They fire twice, first to kill the assailant and then at the ceiling so they can claim they fired a warning shot."

Patrón Pindalo ran each of the ten bundles of cash through the counter. The bills purred smoothly, the LED confirming 50,000 in flashing red digits. Every single envelope intact. The old warrior, *el guerrero* his employees called him, was not obliged to count his loot. This had been done several times by loyal associates, but trust never trumped temptation. A few bills siphoned off here and there. Greed was the grease that fuelled the economy. He could smell it everywhere, even in the reek of cowhide from his briefcase. They called him names but nobody dared steal from Patrón Pindalo.

He heard a tap-tapping at the door. "*¿Abuelo?*"

"I'm working!"

Magdalena rattled the knob. "Why's the door locked?"

Patrón Pindalo shoved the envelopes into a drawer and closed his briefcase. After he unlocked the door, Magdalena ran into the study, inspecting the shelves of polo trophies, the bar with bottles, the coffee table. She made for his desk. "What's this?"

Patrón Pindalo dropped into the sofa. "It counts money." No point in lying, the girl was too damn smart. "Saves the old thumbs."

"Can I try it?"

"Do you have some American dollars on you?" He pulled out his wallet, made a show of looking through its compartments. "Neither do I. Now fix me a drink, my little nosy one."

She skipped to the bar, always eager to try new things, just like Esmiralda. And the girl resembled his first wife, too. Long legs even for an eleven-year-old, wavy blonde hair, blue eyes. Everyone said she looked like Ernesto but he preferred to see the resemblance to Esmiralda who, like their son, had been taller than Patrón Pindalo but sweet enough not to lord it over him. He instructed his granddaughter step by step — the glass and Johnny Walker, the coaster and then the ice in the small fridge next to the safe by the desk. When she was installed beside him on the sofa, slurping from a Coke can held in her fingers, nails smudged with pink polish, he asked what she'd wanted in the first place.

"I've been trying to call Papa. He has to sign my report card."

"Get your mother to sign it."

"Mama flew to Miami yesterday. For shopping."

Patrón Pindalo chewed the ice laced with whisky. He could mastermind the perfect deal, but his family? The adults, selfish and unreliable. First Ernesto had gone AWOL and now his daughter-in-law. Had he known she was in Miami, he'd have asked her to visit Celeste, a case almost as sad as Ernesto. His daughter called only when she ran out of funds. Like his second wife, she'd opened an art gallery somewhere on South Beach that never seemed to make any money, sucking the hard-earned cash out of his pockets.

Magdalena squinted at him. "You sign it. Instead of Patrón, write Ernesto and then Pindalo."

"That, my little schemer, is fraud. You know what happens to people at the bank when they fake someone's signature? We call the police and they go to jail. You want me in prison?"

She shook her head, alarmed at the prospect of another adult failing her. Patrón Pindalo put his hand on her head. "I'll sign it proudly with my name and a note explaining your parents are unavailable."

The bell sounded for lunch and he was obliged to leave the study, Magdalena in tow, having just this morning delivered a sermon to his grandchildren on the virtues of punctuality.

After the midday meal, the house settled into siesta quiet and he returned to the study to lock the envelopes of cash in his safe. He knelt on the carpet and turned the dial clockwise then counterclockwise and clockwise again, the birth date of Esmiralda, may she rest in peace. He felt his back twinge as he strained to reach down, placing the envelopes on a stack of deeds and certificates. Patrón Pindalo felt around for the gold, the watch and jewellery cases, then sat back on his haunches, questioning his sanity.

Eventually he locked the safe and rose stiffly, poured himself another Scotch and lay down on the sofa. He detested inertia but there were moments in his life when he resorted to reflection. The box was gone and he was damn sure he hadn't removed it. But why would someone steal from the safe and leave the cash and gold? It didn't make sense.

He forced himself to think back. It was not difficult to recall the spring burial and twelve-gun salute, the masquerade to cover up the suicide. November 1998, the night before his death, General Galtí had called, asking for an immediate meeting. Appearing some minutes later, he'd handed over a box. "Patrón, I need you to take care of these files. You have a safe place, I'm sure, at the bank or wherever it suits you." A modest favour, it seemed at the time, and Patrón Pindalo had owed him. It was the nature of their relationship, favours traded over drinks and cigars. Here in this study, Galtí had said something like, "You know we had to clean things up, Patrón, remove the troublemakers. The box contains some papers from that time. I wouldn't want them to fall in the wrong hands. Feel free to take a look if you wish. They might come in handy." The General appeared sallow and bloated. A known drinker, he'd not taken well to human rights lawyers and gringos investigating the junta and the rumours implicating his leadership.

Patrón Pindalo advised him to lie low for a while. "Take your wife to Punta del Este, enjoy the beach." Galtí nodded, half-listening. Next morning he was found shot in the head in his garage, slumped over the Peugeot's steering wheel. The widow phoned for help and Patrón Pindalo placed the calls to cover up the suicide and ensure a glowing obituary. Right after the burial, he'd come home to look at the files in Galtí's little box.

He sipped at the whisky, trying to visualize the papers. They'd seemed to contain the comings and goings of military staff, some orders and records. Nothing a good lawyer couldn't discredit or defend with arguments for security and civic order. Ninety percent of the Luscanan population had been relieved when the agitators had been removed. Yes, it had been a clumsy operation, but the job had been accomplished. He'd warned Galtí and his commanders not to overdo it. They'd restored calm and within two years of the coup, Luscano functioned as it always had. Patrón Pindalo remembered concluding that the files were not worth killing yourself over, that Galtí's resolve had collapsed from drink until he'd castrated himself and wound up dead by his own hand, self-inflicted stupidity. How could a person spiral into such confusion and ultimately delude himself into shaming his wife, his colleagues and Barrio Norte friends? He didn't have to look very far for the answer. Ernesto wasn't much of a drinker but he was heading in the same direction. Stealing the files, most probably for extortion. Why else would he take them? Sheer stupidity, for they'd serve no purpose beyond staining the Pindalo name.

His cell phone rang and he fumbled to extract the thing from his blazer. Without his glasses he couldn't tell who was calling and he answered, hoping it was Ernesto. The smooth voice of his young lawyer came on the line. Javier Martinez briefed him on the outcome of the land deal, assuring him that the senators were eager to pass the legislation. Most agreed that the eyesore had to be demolished. Officially, the land and the abandoned prison were owned by the Luscanan military and they needed the cash. Patrón Pindalo instructed Javier and turned the phone off. The casino project was consuming too much of his time. If only Ernesto would work with him, he could delegate, wouldn't have to direct every single step in the process.

Patrón Pindalo reclined on his black leather sofa, too soft to support his cranky lumbar, a prisoner of pain. Ernesto persisted in punishing him. Abandoning his wife and children was bad enough but stealing from the safe, that was criminal. He lay there reproaching himself for never having changed the combination, for trusting his son. All because of a night by Ernesto's bed, waiting for him to wake from the deep sleep of a ten-year-old, same age as Magdalena now, in the bedroom upstairs where she now slept. The boy's blue eyes had opened wide, alarmed at his father's presence. No way to sugar-coat the news. "Your mother's dead. It was an accident. The helicopter crashed into the ocean near Recife." Crushing words to have to say. It was then Ernesto had lost himself, the boy's body convulsing in his arms. Patrón Pindalo never told him that she'd died in his place, killed by enemies intending to assassinate him. The boy must have overheard the rumours and gossip and he responded with asthma attacks, fevers and then the epilepsy. Patrón Pindalo spent years trying to guide Ernesto onto a solid track, but the boy derailed again and again. For Esmiralda's sake, he couldn't abandon his son.

Patrón Pindalo hoisted himself up from the sofa and buzzed Damian on the intercom. "Get the car ready. We're going to find my son."

8

Flaco fiddled with the radio dial, jabbing his elbow into Gabriel's rib cage. If the door malfunctioned, Gabriel would be flung onto the coastal road. Serious head injury, crushed limbs, severed artery. He easily imagined his own burial without his guiding presence. Castillo would handle the job. Gravedigger, gardener, cemetery resident and driver, Castillo was marvellously competent, and rose to unexpected occasions and odd requests, including this one, with a cheerful grace Gabriel deeply envied.

Castillo manoeuvred the pickup truck, a felt hat pushed back on his forehead, one brown arm resting over the open window. He wasn't one to harbour thoughts of his own demise, that Gabriel knew of him. But even after five years of what could only be considered a close working relationship, symbiotic from Gabriel's perspective, he was never really sure what Castillo was thinking. Flaco found a radio signal with flamenco, turned up the volume and bashed out a rhythm on the dashboard to the crashing guitars. From the academic in a tweed jacket behind the desk of his book-lined office, Flaco had transformed into a middle-aged country boy. Wearing a frayed shirt and jeans, he sat squeezed between Castillo and Gabriel on the seat. Early this morning, he'd roped in Gabriel with a phone call, requesting a favour with such finesse there'd been no quick, polite way of saying no to the guy. Luckily, there were no burials this Friday afternoon, or maybe it was unlucky, allowing Flaco to corral the cemetery's *camioneta* for this errand involving a sheet of metal fetched from the port and delivered to a sculptor.

"How far is this studio?" Gabriel asked.

"A few kilometres more. It's on a bluff worth seeing just for the view."

"We can't stay long, have to close the cemetery before sunset, right, Castillo?"

"*Si, Señor.*" Castillo palmed the steering wheel, his form of driving regardless of traffic or road conditions. It made Gabriel squeamish but he couldn't criticize, never having learned to drive himself. The truck hugged the winding road, Gabriel on the inland side. He didn't know how he'd cope on the return trip with the sheer drop to the coves and inlets, felt an impending dizziness at the prospect. At least the pickup truck's suspension handled the craters and its brakes had to be reliable. The new vehicle had been cajoled by Gabriel from the cemetery owner once the old truck had collapsed beyond resuscitation. Señor Bilmo had insisted on buying the replacement from a dealership run by an Italian cousin, another Bilmo of questionable repute. It irked Gabriel to have purchased a product manufactured by the same company that had supplied the military. All those Ford Falcons without licence plates abducting innocents in broad daylight.

Flaco pointed to a cow path up a steep incline. Castillo shifted gears and the truck bucked over potholes and ridges. Gabriel cringed at the shrubs scratching the side of the truck, painted the requisite black and prone to visible markings.

"Who is this sculptor?" he asked.

Flaco described meeting Luis Corva at the university where he taught several courses. "He moved from Buenos Aires after the 1994 bombing of the Jewish Centre. His work's all over the world."

"He's Argentine?"

"Eastern European. Look, there it is." An elevated structure of pale wood and immense glass windows stood on stilts at the high end of a sloping field.

Gabriel stepped down from the pickup truck, his legs feeling wobbly from the drive. Castillo opened the tailgate and the three men slid the titanium sheet down to the ground.

A white-haired man in shorts ran down the field. He held out an old duvet. "Wrap it up in this." The sculptor's face was mottled and his glasses magnified intense blue eyes. Tanned and compact, in his sixties, Gabriel guessed, the man moved with the power of an athlete. Luis Corva put his hand on the titanium. "A beautiful piece, no? I see it's going to work well." His Spanish was unusually accented, overemphasizing the consonants.

Work well for what? Gabriel wondered, helping to wrap the duvet around the industrial-sized rectangle of metal. They carried it across the field, up the stairs into the studio and leaned it against a wall. A small kitchen and living area occupied a far corner of the studio, most of which was taken over by tables and work benches. These were strewn with drawings, pen-and-ink sketches of figures who appeared to be in the throes of death, writhing and contorted. Assorted pieces of wood were laid out along a shelf. Castillo pointed to a small chunk that looked like hardened lava, black but smoother than any rock. "What's this?" he asked the sculptor.

"Grenadilla wood from East Africa," Corva said, "often used for making clarinets."

"He carves," Gabriel explained. "Mostly from wood he finds in the cemetery." At night, Castillo sat on the steps of his cottage overlooking a corner of the cemetery grounds and whittled small replicas of musicians playing the flute or drums, flower vendors, horses and *horneros*.

"It's left over from a commission," Corva said. "You can have it, if you like."

Castillo shook the sculptor's hand. "I hope to return the favour."

"You drove the truck, so we're even."

Before leaving, Gabriel couldn't resist stepping onto the balcony for a view of the blue green sea flecked with sailboats. Flaco joined him, lighting a cigarette, his hand cupping the flame of the match. Gabriel glanced inside the studio. Castillo was examining the sculptor's tools, Corva by his side. "Did you look at the files?" he asked Flaco.

"I'm bringing them to Lalo Martín's office tomorrow. The black book, man, —"

"I know."

Flaco drew on his cigarette. "The dates, the times, the meticulousness of their records, what does that tell you about a place not known for its rigour?"

"That they were trained by Americans?" In the hillside below, olive trees and a few carobs with red flowers stirred in the breeze. It was one of those moments when Gabriel couldn't reconcile the landscape with the ugliness that had occurred here.

Corva walked them back to the truck. "I'd like to visit your cemetery. When I lived in Buenos Aires, I used to go to Chacarita Cemetery for the sculptures and engravings. There's beautiful work to be found in a cemetery."

"There's a sign in Chacarita," Gabriel said. "'Gardel may be dead but he sings better every day.'"

"You've been there?"

"My father's buried there." But Gabriel did not mention the precise location, a simple tomb among a row of suicides, no sculptures to inspire an artist, and far from the famous tenor's wall of plaques and memorials. Instead he quoted Borges, who called Chacarita a "slum for souls," a description that applied equally well to sections of the Cementerio Real.

Gabriel stepped up into the truck and slid in next to Castillo. There was no way he'd sit squeezed against the door going back. They jolted downhill towards the coast. Castillo palmed the steering wheel, his right hand on the piece of black wood on his lap. "Grenadilla," he said. "Never heard of it. Have you, *Señor*?"

"No."

Flaco explained that Corva was working on a memorial for the disappeared.

Castillo glanced at Gabriel. "An important work, eh?"

"It won't bring them back," Gabriel said. His cynicism was a thin disguise. From Castillo he'd learned that a graveyard existed more for the living than for the dead.

As he walked away from the convertible and made his way towards a stretch of sand hidden behind the dunes Ernesto's eyes began to adjust to the darkness. Along the curving coastline of the Bay of Luscano, clusters of lights flickered, intensifying in the city centre, then fading out southwards towards the uninhabited cliffs.

Ernesto sat down on a large piece of driftwood. He took out his pen and the stationery from the hotel room where he'd been drinking gin and ordering room service. His head pounded. He didn't regret the binge, didn't regret anything he'd done of late. Just all that preceded it. He balanced his passport on his knee to support the sheet of paper and began writing. *Querida* Magdalena, *querido* Patroncito.

What to say? Don't screw up your lives like I did. Be honest, think of others, be brave. No, I should tell my children to get out of here. Leave Luscano as soon as you can. But thinking back to the one year he'd lived abroad, a winter in Chicago, where he was supposed to be completing an MBA, he shivered. Icy winds scalloping the snow banks, the chilly indifference of the people and the tough lesson of what it meant to be a nobody. No, he couldn't inflict that on them. He'd apologize. Whatever you do, don't follow in my footsteps. Don't listen to the old man, call him out when he meddles in your destiny, forge your own path.

A couple walked their dogs along the beach, no leashes on the animals. Ernesto waited out these intruders, watching the southern constellation emerge. First Pegasus, its stars connecting the elegant tail, the ears and mane, then Altair, a beacon to the south that would soon define the density of the Milky Way. These were the mythic shapes his father had taught him. Standing on a stool, peering through the lens of the telescope, he'd always wondered but never asked, where is she? His face tensed by the effort of squeezing one eye shut, the other searching that immense sky. God's cathedral lit by thousands, there had to be a constellation named Esmiralda. Long and delicate, as he remembered her, always shiny. But even then, he couldn't recall her face. It frightened the boy, her fading from memory, so he'd sought her in *el cielo*, where the priest promised she resided, so he'd never lose sight of his mother.

But he had. Memory foreclosed by living with one eye shut. Easier that way, fulfilling the expected, following and dispensing orders and ignoring every feeling until he'd become hollow as the *mate* gourds sold in the market. Silver trimming the black exterior, nothing inside, just a vessel. He would float, then, the waves rocking him to sleep.

Ernesto removed his shoes, socks, shirt and belt. Some itinerant would be happy for these gifts. Then he dug a hole in the sand, using a stick to bore down. He dropped the Rolex, passport and pen into the hole. He removed the gold chain from his neck, his mother's and therefore cursed, dropped it in, followed by the crumpled sheet of paper.

The night was unusually balmy for midwinter July. Alma removed her sweater and tied the sleeves around her waist as she waited for Roma to draw down the shutters and lock up the bookstore. They walked down Avenida Primero de Abríl towards the old town. Roma was wearing jeans and a denim shirt, the sleeves rolled up to her biceps, muscular from the drumming. "You have to come hear us play, Alma." Roma described how she'd stumbled into taking up taiko drums. "I never learned piano or guitar," she said without bitterness. Alma had always been aware of how privileged she'd been in comparison with her friend. Roma's parents, dead now, had run a string of businesses into the ground, a flower store, a taxi, then a fruit stand. "Now I know what I missed. Playing the drums, it's a complete escape from my vicious thoughts, my little life." Then she asked after Hannelore.

"She's mostly in bed now. This afternoon, the prospect of a party got her going. She had me parading around her bedroom in my dress and insisted I take this necklace of hers." Alma omitted Hannelore's critique of her black dress. "I'm not saying it's unbecoming," she'd said, which of course meant the very opposite. "I see you wearing it to my funeral. But for Flaco's fortieth, you need some dazzle." Even so, Alma had been reluctant to leave. But Hannelore had insisted.

"Your mother's the one who came up with my name, remember? We were having lunch in your courtyard. I told her I hated it and she agreed, said Rosa Maria was more than uninteresting. 'Why not

Roma?' she asked. 'It suits you, especially spelled backwards.' I'll
never forget being rechristened by your mother at the age of eight.
It gave me the guts to consider reinventing my sense of self. I should
go visit her."

"Soon, Roma. I don't think she's…" Alma looked at her friend.
She understood.

They walked past the cathedral. Water streamed into the plaza
as the flower vendors emptied their buckets over the cobblestones.
A priest switched on the light bulb dangling over a side door, his
private entrance or escape, perhaps a signal.

By the stairs leading down to the port, a series of murals
covered a stone wall. Vivid depictions of Luscano's history, from
the original indigenous settlements and Spanish conquests through
to independence, ending before the junta. Roma said the murals
were created by students commissioned to paint over the graffiti
and peeling stucco of the colonial walls. Entering the city's oldest
streets, narrow and winding, Roma pointed out the landmarks, such
as the second-floor room where Luscano's earliest poet had lived,
vines dangling from a wrought iron balcony. Alma recalled the
epic verses they'd had to memorize in school. She was puzzled that
her friend had researched these details until Roma mentioned that
during tourist season she offered walking tours of the capital. "You
should see the types that come here. Earnest retirees from New York,
rich students from Santiago, French sailors…and they love it, seeing
where our famous writers lived. It doesn't seem to matter they've
never read their works. Plus they tip well." She advertised the
tours in hotels and the bookstore, where she sold an accompanying
illustrated map. "I got Flaco to write a short history of Luscano and
he had it published by the university. It earns him some extra cash
for all his wives and children."

Alma admired this resourcefulness. If Roma had moved to
Canada, she'd probably have adapted faster than Alma had. Perhaps
Roma sensed these thoughts, asking how Alma felt about her new
home. It was the type of question difficult to answer. It required
comparison and she didn't want to criticize Luscano. "The first thing
I noticed was the absence of soldiers, tanks and military symbols.

I can't name a single Canadian general, except for one, Roméo Dallaire." Alma described visiting Ottawa, her astonishment at seeing the Prime Minister's residence with only two cars guarding the entrance. "But that changed after 9/11. Now there are armed guards at the airport, embassies and some government offices. Politicians travel in armoured vehicles, defence spending is on the rise and the army's deployed in Afghanistan. It's too bad," she added, "the militarization of Canada." Luscano and Canada, she'd realized, had more in common than she'd ever considered. In exile, Montréal, its brutal winter, landmarks and idiosyncrasies had seemed so utterly different from the climate and landscape of Luscano. But in truth, a shift in mentality had occurred in the twelve years since she'd been gone, driven by technology and globalization. From that moment in the lecture hall, watching the audience arrive for her lecture, Alma had begun to understand that her students in Montréal were not that different from Flaco's here.

"So what do you consider yourself now, Canadian or Luscanan?"

"Both." Or should she have answered, neither? Alma hovered in that in-between state. She felt affection for the refuge Canada had provided, but over the distance of time and geography, she'd come to identify with Latin America. Many of her students were born to parents from Peru, Ecuador and Colombia as well as El Salvador, Nicaragua and Guatemala. Teaching them, she'd witnessed their transformation, pride edging out immigrant embarrassment as they learned the literature of their roots. She tried to convey to Roma how Canada's gaze was directed to the U.S., followed by Europe, the Middle East and Asia, and how insignificantly Latin America figured in people's minds. "They notice my accent in English or French and ask where I'm from. When I answer, their attention drifts or they say, 'ah, you must speak Portuguese.' It's as if Luscano is an imaginary country I created in a dream world."

Roma laughed. "If they only knew!"

To some extent, Luscano *had* become illusory during her absence. Aside from the weekly phone calls with Hannelore, not much had tangibly connected her to Luscano. The place largely existed in her mind, occasionally Neverlandian in the context of her childhood memories, mostly threatening, an enclosure with the trappings of conspiracy. It was an effort, almost dizzying, trying to match the hallucinatory country to the one her senses now perceived, to reconcile memory with truth, two overlapping circles edging closer.

They passed the naval officers' club, which had been transformed to a boutique hotel with its name, Hotel Colonial, displayed in neon over the arched entrance. Alma remembered skirting the building every time she'd walked to the old market. A plaque on the hotel wall mentioned its history but did not refer to the dirty deeds hatched inside. Two *porteros* in blue uniforms with brass buttons and epaulets leaned against a luggage rack, sharing a smoke. The older one, eighteen at most, flicked ashes off his blue sleeve and grinned as the younger one whistled at the two women. Roma turned back. "In your wildest, *chico*." To Alma she said, "Better to be working as a hotel porter than a recruit in a boot camp."

They crossed the Plaza de los Marineros, walking around the sculpture of sailors brandishing swords. A few skateboarders huddled on the steps of the monument, the smell of marijuana drifting across the plaza. This would have been unthinkable during the junta, when possession of half a joint was enough to solicit a beating, or worse, a night in a cell. "Take a deep breath," Roma said. "It'll steady you for the party." And for Flaco's sake, Alma did, consciously invoking her Montréal demeanour, self-effacing, neutral and light.

Inside El Barco, Alma was kissed and embraced by people she vaguely recognized, as if they'd been waiting for her arrival. There was nothing livelier than a Luscanan party, even early on when the heated chaos was fresh with possibility. A DJ played "Los Desaparecidos," the heavy bass beat vibrating the wooden floor, as guests milled around a long table. The restaurant's marine decor extended to this separate room with photographs of the old port hanging alongside fake brass portholes and nets strung from the ceiling among buoys and wooden traps.

Waiters dressed in striped shirts offered trays of empanadas. Roma handed Alma a glass of wine and led her to a group of musicians. The conversation wasn't limited to formalities of self-identification or tepid exchanges. From Emilio Rodriguez, a violin student of her father's, Alma learned that Luscano's symphony orchestra had survived. They didn't tour anymore, no money for it, but the OSL played a season every year in the concert hall and in smaller venues in the countryside. She told Emilio about her father's composition without revealing it had been inspired from her poem. "I play piano but the piece needs a violin." Emilio immediately offered to accompany her. "Call me at the faculty. We'll schedule some piano time in the studio." On her second glass of wine, Alma encountered professors from the university who'd heard that she was planning a book on Agustini. They promised her names of contacts in the Uruguayan cultural institute and the national library where the poet's writings and letters were preserved. Later a young woman approached, introducing herself as Aurora. Attractive but sullen in a strapless green dress, it took Alma a moment to realize that she was Flaco's second wife.

"He used to talk about you all the time," Aurora said. "I was jealous at first."

"Flaco said you have a son."

"I wasn't even eighteen when Beno was born. Flaco tried to do the right thing but our marriage was a disaster. We're still friends. How can anyone stay mad at Flaco?" She shrugged her bony shoulders.

Roma sidled up and Alma introduced her.

"*Encantada*," Aurora said. "I was just telling Alma about my three-year-old. Beno takes after his father, can't sit still, talks a mile a minute —"

"And bosses everyone around." Roma laughed. Then she spotted someone in the crowd. "What's he doing here?"

Alma turned around. "Who?"

"Gabriel Seil! I can't believe it."

Gabriel stood by the sound system, conversing with the DJ.

"You've had a thing with him?" Aurora asked.

"Are you kidding? No, he used to work at the bookstore with me."

Encountering Gabriel at the cemetery last week, Alma had found him oddly endearing. "What's the matter with him?"

"He's morose. I mean, he's a good guy, just not at a party. Gabriel had a fling with an older European woman, married apparently, but she left Luscano abruptly and…well, ever since, he's taken to coming to the bookstore to cry on my shoulder."

Flaco squeezed through the crowd. "Here's trouble," Roma said.

"Aurora, don't let these women corrupt you." Flaco placed his hand on Roma's shoulder. "If you don't behave, Roma, I'll trash you in my speech."

"Jesus, Flaco. You lure us here on the pretext of seafood to stick us with one of your lectures?" Then she asked how he knew Gabriel.

"I don't really. Is he a friend?"

The code, Alma remembered, for distinguishing opponents to the dictatorship.

"Absolutely," Roma said. "He never got over what happened in the junta. It's one of the reasons he works at a cemetery, my theory anyway." She looked at Alma and without saying a word, her dark eyes behind the round glasses conveyed compassion. Roma wasn't one to mention La Cuarenta directly, but her look told Alma, if you ever want to talk about it, I'm here.

Flaco began seating the guests, directing them to specific places around the table. Yes, he was bossy and controlling, but Alma could forgive him this one night. The anger she still felt after he'd come to the house was relegated to a corner of her mind for now. She was well practised in this ability to compartmentalize, but she'd have to have it out with him at some point. When everyone was seated, Flaco took the last remaining place at the head of the table. Alma counted thirty-nine guests. Unlucky, Hannelore would have said; a party should always be even-numbered. But her mother would have approved of the distribution, men exceeding the number of women, and Alma drank a silent toast to her.

The waiters relayed platters of seafood, paella, salads and baskets of bread. They replenished wineglasses, left sparkling water bottles on the table, brought bowls of lemon slices and salsa. Flamenco music played in the background, the Andalusian lament a little too low for Flaco's liking. Turning forty, he'd outlived Lorca, which entitled him to howl and dance and celebrate life. His worries about combining his friends and random acquaintances seemed unfounded. To his right, Alma conversed with Luis Corva across the table. Lalo Martín and Gabriel, both on the subdued side, were deep in discussion. The musicians, Emilio and the DJ were being entertained by the antics of the gang from the *finca*, the stable and farm hands, true gauchos with whom he'd explored the fields and forests and worked the harvest. They'd all brought wives and *novias*, dressed up with bright lipstick and flashy nails.

One woman stood out, her eyes as round as castanets. She caught him staring and Flaco winked, raising his wineglass. What the hell, it's my birthday. He pried open a crab claw and extracted the pink white flesh, caught sight of Aurora and Roma laughing at the other end of the table. Bless her for coming, that Aurora. He'd not invited his first wife or any of the children. They'd be at the family party Eduardo was planning, a second celebration at the *finca*. Flaco transmitted a telepathic message to Roma, restrain yourself. Aurora's too frail a soul to handle a taiko player, let alone the ardency of a woman. Flaco chewed the crab with a sense of satisfaction. Not a shared drop of blood with any of them, but they'd all come simply because he'd asked. He was itching to make a speech, tie up the frayed strands of his life into one elegant knot. Maybe tonight he'd sleep without a sedative, forty years old and alive, if not at peace.

While the waiters cleared the table of plates, the DJ put on some dance music. Half the crowd rose to work off the main course. Flaco moved to a chair next to the sculptor. Luis Corva always intrigued with his perspective from crossing many borders, or as he himself called it, the perennial refugee.

"No matter how tired you are when you arrive," Corva was saying, "you get a buzz from the motion and energy of Manhattan."

Alma liked his strange accent and agreed with his take on New York. As soon as she'd received a Canadian passport and saved some money, she'd taken a train for hours, far longer than the journey from Luscano to São Paulo. Only then had she appreciated the dimensions of the continent and the features of its towns. Rouse's Point, Schenectady and Saratoga Springs, names as rhythmic as the rattling Amtrak train. Stepping out of Penn Station had been like entering a movie set, the landmarks familiar from books and films she'd seen at the cinema in Barrio Norte. With all the Spanish overheard on the streets, New York connected her back to Luscano more than Montréal had ever done.

"I was there on 9/11," Corva said, "working on a commission. The friends I was staying with had no television, so we went to a bar to find out what was going on." Luis Corva searched the eyes of his audience, the blue of his eyes sharpened by his thick glasses. "I emptied an aspirin bottle and went out on the street to collect the ashes, down on my knees, ambulances and fire trucks screeching nearby."

His scarred face contorted. "The aftershock of violence. I can hear it through anything, the flamenco music, the conversation at this table. It's the soundtrack of godlessness."

"What did you do with the ashes?" Flaco asked.

Luis Corva looked at his hands. "What possessed me to collect them at all? Ashes, you know, cannot be represented in sculpture. Too ephemeral. Like the wings of a mayfly, insect of the genus Ephemera with its miniscule life span.'

"Can't you imply them?"

"I've thought of that. Suggest a fire, an oven or a smouldering aftermath, but attention is drawn to the agent, whereas I want to attest to the effect, the ashes themselves. The arson of humanity, disaster's outcome."

"You could allude to ashes in the work's title," Flaco suggested.

"That's the cheap way out," Luis Corva said.

Alma understood the essence of his preoccupation. Every assault on humanity left scars; the worst were those that left only ashes. Luscano's nightmare began with the burning of books. Not an original strategy to silence resistance, the military had copied the Argentines in the seventies, who had learned from the Nazis in the thirties and forties.

"I need to do research," Corva said. "The inspirational kind. When I come to your cemetery, Gabriel, I'll look in on the crematorium."

"We don't have one." He explained that cremation was the exception in Luscano because of the church. "Anyone who wants to be cremated is sent to São Paulo. The corpse, I mean. It takes a good ten days, and the paperwork to go in and out of Brazil is ridiculous. I've spoken to the owner, suggested he construct a crematorium on an adjacent piece of land he's acquired."

"I'd love to do the facade. A crematorium, imagine that. The business of burning bodies."

"The dead," Gabriel said. "Dead bodies. Who *chose*, or their families did, cremation."

A lull ensued, typical to the topic, the weight and privacy of death turning each of them inwards. Except for Gabriel, whose immunity to abstract notions of death was an occupational side effect. He wondered how to accommodate the sculptor. His boss insisted all the cemetery contracts involve his Italian network of artisans, stone masons and iron mongers. They were good craftsmen, it was true, but Luis Corva's interest in the cemetery had him considering how to make the grounds more artful and interesting.

The lights dimmed and the waiters marched in shouldering a big platter. Everyone belting out, "*Que lo cumplas feliz...*" as Flaco blew out four candles on a chocolate cake, quite massive and baked in what was clearly, if not entirely accurately, the eccentric shape of Luscano. This prompted shouts of "I want downtown!" and "Give me the beach!" as the waiters laboured to cut up and serve semi-egalitarian chunks of cake.

Gabriel was given a wedge of Barrio Norte, prompting him to chortle at the thought that he was literally eating Pindalo real estate. He felt Alma looking at him from across the table and tried to come up with a brilliant line. Small talk was not his forte but he managed to ask about Montréal, admitting he'd been there once. "Made the mistake of going in January, ruined my shoes in the snow." He did not reveal the rest of it, the week in the hotel room with Aude, trying to save their relationship.

Alma laughed. "It's a strangely big deal, coping with winter footwear when you first arrive. We come from a place where only gauchos and fishermen wear boots. But in Montréal, a good pair gets you through the winter."

He was burning to ask about her time in La Cuarenta, assuming the entry in the ledger Ernesto had brought was correct. Except the DJ turned down the music, Flaco rose from his place at the head of the table and bellowed for silence.

He thanked his guests for coming and tried to convey the meaning of having all these arcs of his life joined in one room. As he warmed up, others interrupted with loud toasts. His *finca* friends, the musicians and academics, and Roma, who raised her wineglass shouting, "Never grow up, Flaco!"

Calls for refills from the waiters, then more interruptions and impromptu toasts until Flaco succumbed to the obvious. He'd never hold their attention for a longer speech. They were itching to move to the samba so he grabbed Alma and danced her around the room, felt her body resist his and knew that she'd yet to forgive him. Then he found the beauty he'd been eying. The woman claimed she was married to a stable hand, but she agreed to one dance. Flaco took her in his arms, and they crisscrossed the dance floor as sweat curled his hair and soaked his shirt.

After Flaco's wildness, dancing with Gabriel felt easy, his movements a vague attempt at shadow boxing. He tried to compensate with conversation, lost in the melee of sound. Alma couldn't see what Roma found offensive about him, overly earnest maybe, but well meaning. Then, after dancing a number with Emilio, she was ambushed by Roma for a tango.

Later, when Roma was spinning Aurora inside a circle of dancers, Alma went to the bar in the corner of the room. She drank a glass of water while examining the framed photographs on the wall. Black-and-white shots of ships moored on long wharves, stevedores stooping under loads of trunks and containers alongside greasy coils of ropes. Port scenes from the twenties that could have been taken anywhere. She tried to discern what, if anything, made the scenes unique to Luscano.

Lalo Martín sidled up and pointed to a corner of one of the photographs. "You see that group?" Alma stepped closer and noted the huddle of people, men in hats and suits carrying bundles, women in shawls holding children, their eyes conveying a panicked disorientation. "Refugees from Europe, earmarked for quarantine, most certainly rejection. Buenos Aires didn't want them, neither did Uruguay or Luscano. Some made it into Paraguay. Most starved to death. If I had to come up with a caption for this photo, I'd call it 'Luscano, the last hope vanquished.'" He turned to Alma. "History is ugly…I don't have to tell you that."

Throughout the dinner, Alma had managed to avoid this conversation. Flaco, of course, had seated her next to the man. She tried to catch Roma's eye across the dance floor.

"I'm hoping you'll come to my office sometime soon for a private talk. I want to hear everything that happened to you, every detail."

"It's been so long, I doubt I can —"

"I heard your mother's ill. If it were my choice, I'd wait indefinitely. But I'm losing a battle with time. Please make it sooner rather than later. If you want, bring Flaco for moral support."

Roma came barrelling towards them. Watching from a distance, Flaco tried to intervene but she pushed him off to drag Alma back to the dance floor.

Patrón Pindalo hobbled into the cathedral, one hand bracing his lower back. Not bothering to genuflect, he walked the aisles, hoping to find his son on a pew waiting to be rescued. Damian had cruised the length of Primero de Abríl down to the old market and bus station, west to the bullfighting arena and football stadium, and north on Reconquista, slowing alongside restaurants, ice cream stands and cafés. They'd been to Ernesto's office, his apartment and gym, the polo fields and yacht club. Nobody claimed to have seen him lately.

Patrón Pindalo returned to the car idling by the plaza, determination sliding into dejection as evening slipped into night.

"Where to now, Patrón?"

"The airport." All the overseas flights would take off just before midnight. There was a small chance Ernesto had decided to leave the country. If his son wasn't at the airport, what then? he wondered. For the sake of the children, he'd have to contact Ernesto's wife in Miami. She might have written off her husband, but she had to take responsibility for the children. Patrón Pindalo had no idea how to explain their father's mysterious absence.

Damian drove towards the highway, passing the cemetery. The gates were shut and the graves lay in a dark shroud. It had been years since Patrón Pindalo had visited the family mausoleum. He'd outlived his parents, both dead in their sixties, his father from an infarction in his office at the bank. The old man had bequeathed him the bank, the property in Barrio Norte and most of all, the hard currency of the Pindalo name. His father's motto, "a Pindalo never rests," was a solid work ethic. Too bad his children had proven immune to it. He should probably visit the mausoleum one of these days, but he'd long ago decided his orientation had to be the living and not the dead, including Esmiralda. What good was he to her unless he took care of their offspring?

The car swerved onto the smooth highway, which was illuminated by lights springing from the median. Patrón Pindalo had lobbied for this *autopista*, arguing it would boost tourism, fully aware it would make his own travels that much easier, cutting the trip to the airport from Barrio Norte by a good half hour. Lately, the casino project had him travelling to Uruguay by helicopter from the launch pad at his yacht club. That, along with Ernesto's burnout, had tied him to Luscano.

There was sudden darkness as the car jolted over potholes. "Where in hell are the lights?"

"They ran out of money, Patrón."

Oncoming vehicles illuminated huts and gypsy tents in the fields and the glow of bonfires in the distance. Occasionally the car's headlights reflected the glassy gaze of a cow or dog on a chain. Pathetically Third World. To avoid the sight of it, Patrón Pindalo stretched out on the backseat, hands clasped on his chest as if he were the type to pray.

The party began to peter out and the DJ was packing up the turntables and amplifiers. Six of them, not wanting the night to end for various reasons, left El Barco for the beach. Luis Corva offered to drive Gabriel while the rest of them squeezed into Emilio's Renault because he was the most sober one with a car. The sculptor followed the Renault. Flaco directed Emilio past the plaza and onto the Rambla until they reached a car park not far from the house that had once belonged to Flaco's grandmother.

From the back of his car, Emilio produced a guitar, a blanket and some bottles of wine. They walked down to the beach. Then Flaco opened a box and offered *cohibas*. Gabriel, Emilio, Roma and Luis Corva accepted. Alma, her hand instinctively reaching for her shoulder, declined. Flaco could not know of her horror. He was still in party form and after Emilio tuned his guitar, they sang the folk songs banned during the junta, all the stars as witnesses. Alma surprised herself by remembering the lyrics to the songs of Pedro Malú, Luscano's folk singer and composer who'd escaped in 1991 by seeking refuge in the French embassy. His record label had helped him get to Paris, where he'd died in exile.

The coastline was dark and largely invisible, except for downtown streetlights and the red light on the spire of the cathedral that flashed to warn off airplanes. Nobody was out on the beach at this late hour, the cathedral bell's midnight tolling had long ceased.

In between the singing, Flaco pontificated to his heart's content, planting himself on the sand and waving a bottle like a celestial offering. "If you'd let me, Luscano, I would marry you...as dowry and wedding gift I'd give you Dos Ríos and Campo Gitano." His bastardized version of Lorca's poem had them laughing, even Gabriel, whose brother had loved the poet's work.

Eventually, the banter shifted into the maudlin, that pre-dawn state when the ego's defences have been eroded by drink and sleep deprivation. Emilio described the last days of Pedro Malú in a Paris apartment, cared for by his lover as the HIV corroded his immune system, a slow interior poisoning that, to Alma, resembled Hannelore's lymphoma. As she wrapped her sweater around her shoulders, her arm brushed Gabriel's. He looked at her face and nodded, as if to acknowledge something, her suffering maybe, of which he knew nothing. It didn't make sense.

They all fell silent as Luis Corva spoke of the courage of Soviet dissidents during decades of oppression. Then he told of his past, how he was born in 1944 in Estonia the very day his father was executed for being Jewish.

The surf rolled onto the shore and soon the sky became more sapphire than indigo and they squeezed back into the Renault, stopping to drop Alma off first. Flaco got out of the car and kissed her, holding on a little longer than appropriate for a platonic good-bye. Over his shoulder, Alma noticed the lights inside the house. As she entered the front gate, the door opened to Xenia, her arms outstretched.

9

Back-to-back burials, rare but not unheard of, required the energy and precision of an intricate choreography. Castillo prepared the mausoleum, then drove off on his tractor to the second site, leaving Gabriel to ferry the cordons and brass stands to Oligarchy Alley, his private nickname for the lane of marble vaults. The morning's clarity disturbed Gabriel. He would have preferred a drizzling rain or windstorm to this pastoral scene which only seemed to presage further disaster. The early buds hinted of spring and rebirth, the cheery sunlight disconnected from the cold finality of death.

After arranging the velvet cordons around the entrance of the mausoleum, Gabriel hurried back to his office for his tie and suit jacket. There was just enough time to check on Castillo's progress across the field.

Gabriel found him loading shovelfuls of earth onto plywood planks, immersed in the calculation of soil that would be displaced by the coffin. The planks would be lifted onto the trailer rigged to the tractor, the unneeded soil spread in the new section of the cemetery. Two boys who helped out in emergencies stood thigh deep in the hole marked by a rectangular wooden frame. There was still a good metre of digging required but Gabriel knew enough not to distract them. Hovering never helped a gravedigger, Castillo had often reminded him.

He stationed himself under the jacaranda and smoked a quick cigarette until the pair of vehicles appeared on the crest of the gravel road. He'd not been told whether a mass had preceded the burial but he doubted such a ceremony could have been held without violating the clamp of secrecy. This morning's succinct obituary in *El Día* had emphasized privacy.

Four uniformed men emerged from the hearse and opened the back door, sliding the coffin out. They engaged the springs of the folded legs on wheels and rolled the coffin along the grass, walking in parade step. Their grey uniforms appeared generic, like those worn by security guards, and they carried no obvious weapons.

After the children and adults stepped out of the limousine, Gabriel led them through the *glorieta* to the cordoned entrance of the mausoleum. He retreated several metres, stopping in the dappled shade of what he eventually realized was Flaco's family vault.

He stood in the shadows, sweating out his reaction to Ernesto's death, antagonism towards the deceased ricocheting to pity then terror as he imagined the repercussions, the Pindalo rage and its possible consequences. The news had crept through Luscano in the same manner atrocities had been conveyed during the junta, rumours repeated and confirmed through whispered exchanges.

Gabriel had learned of the death at his mother's house on Saturday evening. His brother-in-law practised medicine in a private clinic and over dinner, Manuel mentioned that Ernesto Pindalo had been unsuccessfully treated for hypothermia that morning. "The body was discovered by some fishermen. Officially, the cause of death is complications from pneumonia." Gabriel had been too shocked to comment but when he returned to his apartment he'd phoned Flaco and during their conversation had learned that Alma's mother had also died.

The next morning he'd gone to the cemetery to alert Castillo and when the calls had come, first Alma's and then Patrón Pindalo's secretary with her list of demands, he'd been prepared. Originally, Gabriel had planned to withdraw from this ceremony completely, wait it out in his office, but he'd decided to witness the interment for Ernesto's sake, concerned that Patrón Pindalo would simply shove the coffin into the vault and leave.

The bereaved formed a semicircle around the priest in purple robes. They bowed their heads as the red-faced clergyman delivered a prayer. Gabriel could not make out the words. Over the years, he'd developed an engaged detachment to his job, treating every burial on his watch as if one of his own were inside the coffin but without the accompanying grief. Today he felt overly invested, unable to invoke the usual nonchalance.

The pantomime unfolded with a terse starkness. There were no flower arrangements or music. No one but the priest spoke a word. There was no squirming, just a shocked stillness. Ernesto's wife gripped her purse, her head bowed, perhaps for the children's sakes, sunglasses covering most of her face. The boy, whose name Gabriel could not remember, resembled his grandfather, with his squat physique and aloof demeanour. Magdalena looked more like Ernesto, fair and slender, but without the arrogance. Her shining hair reminded him of his last glimpse of Ernesto lying in the campus grass by the river.

Patrón Pindalo, his tanned face sagging, kept his eyes fixed on the names engraved on the mausoleum, while the priest presided over the ceremony. The straight line of his dyed black hair above the collar of his jacket defined the old man's perfectionism. The one time Gabriel had met him, years ago, he'd also been immaculately groomed in pressed white pants and a blue striped shirt, monogrammed with a navy *PP* on the pocket. Gabriel had come to the Pindalo mansion begging for help and after smoking a cigar with Ernesto inside the house, he'd been walking past the pool where an *asado* was in full swing. Patrón Pindalo very publicly whacked him on the back. "The past is the past. What are you digging around here for?" The warning delivered with a patriarchal smile and a stinging blow.

The priest intoned a blessing, his purple sleeve swaying as he drew a cross in the air. Magdalena walked to the coffin and grasped the brass handle. She looked up at the adults, her blue eyes perplexed and terrified. The pallbearers stepped forward to deposit the coffin inside the vault but Magdalena wouldn't let go. Her mother stooped to pry the small hand away. Gabriel projected himself into that claustrophobic enclosure, its smelly darkness and chill. In despair, with everything unsolvable, neither love nor compassion within reach, the totality of your life regrettable and meaningless, maybe you can convince yourself there's only one way to end the suffering. Ernesto had walked into the sea to wind up in this marble cell.

The blur of black and purple moved past. A hand grabbed Gabriel's forearm. Patrón Pindalo stared with venomous eyes. The others, in a huddle, stopped and turned back, waiting. Gabriel felt the silent chorus of their blame. The past is the past, remember? The tableau remained frozen until Magdalena came back for her grandfather. "*Abuelo*, we're leaving." Patrón Pindalo took the girl's hand and they walked to the limousine, where the chauffeur opened the car door.

The vehicles drove off and Gabriel lit a cigarette, fumbling with the match. The tractor appeared and he climbed on next to Castillo. They retrieved the velvet cordons and brass stands from the Pindalo mausoleum and drove down through the field of graves.

Burials at the Cementerio Real were rarely so well-attended. But this afternoon, both sides of the gravel road were lined with parked cars, all the way down to the gates and along the avenue. Some people arrived on foot from the bus stop, others by taxi, until the crowd stretched from the arbour of bougainvillea down to the pomegranate tree flecked with splitting buds.

Alma stood on a mat of green carpeting, Xenia next to her in Sunday black, more stooped than usual but smiling. From her own hard life she knew that death brought relief and the spirit must be set free before selfish tears could fall. Alma vaguely wondered how this sea of people would squeeze into the house for Xenia's empanadas and *humitas*. The one step she'd disregarded on Hannelore's long list of instructions was to call a caterer for the after-party. Xenia had insisted on preparing the food herself, baking all weekend while Alma attended to the funeral arrangements. Most details of this day were imprinted with Hannelore's foresight, the ceremony held earlier in the narrow Franciscan chapel with music and ecumenical recitations delivered by favoured students. They read from the texts she'd taught them and some of their voices broke as they repeated how the words had carried them through times like this. But Hannelore had not foreseen the audience size, the chapel overflowing onto the street, where late arrivals stood before loudspeakers transmitting the funeral proceedings. Afterwards, the cortège to the cemetery jammed traffic the length of Reconquista.

A compact man with a felt hat manipulated a contraption of pulleys lowering the coffin into the hole carved in the ground. Hannelore, or the shell of her, dressed in blue silk saved for this occasion inside her box, as she'd called it, was covered by lilies, camellias, azaleas and magnolias. She would have appreciated the floral extravaganza, just as Padre Rubén, with his young narrow face and head of curls, must have appealed to her standards of beauty. He recited a verse by the Sufi poet Shabistari, *"Read the writing on your heart / And you will understand whatever you desire,"* authentically Hannelore with its imperative confidence.

Already, with a suddenness Alma found hard to accept, the memory of Hannelore was reverting to her pre-illness persona, the mother she'd remembered during the years of exile. Alma had been so sure that returning from the beach early Saturday morning she'd find her mother awaiting details of the party. But she'd died alone after sending Xenia to her room to get some sleep. "An ugly thing, dying," she'd said last week. "I'd much prefer to sit it out," words which Alma now translated into "So I will do that, die alone, for you." Her mother's love, complex but ultimately merciful.

The Franciscan invited her to speak. Alma turned to face the crowd, her hand clutching a page. A warm breeze rustled the paper on which she'd copied out the lines that morning. Not the whole poem but an excerpt. The mass of faces regarded her with affection, even the ones she didn't recognize. The last time she'd addressed a group this large, the audience had been expectantly seated in a lecture hall. She lifted her chin so that even those in the back would hear the lines.

> *Je m'abandonne à ce brillant espace,*
> *Sur les maisons des morts mon ombre passe*
> *Qui m'apprivoise à son frêle mouvoir....*

It didn't matter that many would not understand the French, the lines were for her mother. Hannelore would cherish the image, her shadow passing over houses of the dead as a gentle wind. And Alma knew this: if I can find beauty in this scene where so many have gathered to honour you, it is thanks to all that you taught me.

Emilio Rodriguez lifted his bow to Paganini's *Cantabile*, taught to him by Eugen, interred nearby. Such music should be heard *alfresco*, Alma decided, as the sounds seemed to glide along the cemetery grounds, up the tree trunks, through the leaves into the cloudless blue.

There was a jostling and an elderly man emerged from the gathering, leaning on his cane, his free arm cradling a loose bouquet. "*Con permiso*," he murmured and the others gave him room to pass until he reached the grave. He leaned his cane against the brass stand. Swaying dangerously close to the hole, he dropped white roses onto the floral mound, then removed his hat and placed it on his heart. Alma turned to Xenia, who whispered, "*El Professor.*"

The music played through this memorable gesture, the one that defined for Gabriel the burial of Hannelore Álvarez, just as Magdalena's hand gripping her father's coffin defined the burial of Ernesto Pindalo. Gabriel stood on a knoll, a fair distance from the grave, ready to smooth over any glitch. He guessed what all those around him were thinking, the one question everyone secretly asked themselves at a post-mortem event this well-attended. How many would come to my burial? When he harboured this thought, an image materialized at his future grave, the small group, his mother and sister with her husband and children, and Castillo, of course, all in various degrees of mourning. Gabriel knew his interment would resemble Ernesto's more than Alma's mother's. Burials were theatre of the highest order; some were one-act plays, short and stripped of only the necessary, like Ernesto's had been. Others, like this one, were Shakespearean, sometimes celebratory or even comedic, but usually tragic. The sighs he overheard today were not of relief but of authentic sadness.

Later, as the crowd drifted towards the parked cars, Gabriel waited beneath the jacaranda tree, hoping to ambush Flaco. He spotted him walking with Roma and the violinist towards a car and hurried over. "I need to talk to you. Can you stay back?"

"What is it?" Flaco asked.

"Ernesto's burial this morning...not like this." Gabriel gestured to the people walking on the gravel road.

"Why did he kill himself?"

"How do you know?"

Flaco shrugged ambiguously. "You realize the files might be worthless."

"He killed himself for nothing? That's..." Gabriel stammered, searching for the words.

"Where's Lalo Martín supposed to say he got them from?" Flaco noticed Alma walking towards them and went to embrace her.

Gabriel wished she'd come over to embrace him, although nobody ever lingered to embrace a cemetery administrator. He'd observed Alma at the party, surreptitiously he'd thought, until Roma elbowed him. "Stop staring, Gabi. You'll freak her out." But he was grateful that Alma had invited him to her house. After two burials, a strong drink and company were preferable to waiting alone in his apartment for the next disaster.

Still wearing her sleeveless black dress, Alma sat in the courtyard and stared into the night sky, too tired to contemplate moving. Xenia, also spent, had gone to bed, leaving every glass and plate to be washed in the morning. It seemed as if hundreds had come, many staying for hours. Hannelore's students, their parents, all the musicians from the OSL, neighbours and friends, as well as acquaintances, nurses who had treated her mother at the clinic, shopkeepers who'd served her in their stores, the dentist's receptionist, strangers compelled to share anecdotes and praise for her mother. Flaco and Roma had helped to deflect some of the well-meaning mourners. Hannelore would have laughed, "So typical of Luscano, they arrive late in droves and never leave."

The day circled in Alma's thoughts, a spin of conversations and scenes, the ceremonies at the chapel and the cemetery. "You'll thank me," Hannelore had said, handing over her instructions a few days ago. She'd been right about everything, even the insistence, underlined three times, No eulogy! At some point she'd said, "I hate those summing-ups. Whitewashes or thrashings, they never truly represent the deceased." Although she'd spared Alma the struggle of creating an appropriate text that would capture Hannelore's essence, the impulse to record something remained. The few lines from Valéry were not enough.

Hannelore's life had been interesting but not easy. The child of immigrants in Argentina, exiled again during the Perón years, she'd observed Luscano with an outsider's objective eye while participating in its essence, the music and art. What was it about Hannelore that inspired so many to come today? She'd been controversial and critical, but rather than taking offence, many had spoken of her authenticity and grace. For Alma, it was her mother's courage that stood out, even during the last days of her life, as she railed against her imminent death. The same courage Flaco was counting on Alma having when he'd implored her to testify. That was the lifelong burden of being her mother's daughter: not living up to expectations. Flaco hadn't mentioned it again, but his eyes when he looked at her conveyed a pleading. He probably wasn't aware of it himself, carefully avoiding the subject at his birthday party and again today. Alma could feel it and, for the sake of their friendship, would have to find the right words to explain how deeply she'd interred the horrors of La Cuarenta.

The lights of a jet crossed the sky heading south towards Uruguay. All her plans when she'd first arrived, of going to Montevideo to research Delmira Agustini, of writing about the poet and her works, were diverted, first by her mother's illness and, now, the daughterly duties that lay ahead — visiting the notary, closing bank accounts, notifying authorities. Her northern home seemed distant and fictional, trading places in her imagination with this reality. Luscano had ensnared her faster and more tightly than she'd anticipated.

Part II

Love, the night was tragic and sobbing
When your golden key sang in my lock...

From "The Intruder" by Delmira Agustini,
El libro blanco (1907)

10

Certain lives, especially those of the feisty, the resisters, are best understood played out backwards. Begin with death, then follow the life as it coils, turning into itself, repeating and developing, complications giving way to clarity.

Amor y muerte

A winter day in Uruguay, a small country often considered dull by its neighbours, yields a windfall for the tabloids. Reporters work through the night and the capital wakes up to the headline, "Love and death! The ideal couple dead!"

El Día spares no details. A front-page photo displays the poet lying in a pool of blood. She, murdered at twenty-seven and he, shot by his own hand at thirty. A tragic finale to the Reyes-Agustini love story. The pages of details thrill Montevideo out of its stodgy complacency.

What was she wearing?

A silk slip, can you imagine, in blue so pale that in the photograph it looks white and the blood black.

Had they, you know, before?

She was wearing nothing else.

Whispers behind gloved hands, while to the bereaved family, respectful silence or murmured condolences.

No one asks, who loved her and whom did she really love? No one asks, how could this creative force have lived among us and suffered without any of us knowing?

She was beautiful, they agree, and gifted. All those languages, an autodidact who recited Verlaine and Baudelaire from memory, painted watercolours and acted in plays. A charmed life, an established family, success. A poet with three books published to critical acclaim, a prominent player in literary circles whose works were praised by the great Rubén Darío.

Her wedding to Enrique Job Reyes had been celebrated by the elite of Montevideo. Why did she divorce him, then secretly meet with him? And why did he kill her? Don't they know that given the opportunity, people choose the moment of their death? Usually night or early morning, the fewer witnesses the better. The sacred act requires privacy and a perfect alignment of stars. As for why, don't they know it's possible to die of sadness?

¡Prudencia!

The voices of her relatives mingle with the buzzing of cicadas. In the Uruguayan countryside, she sits at a long table in the shade of an ancient *palo borracho*. A raven circles the tree. Lush vegetation droops with humidity. A sprig of yellow flowers falls onto the spongy grass. *Muchachas* come and go, bringing salads and pitchers of lemon slices floating in ice water. Delmira catalogues the images.

Here in Villa Maria, the Agustini summer home in Sayago, she partakes of this Christmas Day tradition, an obligatory midday meal in the garden. Like most Uruguayan families of their class, the Agustinis summer outside the city for relief from the stifling heat. Delmira, more observer than participant, performs her role perfunctorily. The dutiful daughter smiles at her father, agrees with her mother, appears to listen to her brother's insipid monologue, his face as red as the cabernet in his goblet. Estrangement has her fluctuating between reality and fantasy.

Smoke drifts from the brick chimney across the terraced lawn. A shirtless *asador* attends to the barbecue. The muscles of his back contract as he prods the burning wood with a branding iron. Flor appears from the kitchen and crosses the lawn, her black braid swinging across her shadow. The *muchacha* hands the *asador* a glass of water, which he lifts to his lips, tendons working his brown neck as he swallows. The man returns the glass with a quick word, something provocative that elicits a smile. Flor glances up at her employers seated around the table and hurries back to the kitchen.

After the coffee is served, Delmira rises. She kisses her father good-bye and, ignoring her mother's admonitions, makes for the house to prepare her escape.

As the carriage pulls out of the corridor of cypress trees, the rain pelts down in one of those sudden subtropical drenchings. The downpour makes muddy trenches of the road. The coachman whips the hindquarters of the horses. Inside the carriage, Delmira empathizes with the beasts, their struggle to plod through sheets of rain, to endure the *tierra* and its inhabitants. In this heat, she's wearing an ankle-length dress, a corset, garters, stockings, shoes, gloves and a hat. Only the skin of her face and throat is free. Queasy from the heavy food, she considers unfastening the bindings and frills, dares only to unbutton her gloves, remove the hat and lift the crinoline to her knees. She turns to Flor, who's staring at the line of *ombú* trees along the road, guarding the fields like warriors. "What's his name?"

"Who?" But Flor can't pretend for long, not with her beloved Nena. "Amado."

Delmira laughs. "Is he true to his name?"

"He's a man, that's all I know." Flor closes her eyes, exhausted from serving the family through the fiestas. Her head falls against the velour seat cover and she folds her sturdy hands in her lap.

Flor's head rolls until it leans against Delmira's shoulder for the rest of the bone-jolting journey into Montevideo. Delmira doesn't mind the intimacy. It is Flor who taught her the facts of life, it is her daring that Delmira draws on to take the steps to file for divorce. But lately even Flor has warned, *¡prudencia!* Convention limits the immunity Delmira can draw around herself.

Imagine existing as a free spirit in the wrong time, an exile in your own country.

Venganza de sangre

Seven months later, Delmira Agustini lies dead on the floor next to the killer in his underclothes, their blood commingling on the floor.

Just after six in the evening, Germán da Costa, the only other resident in the house at the time, is in his room reading when he hears four gunshots. He runs out of the house and returns with two policemen who break down the door of the room off the hallway. Germán da Costa identifies the man with the revolver in his hand as his friend, Enrique Job Reyes. He's murmuring, "Delmira, Delmira." An ambulance transports him to Hospital Maciel where he dies that night.

Uruguay's celebrated poet is pronounced dead immediately. In the rented room, the policemen establish that two bullets struck her — the first by the ear with an exit wound, the second lodged in the left side of her skull. A projectile embedded in the bloodied wall by a framed photograph of Delmira indicates that the killer's first attempt at shooting himself went wild.

Delmira's father arrives by carriage and arranges for her body to be transported to the Agustini residence along with her blood-splattered belongings — the dress, velvet hat and small leather purse.

Mística, asexual

Delmira Agustini lies covered in black silk inside an open coffin the day after the murder. Visitors enter the bewildered hush of the family home with bouquets of *junquillos* and *azucenas*. A journalist from *La Razón* reports that the poet's mouth appears mystical, asexual, unlike, he's insinuating, her poetry or the death scene.

The mother clutches a rosary, her thighs overflowing the narrow seat of her chair. Her life's work dead, murdered by that low-life horse-trader. Señora Agustini, half German, half Argentine, who home-schooled her daughter, nurturing her talents, guiding her morality, cannot fathom how this tragedy has befallen her. What can be worse than outliving your child?

The father hovers behind her, shaking hands with the well-wishers. He's afraid of his wife and his son, Delmira's older brother, their only child now. Antonio Luciano Agustini paces the living room. He is livid with anger at his sister, discerns the innuendo in the whisperings, the interviews and photographs, the morbid curiosity drawing strangers to the living room. In a few days, revenge has him packing her things into trunks. All her manuscripts and papers, her paintings and the infamous doll, mascot of the fake infantilism of her life at home, will be transported to Villa Maria and stored in the basement for forty years. Antonio will spend the rest of his life disavowing his sister and her scandalous behaviour.

During the solemn *velatorio* in the living room, no one notices Flor in the kitchen. Grief for La Nena wells from her core as she arranges the lilies in the family's crystal. Stem by stem, the flowers are trapped inside the vase and she weeps for the woman she raised, for the poet who read her the early drafts of her work. Flor, the only person in the household unable to read the poems, is the only one who understood them.

Later, she climbs the stairs to help Señora Agustini dress for the cortège to the cemetery. From the bedroom, the women hear a commotion outside on Calle San José. They look out the window onto the procession of carriages and cars, the horse-drawn hearse with the coffin of Enrique Job Reyes proceeding slowly towards the Cementerio Central. Flor heaves the window open and screams, *¡Asesino!*

At four in the afternoon, Delmira's coffin is brought to the same cemetery as her ex-husband's. The poet herself was not religious, but her mother's piety is unquestioned. As the priest delivers the benediction, the writers of Montevideo huddle together, silently reviewing their assumptions about her. The separation from Reyes so soon after the wedding led them to understand she never loved the man. Now it emerges she's been meeting him in secret for months. These writers remain silent, claim they're too shocked to deliver any words.

The poet is spared a summing up, the predictable chronology with its absurd avoidance of the word "dead." A eulogy says: this person was born on this date in this place, had this sort of childhood enhanced with memorable anecdotes, married this man, accomplished these things. None of it captures a person's essence. What scars did she carry and what brought her to this specific death? Priests dissuade, even prohibit, the delivery of eulogies during funeral masses, aware that the most interesting depths of the dead are controversial and their secrets, blasphemous.

The cemetery employees deliver the coffin to the morgue, laying it down next to Reyes's. Two years will pass before she's buried in the family tomb, plot 311. In 1992 her remains are relocated to the Panteón Nacional in an official ceremony.

La leona

For decades following her death, tributes are published by authors whose motives are suspect. Are they cashing in on her fame to benefit their flagging careers? Or perhaps it takes time to make sense of an unusually violent death.

In 1924, an Uruguayan writer reveals "How I knew Delmira Agustini." In the article, Alberto Zum Felde quotes from the poet's letters. "I feel so alone and isolated," she wrote to him after he'd published a favourable review of her book. "Please come to visit me." He finds her sitting on a sofa under a mirror. Long hair, small hands with rings on every finger, she's wearing a pale silk dress. The mother chaperones from a chair in a corner of the living room. Zum Felde is transfixed by the poet's beauty, revels in her purity, cannot fathom how this girl is capable of the eroticism in her poems. When he leaves, the mother accompanies him to the door. Delmira, she confides, is damaged by a crisis of sensitivity and tormented by her poetry. Zum Felde sees the poet as a beautiful lioness imprisoned in a domestic jail.

A childhood friend reminisces in *La Revue Mondiale* in Paris. André Giot de Badet remembers Delmira sitting under an *ombú* tree practising French with him in the countryside. They commuted together in the *ferrocarril* to Montevideo where Delmira attended piano and painting lessons. De Badet maintains his disbelief in her tragic death although he left for France well before the poet married. Half of his memories are later discredited as inaccurate.

Every decade, new recollections and opinions emerge. Delmira Agustini was a lyrical genius. She possessed a singular violence or a savage happiness, her poetry seeping into biography. In 1967, Zum Felde is again compelled to defend her chastity, writing that her eroticism was pure myth, a poetic invention. She was chaste, he swears, living in the protection of her parents' guardianship.

People cling to what they want to believe. Their memories reveal more about themselves than the deceased.

Acto mágico

Every day Delmira would write in her room until late afternoon. Then she would bring her poems to her father. In the evenings he would transcribe her disorderly script into his neat handwriting. From the first poem published in 1905 when Delmira was nineteen years old, Señor Agustini copied her lines of anguish, eroticism and imagined sexuality. So complete was his respect for his daughter's vocation, the man never commented on her poems, blind to their audacity, oblivious to their collision with the morals of his puritan world and his wife's strict piety.

It is the writer's curse to be judged on the printed word, phrases or stanzas imagined at some fixed point in time. The poet moves on, yet the words stick like filaments of a web. She's elsewhere weaving a new creation and giant hands conspire to move her back, defining her according to the arduous moments in which she created a universe. She wrote this. It must be her.

Throughout her life, Delmira repels this curse by maintaining she writes in a trance, that her poems emerge by sleight of hand in an act of magic. The writers and critics in her circle never probe her claims of sleights of hand and self-described magic. Delmira chose to propagate rather than dispel the systemic refusal to recognize that the painful process of revising and editing is intrinsic to artistic integrity.

The poet's self-propagated myth is finally unmasked in 1950. After the brother's death, his wife sells Villa Maria. The new owner discovers the trunks of Delmira's possessions and papers and donates them to a cultural institute in Montevideo. Researchers unearth the letters, manuscripts and lucid improvisations written on any available paper: sheet music, notebooks, envelopes and inside books. These scraps reveal the meticulous revisions Delmira made to her poems, the iterations and repetitions preceding the published works. This is the paper trail of truth.

Bello gesto de libertad

And the letters discovered in the trunks! Love and seduction playing
out in her correspondence. Letters from the poet's heart composed
after an intense day of writing.

Flor brings her tea and rests on the bed as they talk. Delmira
has seen the men entering or leaving the *muchacha*'s room when
the parents are in the country. Flor willingly satisfies her curiosity,
tells of the touch of a man, when it feels right, when all the senses
engage towards the ecstatic shiver of satisfaction. Delmira reads
her drafts of the poems and Flor nods, says, "Yes, Nena, that's
how love is, all those things and maybe more. You'll find out soon
enough."

After Flor leaves, Delmira sits down at her desk beneath
the sloped ceiling of her room. She composes letters, quickly in
succession, as if stringing beads to establish the long connections
that will become her legacy to literary history, the correspondence
with critics and writers in Latin America.

Manuel Ugarte, what did she see in him? It began on his side
with a 1912 letter in which he compliments her books. "You are
an exceptional talent," he writes. Maybe she can be forgiven for
falling for his flattery. Manuel Ugarte, the literary Don Juan of
Buenos Aires, is known for seducing with his looks and words.
Much later, he befriends the Argentine poet Alfonsina Storni, who
ends her life by walking into the sea. Perhaps Ugarte has that effect
on women; perhaps he stirs a suicidal impulse. Nothing wounds a
serious writer more than witnessing the success of a dilettante.

After a few letters, Ugarte shows up in Montevideo and
meets Delmira in visits supervised by her mother. These are
chaste discussions on the sofa in the living room. Delmira plays
the piano for him. Meanwhile, in the background, Enrique Job
Reyes is courting the poet. When she finally accepts the horse-
trader's proposal to marry, Ugarte does not have the wisdom to
withdraw. He hangs around Montevideo and attends the wedding
on August 14, 1913 at the Agustini residence. The celebration is,
by all accounts, a disaster.

Guests mingle, drinking champagne while a quartet plays in the living room filled with flowers arranged in vases by Flor, lavish bouquets of winter roses and ferns. At some point during the celebration, Ugarte ambushes Delmira in an alcove by the kitchen. Something happens, one kiss or more, enough to throw her off. That night, in her new home, she cannot consummate the marriage. Unaware of Ugarte's effect on his new bride, Reyes blames the mother and her repugnant advice, claiming in a later letter she warned Delmira not to bear his child, not to let him touch her.

Ugarte returns to his debonair life in Buenos Aires but Delmira can't leave him alone. "You tormented my wedding night and honeymoon," she writes. "I can never say how much I suffered...your spirit so close to me among all those people...I am deeply wounded." He replies with a formal letter, disregarding her passion, unwilling to acknowledge his obvious efforts to thwart her marriage. But in 1914, less than one year after the wedding, Ugarte reads of the Reyes-Agustini divorce in the newspaper and sends her a note. "Congratulations on your heroic deed of liberation." Delmira replies, admitting the cost of the divorce to her spirits, and begs him to visit her. Ugarte maintains that his work requires him to remain in Buenos Aires. When Delmira sends him "Serpentina," he replies with a poem of his own, insipidly infantile. Delmira's poem will be published in a posthumous collection. No one reads Ugarte anymore.

La inmensa ansiedad

Of all her letters, the correspondence with Rubén Darío stands out for its pure exaltation. In the 1890s, when Delmira is beginning to write, the Nicaraguan poet is in Paris cavorting with Verlaine and the symbolists. *Modernismo* is catching fire in Latin American letters, lit by Darío's commitment to denounce obscurity, embrace the cosmopolitan, celebrate language as spoken in his hemisphere.

Delmira's early poems draw from Darío's verses. She too poeticizes the supernatural, leans on mythology and idolizes the grotesque. And, like him, she writes of the swan, overused symbol of poets, particularly the *modernistas*. But doubt of Delmira's agility and brilliance as a poet is laid to rest in her handling of the symbol. In her poem "The Swan," the "soul of the lake," the "candid and solemn bird has a wicked charm."

For Darío, the swan is an emblem of beauty. In one of his poems, more heavy-handed than deft, the swan's neck takes on the form of a question mark. His overreliance on the symbol prompted another *modernista*, a Mexican, to attack the Nicaraguan in his poem: "Wring the swan's neck who with deceiving plumage / inscribes his whiteness on the azure stream; / he merely vaunts his grace and nothing feels / of nature's voice or the soul of things." This provocation by Enrique González Martínez, translated by Samuel Beckett, appeared in a 1958 anthology edited by Octavio Paz. By that time, the *modernistas* had been succeeded by the *vanguardistas*, *creacionistas* and *post-modernistas*.

But at twenty-six, Delmira's admiration for Rubén Darío is unreserved. She records that her greatest happiness is the day in 1912 in Montevideo when she meets the forty-five-year-old poet on his book tour. And gift of all gifts, he agrees to write introductory words of praise for her third book, published just before her wedding. In the last collection of poems before her death, Darío proclaims, "Of all the women writing verse today, no one has impressed me like Delmira Agustini for her unveiled soul and her floral heart…. If this beautiful girl continues in the lyrical revelation of her spirit as she has done so far, she will astonish our world of Spanish language….she says exquisite things that have never been said. May glory, love and happiness be with her." How can she not recoil at his sexism, the condescension of his words? Or has she become immune to this treatment by her mostly male colleagues?

When Darío travels on to Buenos Aires, Delmira can't resist firing off a letter. Crossing professional boundaries, she confesses her torment. "I have reached a moment of calm today in this eternal, painful exaltation and these are my saddest hours. I don't know if you've ever looked insanity in the face and fought the anguished loneliness of a hermetic spirit…the anxiety, the immense anxiety."

"*Tranquilidad,*" Darío advises. "Believe in destiny above all else. To live, to live, to have the obligation of happiness." The poems in her book, he says, are "*muy bello*" but urges more sincerity, signing his letter *El Confesor.*

Delmira's response is immediate. She exalts his verses, crowns him king of poets, "god of *El Arte.*" Then she plays the next card in her epistolary game. "My letter should be secret. Do not write back. Surprise me. I will wait. Let it be spontaneous." The master is travelling extensively, busy transforming Latin American poetry and nurturing his hemispheric dreams. Finally Delmira breaks down and sends him some new poems. He responds with detached encouragement. "Be optimistic, Delmira, and receive your destiny smiling." The patronizing tone of his letter must have scalded her soul.

Tanta vulgaridad

Unlike the crafted epistles to Darío, the words she writes her future husband are silly and childish. "*Yo tiero*"...I wove you. Her letters to Enrique Job Reyes expose the enigma of her dual personality.

Reyes is not her first boyfriend. She meets him in 1908, probably through mutual friends. Montevideo is small and the bourgeoisie's circle is tight. In between chaperoned visits with Delmira, he spends his days at auctions, his nights drinking and playing cards with other horse-traders. Their courtship lasts five years before they marry. All along they're seen as the ideal couple with love, money and glory.

After the wedding, they move into a house on Calle Canelones. A love nest with new furniture, the house should represent a new start at a safe distance from interfering families. But it unravels quickly. One month and twenty-one days after her marriage, Delmira returns to her parents. "I cannot take so much vulgarity," she famously declares. Montevideo gasps at her audacity.

What happened? Delmira is a young twenty-six-year-old, accustomed to a disciplined routine around which her family and Flor revolve. Enrique Job cruises the town, brings his cohorts home for games of cards. They drink whisky and smoke cigars, make lewd jokes and take no interest in the needs of the precocious poet in their midst. There's also this: shortly before the wedding, Delmira's third and most important book is published. *The Empty Chalices,* with a short prologue by Rubén Darío, includes twenty-one new poems of shocking eroticism. "To Eros," "Your Mouth," "Oh You!"...the titles and verses glow with desire and sexuality. During the intense period preceding the wedding, Enrique Job probably never got around to reading the book and when he does, he's shocked. The lovers in Delmira's poems do not resemble him at all.

His fury escalates when she leaves him. A *caballero* of the old school, where appearances count for everything, he adheres to Uruguay's machismo. Angry letters accuse Delmira of staining his honour. In the Iberian cult of tradition, this is a valid motive for murder.

Enrique Job sells the furniture and rents a furnished room in a house on Calle Andes where his friend Germán da Costa is living. Around the mirror in his room, Enrique Job hangs portraits of Delmira and her many drawings and paintings. In a ranting letter, he claims to have always behaved like a gentleman, refers to a night before the wedding when she wanted to make love and he refused to do so out of wedlock. He takes on his mother-in-law, whose "repugnant advice" created Delmira's terror and panic the night of the wedding. "Your mother is hateful," he says, the first pass in a duel, a glove thrown to the ground.

Señora Agustini's influence, her tutelage and authoritative devotion are no match for the husband. At home again, Delmira submits to her mother's care. The woman tends to her daughter's shattered nerves, indulges her with unconditional love and, along with Flor, steers her back into the family fold. Delmira resumes her routine, writing intensively by day, corresponding and flirting with men she meets in Montevideo. She also takes advantage of her provincial country's one progressive law. Back in 1907, almost a century before divorce is legalized in Argentina, Chile and Luscano, the parliament of Uruguay enacts legislation allowing divorce. Delmira initiates legal proceedings and newspapers report on her impending divorce.

During the nine months between their separation and deaths, Enrique Job Reyes is tormented by jealousy and passion. Nights, he is seen raging outside her home. His sister blames Delmira for trying to make a lover out of a husband.

Twice a week until her death, Delmira secretly visits Enrique Job in his rented room. Amid the speculation as to why she continues to see her ex, defenders of her will to live swear she was merely trying to get him to sign the divorce papers.

Doble personalidad

Was her death the result of a suicide pact? According to his friends, Enrique Job Reyes is crazed with anger. He possesses a gun. The tickets to Buenos Aires found in his nightstand might be a decoy, a planted distraction, or a final effort to save them. He is consumed. If he cannot possess her, he will kill her to silence the gossip, put an end to the embarrassing poetry, save his family and his reputation from further stain. And destroy the mother.

At dusk on July 6, 1914, Delmira Agustini leaves her parents' house. In one hand, she is holding an umbrella against the winter rain. In the other she carries a purse with a hand mirror and an unsent letter addressed to the editor of a periodical in Buenos Aires. She apologizes for her silence. "I've been ill," she writes and promises to collaborate with his magazine in the future.

Her spirits have been drawn and quartered by the pull of her husband on one side, her mother on the other. Abandoned by all those she respects, the lovers and mentors who dismiss and patronize her, and suffocated by the unbearable burden of existence, she knocks on the door to 1206 Calle Andes...

11

Xenia staggered into the courtyard with an armload of blankets and towels. Alma closed her laptop. "Let me help!" Hannelore had been so stubborn Alma had never realized how single-minded Xenia could be. She refused to allow Alma to throw out any of her mother's belongings, insisted on airing them out before packing them in suitcases. Yesterday they'd gone to the station to purchase the bus ticket to Todos Santos and the agent had emphasized the two-suitcase limit per traveller, particularly in Xenia's case. Her journey involved several stops and transfers, first in Asunción, then, after crossing the border into Bolivia, in Sucre and Cochabamba. Alma took the largest blankets and spread them over the table and chairs while working to convince Xenia to send the bedding by mail.

The overhead sun was searing and Alma's eyes burned from the effort of typing and squinting at the little screen. She wasn't sure about what she was writing, the work hadn't taken form yet, but Alma hoped that in the creating of it, she'd find out. It was a struggle to restrain the years of academic training and let the poet's story emerge as confession more than reportage. But now that over a month had passed since her mother's death, it seemed essential to be reclaiming a daily rhythm of work.

After carefully arranging Hannelore's best blanket over one of the wicker chairs, Xenia sat down on the stoop to the kitchen. "What are you going to do with this place, *m'hija*?"

"I have until Christmas to figure it out." Before returning to Montréal, she'd have to sell or rent the house.

"You should keep it. There are no houses like this one in Todos Santos."

"I can't afford to keep the house and my apartment in Canada."

Xenia pointed at the stacks of books and notes next to the laptop. "Work hard, write your book, you'll be able to keep the house. That's what your mother would say."

Alma went to sit by Xenia's side just to feel the strength of her and smell her scent of sweet grasses. She'd miss Xenia, her resilience and clarity, but most of all her intuition. Alma told her of the poet and her enigmatic death.

When Xenia heard of the murder in the small rented room, she placed her hand on her heart. "It's because she didn't have children. Or maybe she was pregnant and desperate. When I was pregnant, I was not myself. Already in mourning, as if I knew my children were not for this world, that I was just their temporary coffin."

Alma had read of a theory somewhere that Delmira Agustini had miscarried in the months before her death and that this loss had shattered her completely. But it was only conjecture.

"Each time I lost my baby, I became mad," Xenia said. "*La Loquita*, they called me. I had to leave Todos Santos to recover my mind. I chose life in the end because who else would pray for and remember my babies and my husband?" She placed her sturdy hand on Alma's knee. "You know, *m'hija*, when you came home that night, I was very worried you'd choose not to live."

The day of her release from La Cuarenta, Alma had been gripped with a feverish energy. She'd locked herself in the bathroom, drawn a hot bath and scrubbed her skin with a rough sponge. Soaping and scrubbing her body, stepping out of the grimy water, draining it from the bathtub, running water again and again until the hot water tank was depleted. And her mother knocking, threatening to break down the door. Alma had asked for Xenia. When she saw the infected burn on her shoulder, Xenia opened a towel, patted her down, found an antibiotic salve, talking to her quietly, murmuring "*m'hija*" with such calm and resolve, Alma had been able to dress, eat and pack her things before her father drove her to the airport.

"When I saw how you packed your suitcase, when I heard the anger in your voice, I knew you'd be all right. If your poet had found her anger maybe she would not have allowed this man to kill her."

It was true. There was little rage even in Agustini's most passionate poems. The letters where she'd shared her deepest thoughts showed profound distress but not rage. Alma thought of her own anger. Inside the prison, fear had suffocated anger, but once released, she'd become indignantly angry. For lack of a specific target, she'd been angry at all of Luscano. Her anger was made even more potent by guilt that she'd survived while others had been tortured to death. This kind of rage, unexpressed, could engender the most despicable thoughts and lead a person to question the value of living.

In the afternoon, Alma packed up the blankets into parcels and took a taxi to the post office. She lugged the packages up the marble stairs of the colonial building and waited in a long, disordered lineup. Above her, on the domed ceiling encircled with gold leaf, cherubs floated in a garishly blue sky, some failed Iberian painter's rendition of Renaissance art.

Finally, she made it to a wicket and hoisted the parcels onto the counter. "Bolivia?" the woman asked. "No, no, you have to come back on Monday. We're closing now and it takes time to complete the forms for Customs."

"They're just some old blankets."

"A gift?"

"You see, my mother died and we —"

The woman grabbed and squeezed Alma's hand. "I'll see what I can do." Soon enough, the parcels were stamped and dropped into overseas' bins.

Alma left the post office just as the guards were locking the entrance. She walked across the Plaza Federal, reflecting on the random kindness she'd encountered since her mother died. Almost every time she faced an official behind a desk to obtain the certifications, annulments and other official documents she needed in connection with Hannelore's death, she'd been offered coffee, handed tissues, embraced and consoled. "How hard it is to lose your mother," strangers would say. "Mine died two years ago and I'm still devastated." While Alma tried to steer the discussion back to the purpose of her visit, the person would go on and on until they either botched the work or redirected her elsewhere. Still, the humanity she encountered transcended systemic incompetence.

Alma approached the bookstore and peered into the sooty window of La Librería Internacional. A few customers browsed in the narrow aisles and further back, Roma stood behind the counter. She hurried to greet her at the door, slinging her arm over Alma's shoulder. "Gabriel Seil's back there, morose as ever," she whispered. "Help cheer him up, will you?"

Gabriel struggled to rise from a low plastic chair. Alma kissed him on one cheek, then went for the second, not yet cured of Montréal's double kiss. "Sorry," he mumbled, after their heads collided. In jeans and sneakers, the only trace of his cemetery persona was the colour of his T-shirt, jet black and logoless.

The high shelves were jammed with books, no signs of the candles and cards taking over Canadian bookstores. It was as a bookstore should be, Alma thought, the hallowed domain of books and books alone.

Roma dragged a chair from behind a frayed green curtain and left to make coffee. "Gabriel, you handle the cash." He sat on a stool behind the counter loaded with an antique cash register, a rotary telephone and baskets of receipts.

Gabriel rubbed his hands over his knees. He did not make conversing easy.

"Do you miss this place?" Alma asked.

Roma stuck her head out from behind the curtain. "Of course he does. Why else would be come here all the time?"

"To buy books?" Gabriel laughed in a quick exhalation.

Alma asked him how he wound up working at a cemetery.

"The fellow I replaced was an acquaintance. When he decided to leave, I applied for the job. It's been interesting at times, a magnifying glass on Luscano. My boss is tough but thankfully absent." Then he spoke of a man he worked with, how much he'd learned from him. "I'd be dead without Castillo." That strange laugh again.

Roma brought espresso cups on a little tray. "I need the caffeine. We played at the club last night. It went on late. You've got

to come and hear us play, Alma." They drank the gritty coffee while
Roma told Gabriel stories about her escapades with Alma during
high school. Customers came and went, Roma ringing up their sales
or answering questions. There was no computer in the store but she
seemed to know of all the books, their publishers and authors, and
their precise location on the shelves.

At one point she showed off the new tattoo on her ankle,
a drum she'd designed herself, and tried to convince Gabriel he
needed something, a piercing or a tattoo. "You're too drab." He
writhed and blushed.

Before Alma could defend him, Roma asked, "What's up for
you after Xenia leaves?"

"I'm used to living alone and —"

"You're going back after Christmas, aren't you?"

Flaco must have told her. "I'm just dealing with everything step
by step. See Xenia off, work on my book, then I'll —"

"You can't sell that place, Alma. Why don't we come live with
you? Pool our resources. You could rent out the rooms. I'd love to live
near the beach. Better than the dive I'm in now. I pay rent in dollars,
get paid in pesos. I'm always broke. So's Gabriel. I bet he'd be in."

He mumbled something like, "Barrio Norte, bastion of the
bourgeoisie."

"You mean the oligarchy. It's not the same thing. You're about
as bourgeois as they come, Gabriel. Alma's street is on the border, no
mansions to be found, just middle-class homes. We could make it a
collective. Take turns cooking, grow a garden in the courtyard, have
literary soirées. You could write your book, Alma, while everyone's
at work."

"Literary soirées?" Gabriel asked. "Like readings?"

"Poetry and taiko drums. A double billing, out in the courtyard
where your mother staged our plays, Roma and Alma live from
Luscano, remember?"

"Really, Roma, I need some time on my own."

"You've had too much time on your own."

A customer approached the counter, asking for a certain
blockbuster, one of those American thrillers published in quickly

rendered translations. Alma tensed at the nasal voice, the cropped hair. Memory couldn't find a match for the jowly double chin and bloodshot eyes, but twelve years had passed and he might have aged this badly.

When he left the bookstore, Alma grabbed her purse and said her good-byes. She slipped into the sidewalk stream of pedestrians hurrying to pick up all that they needed before the stores closed. The man's height kept him visible, as did the purple and yellow stripes of his polo shirt. Alma followed him down Calle Florida and into a shopping galleria, where he entered a *tabaquería*.

Through the window Alma observed him purchase a box of cigars. He slipped it into the bag with his book, pulled a money clip out of his pocket and threw down some pesos. More than his purchase, the arrogance of his gesture, that demeaning toss of money at the clerk, convinced her.

When he left the shop and returned to the street, Alma followed until he entered a restaurant and took a stool by the counter. She paced the sidewalk, watching him through the windows. He removed the book from the bag and slouched over the counter to read. A carafe of wine and a plate of pizza were brought to him. He put down the book and sliced through the cheese and tomato sauce with sawing incisions. He ate, wiping the grease off his chin with his hand. Behind him, small tables were occupied by older men, smoking, drinking and talking football or politics. She could hear their voices when they argued but he did not turn around or engage with them.

The streetlights came on. Xenia was waiting at home. But now that Alma had found him, she couldn't leave. The bar's lighting showed the sallow skin of a cigar smoker, thinning hair, the polo shirt tucked into light khaki pants. His paunch bulged over a leather belt, his legs pressed against the counter and on his feet, dusty loafers. She remembered the revolver he'd carried in a holster around his waist. If he had a weapon now, it was concealed, strapped to his leg or under his shirt. Someone jostled her shoulder. Alma held her purse close. A kid tried to sell her a newspaper, lottery tickets, ballpoint pens.

The man stood up, dropped two bills on the counter and made for the door. In the brief halo of light by the entrance, Alma saw the mole on his high forehead and she was absolutely sure. She turned her back, stepped into a doorway and waited until he'd continued down the street.

The wine did not affect his gait. Between the intermittent streetlights, his black hair and brown skin blended into the shadows. He turned down a narrow alley. Alma hesitated. There were bins of garbage. A stray dog sniffed the gutter. The alley led towards the *villa miseria* by the river. If he lived in the shantytown, there would be some satisfaction in knowing the former officer had paid for his cruelty with poverty.

She followed him, walking as quietly as she could, holding her breath against the stench of garbage. He turned onto a wider street with rows of low adobe houses. Halfway down the block, he passed through the gates of one of those houses and she heard a screech, "Papa!" He gathered a tricycle and went inside. The curtains were drawn on the window and she lost sight of him. Alma walked by, noting the number. At the corner, a light dangled over the street sign, Calle Libertad.

When she came home, Xenia was waiting with dinner. Alma opened a bottle of wine. She wanted to tell Xenia but couldn't let him poison their farewell dinner.

Flaco double-parked on the crowded street and lifted the suitcases onto the sidewalk, whistling for a porter among the boys sitting on their trolleys. He removed a piece of paper from his pocket and handed it to Xenia. "My sister's phone number in Sucre. She works for the Bolivian government. If you need anything, have someone call her."

Xenia nodded and put the paper in her purse.

"I'm going to miss your *humitas*," he said.

"Alma will make them for you. Señor Flaco, you'll watch over her?"

"Of course." He stooped to embrace her. "You know," he said looking over his shoulder at Alma, "I've never been to Cochabamba. Maybe we'll take a road trip, Alma and I."

"We're going to drive into the Andes in that jalopy?" Alma laughed, but she was moved by his attachment to Xenia. Flaco had insisted on driving them to the bus station even though he was teaching a class in a few minutes.

"La Vieja could make it to Todos Santos, couldn't she?"

"*Si Dios quiere.*" Xenia reached for his hand. "Be careful, the x on your lifeline, that's the shadow of a condor." She blew on his palm, blessing him.

Alma took Xenia's hand and they followed the porter into the terminal. It reeked of urine, tobacco and rotting food. They plunged through the turmoil of hawkers and passengers until they reached the loading dock for the bus to Paraguay. The porter put down the baggage of scratchy Argentine cowhide, the same suitcases her parents had brought with them to Luscano over forty years ago.

Couples with babies in their arms lined up alongside workers heading to the mines and soldiers in fatigues. Three elderly women waited near the front. "Try to sit next to one of them," Alma whispered. "And no matter what, don't let go of your purse." Inside the lining of her sturdy handbag, Xenia had hidden the three thousand U.S. dollars bequeathed to her by Hannelore.

As they stood waiting for the bus to begin loading, Alma tried to memorize every detail of Xenia. She wore her Sunday black, a woollen cardigan covered with Hannelore's pink mohair shawl, her silvery braid lying neatly along her spine. How she'd manage the trip with these heavy suitcases was beyond Alma's imagination. She'd tried to convince her to fly to Sucre before continuing on the bus north through Cochabamba. "In the sky like the birds? No, *m'hija*, I want to feel the ground with my feet."

Xenia's bus would drive west for a day before stopping in Asunción. Flaco had reminded Alma of the tensions between Luscano and its neighbours. "Paraguay once placed landmines in the region. It's pathetic, arguing over a hillside of tangled forest." These were turbulent times in Bolivia. Xenia swore allegiance to the country's emerging leader, a former coca grower. "One of us," she'd repeated last night. "He'll be president one day. Remember, the universe can be just, but it takes a very long time." Alma didn't have the heart to explain how many Bolivians, especially the oligarchs in Santa Cruz, opposed Evo Morales for his skin colour and lineage.

The crowd grew into a squirming mass. Alma held onto Xenia's arm. The time for words had passed. Last night during their farewell dinner, Alma had conveyed all that she'd needed to say, feeding off Xenia's quiet determination. A surge pushed them towards the chained gate. Alma reminded Xenia of the three pre-addressed postcards in her purse. "As soon as you arrive, ask your nephew to write me a note with your phone number and mail them." Alma could not consider the possibility that she'd never hear from Xenia again.

A Mercedes bus pulled up and the door cranked open. Inside, bright upholstery covered the seats. Alma had been dubious when the ticket agent had promised comfortable seating and a television. But it didn't look bad and she grabbed the suitcases and lurched them to the hold where the driver was loading baggage.

Xenia turned, her eyes welling, and reached her arms out.

"*Adios*, Xenia, *adios*." Alma embraced the small woman wrapped in pink mohair, and slid a packet into her pocket. Alma watched through the tinted window as Xenia climbed onto the bus and found a seat next to a woman near the front.

Alma imagined her opening the packet, a small album with photos of Xenia with Alma and her parents that she'd put together from her father's collection of photographs. So Xenia could show the others in Todos Santos where she'd been living since 1967, the year Che Guevara had been executed in the *altiplano* of Bolivia, the year Xenia's husband had been crushed in the tin mine. Todos Santos had changed. Xenia knew that many of her friends were no longer alive, that federal agents funded by the American DEA had burned out the coca growers' fields. Her determination to return defied reason. But Xenia deserved to realize every capricious yearning, having put aside her own needs for over three decades.

The door closed, the bus backed up and Xenia pressed her hand against the window. As the bus lumbered down the street, the small palm on the glass became distant. Alma hurried to leave the stench and chaos of the station.

Twelve years ago she'd left Luscano with barely a backward glance. If the terms of Xenia's cosmic justice were true, it was rightly her turn to be left behind. Alma walked uphill towards Calle Libertad.

12

The desks had been ransacked. Coffee cups and paperweights lay shattered on the tiled flooring. The computers were smashed and a fax machine knocked over. Lalo Martín had removed his gabardine jacket, the first time Flaco had seen him in shirt sleeves, and was systematically looking through the files and cabinets to find out what, if anything, had been stolen.

Flaco collected the documents strewn around the office and handed them to César, the prosecutor's assistant. Then he found a broom to clean up the shards of glass. The sweeping channelled his rage at the Ministry of Justice for their lax security, for enabling this destruction. He filled two garbage bags with rubbish and tied them shut. César took the bags on his way out.

"Lalo, have you figured out what's missing?" Flaco brushed his hands on his jeans, felt splinters digging into his palms.

"Nothing, as far as I can tell."

"Your laptop?"

"I've taken precautions." He pointed to the ceiling lamp, at the telephone and laid his finger on his lips. Flaco felt foolish. Of course the place was bugged.

It was dark when they left the building to cross the Plaza Federal. They sat down at a table outside La Loca. With nobody in earshot, Flaco asked about the box of files Ernesto had brought.

"Safe."

"At your house?"

"You don't need to know. But I do have a guy watching the house. I'm going to have someone posted at the office, too. It eats into our budget, all this security, but we can't make it easy for them."

"Who do you think is behind this?"

"It's a scare tactic."

The answer too vague for his liking, Flaco repeated his question.

"The military, former and present."

The waiter arrived. Flaco requested two whiskies and some pasta. When they were alone again, he asked, "What about Pindalo?"

"Possibly."

A few weeks ago, at the *finca*, Flaco's brother had warned him to be prudent. "Flaco, you've got to give up this plan for a memorial," Eduardo had said. "Patrón Pindalo's negotiating to purchase the land."

Flaco told Lalo about the casino Pindalo was planning to build on the La Cuarenta property. "I'm sure they're going to oppose any sculpture going up on their land if the deal goes through."

"My focus is on preparing a case," Lalo said. "I can't worry about Pindalo, his arms trade and money laundering." Then he asked about Alma. "When's she coming to —"

"A little more time."

"Her mother's death. I understand but —"

"The family *muchacha* just left for B,olivia. Alma was close to her."

"At your party, I sensed a willingness."

"Not if she hears of your break-in or the phone tapping."

"I'll address that with her. She's not the only victim who —"

"You've found others?"

The waiter brought the drinks and a bottle of water. Lalo Martín waited him out. Then he leaned in towards Flaco. "The ledger that Ernesto brought...it's helped us trace some families...I can't say more."

Flaco understood the prosecutor's secrecy was not about trust but safety. Still, it troubled him not to be on top of all developments. He'd appreciated Lalo Martín's call this morning informing him of the break-in. At least he knew what they were up against. With his students, Flaco had to show an unfaltering determination, but with Lalo he could express his doubts. The waiter brought their meals and Flaco ordered another whisky. The candle flickered on the table between them. Flaco forced himself to eat, aware of people on the benches in the shadowed plaza, their faces obscured in the dark. He'd hated the paranoia planted by the junta. It brought out the worst in people, the perpetual fear. It had made them sick, him and his friends. For some, it was physical, with strange outbreaks of skin rashes or inflammations, sudden hearing loss or speech impediments like lisps and stuttering. In our twenties, he thought, we were so vulnerable and clueless. Some developed weird manias. Never take the same route home, don't use the phone, never speak to a stranger degenerated into never wear red, they'll think you're a communist, always carry a toothbrush and a full pack of smokes in case they kidnapped you, and, his specialty, fuck as often as possible because, hey, it might be your last chance until you get into heaven.

The break-in at Lalo's office resurrected the dread and mistrust. The only solace in sweeping the shards in the office had been the realization that cleaning up Luscano had become the most important purpose of his existence. Flaco had faith in his students as far as his leadership could take them. And that made him falter. How far could he go? Across from him, the lawyer sat unperturbed, quietly eating his meal.

"Don't forget the names for the sculptor."

"César's working on it."

He wished he could siphon some of Lalo Martín's single-mindedness. It was a good example. Flaco resolved to focus on organizing the memorial and let Lalo handle the prosecution. But what if something happened to the man? When Eduardo had told him about Ernesto's suicide, Flaco had felt things starting to go wrong. Now the break-in. What was he getting Alma into?

13

Patrón Pindalo's power and grief were a lethal cocktail. Since their encounter the day of Ernesto's burial, Gabriel had anticipated retribution, waiting anxiously for the moment in order to put it behind him. When Patrón Pindalo finally showed up in his office, Gabriel adopted the same attitude he'd reserved for Ernesto, restrained contempt.

"I want you to know, Seil, that we've reconstructed my son's last days," he said, installing himself on the chair across from the desk. "He was here at the cemetery."

Gabriel looked out the window, wondering who the "we" included. The police, the military or the band of gangsters in Pindalo's employ? Outside, Castillo stood spraying the bed of white camellias with a hose. The gravel road was full of cars that morning. It was the beginning of the Jewish holidays and many had come to visit their dead. Their presence reassured.

Patrón Pindalo crossed his leg, clasping a tanned hand over the knee of his grey trousers. The casual posturing gave him away. Gabriel reminded himself that if Patrón Pindalo had really wanted to harm him, he'd have dispatched an emissary to ambush him on a downtown street some night.

"What was his state of mind?"

"Anxious."

"Suicidal?"

"Not that I could tell."

"He left his wife and children a month before he died."

"I didn't know that…he didn't say." Gabriel couldn't pretend that he didn't care. No, it haunted him, Ernesto's agitation the day before his drowning. If he judged himself harshly, he could argue that if he'd spoken to Ernesto as he lay in the campus grass, the guy might not have flipped out. "I didn't know him that well. He was a friend of Roberto, my brother."

"I know that. So what did you talk about?"

"Regrets." Not exactly a lie. There had been remorse in Ernesto's desperation. Why else had he stolen the files?

"What regrets?"

"Nothing specific…he just seemed…agitated."

"How long's your brother been gone? More than a decade, right?"

The man's eyes, narrow as a viper's, bored into him. He was soulless. To display this level of arrogance here where generations of Pindalo ghosts, including Ernesto's, resided as witnesses. The heavy stapler on Gabriel's desk would be the perfect weapon. But why stoop to his level? "Maybe he regretted his inaction. He might have saved my brother."

"Yes and no. Not on his own."

Gabriel's stomach churned.

"Did he mention any documents?"

"No." Now that the bastard had indirectly admitted he could have intervened to save Roberto, it was easy to lie.

"Ernesto was seen at the university the day before his death. Why?"

"No idea."

"Do you know Professor Molino?"

"Yes."

"Did you introduce him to my son?"

"No."

"I ask you again, Seil. What was he doing here?"

"Maybe he came to visit his mother's tomb."

"She's been dead a long time. Why would he come to the mausoleum now? Unless…he was contemplating taking his life and came to face his ultimate destination?"

It struck him that Pindalo was improvising.

"Death, you see enough of it here. Can't you smell it coming?"

Gabriel stared out the window so as not to see what he understood intuitively, Patrón Pindalo's need to know, the importance of detail in an unexplained death. He was admitting that Ernesto had killed himself. That's the distance he'd come. Now he was haunted by guilt.

"Ernesto left two shattered children in my care. All of us, his wife, his sister, would have wanted to prevent his death. It's too late...but something smells here, Seil. There's some link between you, Ernesto and this Professor. I know the brother, Eduardo, and I knew their grandmother. *Buena gente.* Although the father was a gambler of the worst sort. Maximilio Molino...I imagine he'd approve of the deal I've been hearing about."

A crafty move.

Patrón Pindalo regarded him with a smirk.

"What deal?"

"La Cuarenta's going down. It's being demolished for a casino." He sprang from his chair and reached across the desk to shake Gabriel's hand, then changed his mind. Instead he asked, "How's Bilmo? Remember me to him, will you? And if he ever fires you, let me know. I'd be happy to help." Patrón Pindalo left the office. The screen door to the building swung shut behind him.

As Gabriel stood at the window watching the car recede down the gravel road, he realized it had been an interrogation, pure and simple, although he wasn't sure whether he'd passed or failed. He'd been like an actor in a film noir detective story, one who kept forgetting his lines. Gabriel fluctuated from pride that he hadn't capitulated to regret that he hadn't taken a stronger stand. What if he'd tried to barter? Trade the information that Ernesto had indeed given away documents stolen from his father for details on Roberto's last days? But that would be colluding with the devil himself. And the parting threat, so typically couched in oligarchic charm. Let him have Bilmo fire me, let him try. Then despair at the thought of it. What sickened was the indifference to Roberto's disappearance. Patrón Pindalo could have helped but chose not to. That persistent negation, symptom of Luscano's endemic indifference, made his brother disappear again and again.

14

The official gathering at the Hotel Colonial was a formality. All members of the consortium convened to sign the documents with the arsenal of Mont Blanc pens ordered for the occasion. Patrón Pindalo was the last to enter the conference room. He ignored the offer of a seat at the head of the table and sat down next to his lawyer.

Javier Martinez conducted the meeting with a courteous but curt delivery. Patrón Pindalo admired the fellow's efficiency. Educated at Yale, he brought an American directness to negotiations. The old guard loved to talk, but in the presence of the young lawyer they kept themselves in check, admiring the gold souvenirs in their hands like children. Patrón Pindalo found them pathetic as his eyes went from one to the other, the former ambassador, the mayor's brother, an ex-colonel, the Galtí widow, a retired cardiologist, the university rector and a so-called philanthropist who'd made his fortune off gangs of moneychangers loitering on street corners.

Since Ernesto's death, his patience with everyone except his grandchildren had evaporated. At the same time, the casino deal kept him from wallowing in grief, with all the meetings, attended with or without Javier, depending on the situation, to get the government to approve the development and transfer ownership of the land. Selected senators and officials had received their envelopes of cash. The sale had been registered and transacted. The bishop had promised not to invoke questions of morality in return for renovations to his rectory. "We can't condone gambling, Patrón," he'd said over one of their dinners, "but we support any initiative to alleviate poverty and create prosperity."

Leather-bound contracts were passed from signatory to signatory. Patrón Pindalo handed them on. His name was not directly linked to the deal. Instead, he'd acquired a controlling interest in the corporation created to manage the casino and eventually, the hotel and golf course that would be built on the site. It was the cash flow, not the land, that appealed to him. The casino represented a profitable laundromat. The sooner it was up and running, the better.

Patrón Pindalo scanned the press release Javier had had drafted for tomorrow's news. Nicely upbeat, with the number of jobs to be created and the millions of pesos the development would generate in annual tourism revenues.

When the signing was done, waiters were summoned into the conference room with trays of champagne glasses. It was eleven in the morning, too early for any decent person to be drinking. What hope was there for Luscano with this degree of decadence? Patrón Pindalo smiled and accepted a glass. The men and women toasted the prospect of their increased wealth. Some lit cigars and stood by the French doors that opened onto the Plaza de los Marineros.

Patrón Pindalo left his champagne flute on the table and worked the room as quickly as possible, shaking hands with the men, kissing the women. The pity in their eyes was intolerable. It had been four months since Ernesto's drowning, but it didn't get easier. For the first time in his life, Patrón Pindalo sensed the others knew more than he did, that ugly rumours were circulating behind his back. The confrontation with Seil had yielded nothing. He smelled lies but couldn't prove them.

He approached Javier Martinez, a type commendably more absorbed by his work than the emotional states of others, and directed him to the outside hallway. "Well done. Looks like everything's in order."

"The credit goes to you, Patrón. A brilliant plan. 'Win-win,' as they say in English."

"When will the demolition take place?"

"By the end of the month, provided there's no glitch." Javier smiled a perfect row of white teeth.

"There's always a glitch."

"Right. The question remains: the reaction to the news release? I don't foresee problems. We make a good case for the country."

Patrón Pindalo took in the lawyer's tightly knotted silk tie, the snug, tailored suit. He preferred to find some defect in his employees. In Javier's case, the young man cared too much for his own appearance. That vanity could get him in trouble.

"It's not Luscano you need to worry about, but our neighbours. This is going to eat into their gaming business."

"Brazil and Paraguay are on side."

"And Uruguay?"

"Lukewarm."

"You work on that."

Patrón Pindalo left the Hotel Colonial without any sense of achievement or jubilation. Why couldn't Ernesto have been more like this Javier? Such questions were a waste of time. He couldn't let bitterness corrode him; it was a battle, one of the tougher ones in his life.

15

Alma had expected that the silence of the house with Xenia gone would induce her to write long hours. She'd thought her days would revert to the routine of her life in Montréal, less the pressures of teaching and marking, and she could bask in the luxury of coming and going as she pleased without explanation or obligation. But she found herself going out, visiting Roma at the bookstore or spending time at the university library, where she read texts on Delmira Agustini. Encountering the theses written by others since her departure proved there was sustained interest in the poet's work.

As she browsed the stacks in dusty rows inside the old ivied building, the faces of her fellow students returned to her. At the library's long tables she'd shared lecture notes and books with them, and their idiosyncrasies emerged from memory. How naive and young they had all been. One night, watching Roma play taiko drums, she asked Flaco what had happened to them, naming the ones she remembered specifically. He told her what he knew, that many were in exile in Barcelona, Paris, Santiago or Buenos Aires, four had disappeared, two others committed suicide. "Worse than a brain drain," he said, "a generation decimated." And that, he explained, was what made his students so important. "They have to bridge a huge gap."

Alma studied them, the students in the library, hunched over books and laptops, texting on their phones. Much like her students in Montréal, their easy interactions and generous doling out of hugs, their openness and absence of angst made her hopeful. They seemed wiser, too, and this she thought would protect them. On the other hand, a person's courage remained unknown until tested. What would they do if their friends began to disappear?

On her way home from the university, she usually detoured to Calle Libertad and the nondescript block of houses where Carlos Cruz lived. Daytime, a woman swept the front path or wiped windows in circular motions with a white cloth. How easy it had been to attach an identity to the man, his name obtained from the credit card receipt in Roma's register, his workplace discovered by tailing him to the industrial barrio, south of the old market, where he worked in an auto parts factory. Alma didn't know what he did all day inside that brick building. Perhaps he was in sales or accounting. He didn't wear a suit or tie to work nor were his hands stained with grease or dirt when he returned home. Observing the routine of this family man with a penchant for thrillers prompted Alma to wonder whether he even remembered what he'd done, whether he ever woke up haunted or ashamed of the suffering he'd caused. Every time she watched him, his house, his wife and children, or followed him through Luscano, she felt closer to some sort of understanding. He was so absolutely ordinary that her fear of discovery receded with each session of spying. He wouldn't recognize her and if he did, what could he do?

Roma, when she'd asked for the man's name, had said, "Do you want to tell me why? If not, don't say anything. I'd rather you didn't lie." Roma might have guessed her motive had to do with recouping something she'd lost, a sense of control. The power of the watcher over the one being watched. As if Carlos Cruz, in all his banality, was at her mercy now. She knew it was an illusion, but the role suited her, the temporary feeling of empowerment she had when she followed him.

One hot afternoon she sat sweating at a piano inside the music faculty. Emilio Rodriguez held the violin to his chin and, working his bow, deciphered the piece her father had written. After hearing it played through several times, Alma worked out the fingering with her right hand, improvising chords with her left, Emilio keeping time with his bow. He gave her some blank sheet music and helped her transpose the score for piano. They tried to sing the words of the poem but their voices could not sustain the long notes. Emilio suggested a singer he knew, and before leaving for a rehearsal, promised to organize a session for the three of them.

Sweat trickled down her forehead as Alma replayed the piece, stopping to write the notes on the sheet. Her father had not always respected the rhythms of her words with a beat per syllable. The piece represented more than a chanting of the poem but a reworking of her poem in a new dimension, all the false starts, notes written and erased, the meticulousness and focus drawing her inward so that time and the present became irrelevant. The sounds transcended her words and she began to feel an affection for the music she'd never felt for the poem itself. The rhythms and syntax that she, the young naive student, had created, on which her father had built these sounds, the long legatos of the couplets and slow building of resonance that turned into itself fugue-like, as if echoing off the walls of the cathedral itself. It was beautiful, the music and act of playing the piece, even as droplets of sweat fell on her knuckles and her fingers slid on the keys.

In this heightened state, all the *if onlys* that had coiled themselves so tightly began to unravel. If only there hadn't been a coup in 1990, if only she hadn't witnessed the tanks in the Plaza Federal, if only she hadn't smelled the books burning, if only she hadn't written the poem, if only she hadn't handed it to Flaco for the university magazine, if only she hadn't been at home the night of January 6, 1991. Futile conditional clauses that introduced her most self-damaging thoughts. She'd trained herself to cut them off before their completion.

Sweating over the keys bent her thinking elsewhere. She *had* written the poem and it had been set to music by her father and now she was playing it herself on the piano. The clauses rearranged themselves. If only she hadn't left Luscano, if only her father hadn't died before she returned. She repeated the piece, warming to the sense of it, whispering the words, "*En la Plaza Federal tenemos una iglesia, La Catedral de Luscano, edificio de gracia....*"

16

A few weeks after Xenia's departure, the phone rang early one morning. Alma recognized the man's *madrileño* accent from the one time she'd heard him speak. The Professor invited her for tea and she accepted, curious to hear what he had to say about her mother.

The Professor's apartment occupied the top floor of a low-rise building on a cul-de-sac in Barrio Norte. When Alma stepped out of the elevator he was waiting to greet her, leaning on his cane and peering at her through his glasses. His frame was frail and his bald head the same hazel colour as the woollen vest over his white shirt. The Professor led her through a large sunny room with bookshelves, a leather settee and desk by a wall of windows between panels of velvet curtains. He was obviously a meticulous man, as not a book or newspaper lay strewn about. They sat at a table that looked over his terrace and onto the sea. He'd set out platters of fruit tarts and pastel puffs of meringue along with the plates and teacups. He prepared the tea while Alma filled her plate. Since Xenia had left, her meals had become sporadic, and she was hungry.

As if to establish his credentials and gain her confidence, the Professor described his origins and career. Born in Madrid, he'd left for Luscano during the civil war. He wrote books that were published in Spain, lectured in various universities in Europe and Latin America and eventually taught philosophy at the University of Luscano. "In 1991, during that period of turmoil you know all too well," he said, "I was invited to replace some professors who left the country and wound up teaching until I retired, five years ago, at the age of seventy-three." He sipped some tea, his hand shaking slightly. He put down the cup. "Ethics were my specialty, especially

Nietzsche and his teachings on the will to power as the basis of true morality."

Alma waited for an opening. A craving had been building in her, the need to speak of her mother with someone objective. The man was quite a raconteur, not at all the self-effacing presence she remembered from Hannelore's burial, and she consumed several pastries before she was able to interject, "My mother...you sent her flowers every week. And let her enjoy the mystery of having a secret admirer."

"I hope you understand, given your loyalties to your father, whom I never had the opportunity to meet, although I witnessed many of his concerts. A fine violinist. The orchestra was never the same after he died."

"When did you meet my mother?"

"My dear, I feel I've known her all my life."

Perhaps the sugar in the pastries was taking effect, making her feel agitated. Alma rephrased the question. "How did you meet her?"

"At the Spanish embassy here in Luscano, just before Franco died. It was an evening on Cervantes. Some of us, the Spanish émigrés, were asked to read. I noticed her sitting in the audience. The green eyes cast their spell on me." He went on about the evening, how when drinks were offered, he made sure to seek out Hannelore and described her, the yellow dress she wore and her black hair. Alma calculated that the meeting must have occurred when she was a child, about eight, given that Franco died in 1975. It was strange that she'd never encountered the Professor at the house, that Hannelore had never mentioned him. She began to regret this visit. Coming here might have been disloyal to her mother's privacy and her father's honour.

Alma asked for a glass of water and when he returned with the sparkling water, he stood beside her, pouring from the bottle, and she felt the brush of his trousers, smelled his cologne. She moved her chair over and he took his seat.

"I invited you here to confess. I loved Hannelore for many years, not the way you would know or long for at your age...the kind of love an old man might permit himself without having to change his ways. Your mother understood me. I was fully aware the flowers were a cliché, but when she was first diagnosed I had to come up with something. Hannelore was so demoralized. Taking her dancing, well, that was not a possibility in my advanced years and her weakened condition. Although I like to think that we danced conversationally, that she enjoyed our exchanges almost as much as a turn on the dance floor."

"Did she visit you here?" Alma tried to imagine her mother leaving the house, her husband and child, for secret rendezvous with this man. It was easy enough to conceive of, but harder to fast-forward to the time of the junta, after she'd left Luscano, to think of her father waiting at home for Hannelore, or worse, hearing snatches of the rumours swirling around. Luscano's specialty, the gloating repetition of innuendo and gossip.

"Your mother preferred livelier, stylish locales. The Hotel Colonial for drinks or the Café Prague, where I bought these pastries. But in your case...I must tell you that she spoke of you with great pride. Look what she gave me for Christmas some years ago." He reached for the book he'd set aside for this moment. It was Flaco's anthology, a thin book with a black cover, the title, *Voces acalladas,* in white, blood-spattered lettering.

"I wrote the poem a long time ago...the words are not what I would write today."

"Many authors feel that way. Even Borges fantasized about the erasure of his work. The words disappearing as he wrote them, a liberation of sorts, no holding of account, no quoting out of context." He put down the book. "You paid dearly for that poem."

"A week in prison. I survived. Others paid with their lives."

"Your mother paid, too."

The blame in his voice was unmistakable. He didn't seem so frail anymore. No, he seemed grotesque. Alma pushed aside her cup and saucer. "Every thinking person paid. The insult of the junta...my mother resisted in her way, she always had." Unlike you, she could have said, an opportunistic collaborator.

"She resisted me, I can tell you that. She stood by her daughter and her husband and I had to take second place. Another reason I invited you here today, to remind you how much she loved you.

Even after you left, she spoke of you, not with regret but with respect for the life you created for yourself in exile. One aspect in particular that she admired was your independence. I think she would have wanted more of a career than tutoring the children of prosperous Barrio Norte residents. She abhorred the domestic and the type of women who rely on men to define their existence."

There was an element of truth to this. Hannelore had repeated the words "value your freedom" to Alma throughout her life, a mantra that became loaded after her time in prison. But he was overlooking Hannelore's beauty and the way she used her appeal to her own ends, the manipulative coquette inside of her. Alma didn't want to redefine her mother after death, to idealize her. She'd been careful with Xenia not to criticize Hannelore; it would have been tacky. And so she said, "My mother's countenance, the impact she knew she had on men especially, contradicted her feminist ideals."

"It's true that in the machismo culture of this continent, doors opened easily for Hannelore. Her beauty and her European aura... Alma, I've observed many women in my life. You have no cause to suffer under your mother's shadow, you're quite the graceful swan yourself."

She left soon afterwards and walked down to the beach, kicked off her sandals and splashed through the shallows. The salt water was warm, pulling her in. She waded to her knees until a wave chased her back to shore. She saw him then, the Professor on his terrace, lifting his cane in a final salute. He was repulsive but he had touched a nerve. It was ridiculous competing with a dead mother but so ingrained, a Freudian case study irrelevant now that both her parents were dead. That small triangle, Alma, her mother and father, did not include the Professor, a traitor and interloper. No wonder Hannelore had chosen not to speak of him, had never admitted who was sending her flowers every week.

The first postcard from Xenia arrived in the mail at last. Someone had printed the message that she'd arrived well in Todos Santos, adding the instructions, "Visit your mother's grave for me." Alma celebrated with a breakfast of scrambled eggs, avocado and toast.

She left the house, walking briskly towards the avenue. The gods were living up to their end and she'd live up to hers.

A hearse and several cars were parked on the gravel road outside the cottage. Somewhere a burial was in progress but the field with her parents' graves lay quiet. The lemon and pomegranate trees had flowered since Hannelore's burial. Spiders had cast webs over the grave and the sod where the casket had been lowered had meshed with the surrounding grass. Alma sat on the ground. How quickly nature absorbed its dead and regenerated growth. The cemetery served to compost. Burial grounds transformed into parks with markers for the dead. Here we lie, exactly here. Two lines etched on the grave, *Hannelore Stern de Álvarez* followed by *1927–2003.* "Just the facts," she'd stipulated. "No quotes or religious symbols." The maiden name, Stern, had always struck Alma as enigmatic. Meaning strict in English, star in German. Hannelore deserved to have an astral body named after her, an intense flare in the southern constellation burning across billions of light years. Alma didn't believe in an afterlife. The spirit lived on in the memories of those left behind. And it consoled her that the two graves, her father's and mother's, lay side by side.

Alma stretched out on the grass and regarded the sky. She didn't miss her parents, absent from her life since she left Luscano, but she felt a sadness and regrets of various kinds along with gratitude for having spent the last weeks of Hannelore's life by her side. The experience helped demystify death. It had deepened her understanding of the complexity of her mother's character, witnessing her as an adult, how she'd looked at her own life with clarity, facing death without self-pity. Hannelore had railed against her husband, foisting her suspicions of adultery on Alma, but she had loved Eugen, weak as he was, for bringing music into her life. It was clear, if the Professor was not completely deluded, that there had been hypocrisy in Hannelore's accusations, but Alma was certain that even if divorce had been legalized before 1995, her mother could not have left Eugen. Not for the Professor, in any case. But she was falling into a trap she recognized from her work on the poet, that post-mortem phenomenon of re-examining personal history and in the process, formulating conclusions to replace what was with what might have been.

"Alma?"

She sat up, brushing blades of grass from her hair.

Gabriel held out his hand and pulled her up. "Are you all right?"

He must have thought she'd collapsed with grief. Alma tried to reassure him.

"We've just finished a burial," he explained as he accompanied her towards the gates. "A ninety-two-year-old who died in her sleep, the family subdued but relieved. Her children in their seventies, the grandchildren and great-grandchildren, a whole clan of them, close-knit and supportive. My favourite kind of burial." Gabriel suggested lunch and they dodged traffic on the avenue and walked to the adobe shack with the Coca Cola Lite sign on the roof. Tables outside were occupied by men in coveralls and students with knapsacks at their feet.

"It doesn't look like much," Gabriel said, "but the empanadas are the best in Luscano." Inside the shack, a woman behind the counter greeted them. Gabriel introduced her as Juanita, Castillo's girlfriend. They ordered chicken and cheese empanadas, red wine and sparkling water. Gabriel carried the bottles, Alma the glasses, setting them down on an empty table beside a wall covered in a tangle of crimson bougainvillea.

"You should see this place on Sundays," Gabriel said. "There's a lineup down the street by noon. Everybody buys empanadas here for their *asados*."

"I haven't been to an *asado* since I left Luscano," Alma said.

"They have barbecues in Canada, don't they?"

"Not the same." She couldn't express the difference succinctly but surely it had something to do with frequency and the notion of time. Her teaching job didn't allow her to fritter away her Sundays, eating and drinking from noon to midnight.

Juanita brought the empanadas, plates, cutlery and a bowl of salsa. She set the table and poured the water and wine for them, shyly checking out Alma from the corner of her eye. Instead of an apron, she wore a *guardapolvo* like the ones Alma and Roma had worn to school, navy lab coats of durable cotton. Her black hair was pulled back into a thick coil of braids and her eyebrows met in a V above the bridge of her nose. She moved with grace, every gesture gentle and determined. After placing the sauce between Gabriel and Alma with a warning, "Careful, it's piquant," she left to clear tables of plates and glasses.

Alma took an empanada and blew on it. "You can't imagine how I missed these in Montréal," she said. "Our *muchacha* used to make them." She told Gabriel about Xenia's long bus trip and her relief this morning when the postcard arrived.

Gabriel expounded on the regional differences of empanadas. "The best," he confirmed, "are from the Andes, northern Argentina and Bolivia."

Alma laughed. "You remind me of the Latinos in Montréal, arguing over tamales, ceviches, empanadas and coffee, everyone claiming their country's as the best."

Gabriel asked about Montréal. Alma told him of the intriguing mix of immigrant cultures, the unbearable, long winters and the unrelenting influence of the gringos to the south. He seemed unusually aware of local politics, how close Québec had come to winning independence in the nineties. Alma asked how it was that he knew so much about Canada.

He chewed slowly, weighing the question. "I thought of moving there at one point. But I probably couldn't find work, would have trouble adapting."

Alma silently agreed with him. "You've lived here all your life?"

"My parents came from Argentina. My mother was born there, my father emigrated from Belgium. He died when I was a baby, my mother remarried and we moved here. I've often thought of going back to Buenos Aires. There's so much going on there. But there's something to be said for Luscano. I'm not sure what it is. Maybe you know, having lived elsewhere."

Alma sensed what he was getting at. "It depends who you are. If you're an immigrant from Brazil or Bolivia or if your skin is dark, it's rough. But if your family's European, and your skin is white, doors open because of Luscano's inferiority complex. Canada has a similar complex of being a former colony but it's more subtle and evolves more quickly. A lot of immigrants suffer, especially if they don't find work." Her parents had arrived with next to nothing but they'd been received in Luscano like minor celebrities.

"But you feel more exposed in a small country. Aren't you glad you left?"

"When you live in a place where you spent your childhood, it gives you a certain confidence. The reverse is like performing in a play without a script. You improvise." Alma wanted to articulate the ambiguity of her feelings towards Luscano but she stumbled, as usual, concerned that criticizing the country would offend him. "Canada is far from perfect but it's safe." Alma paused. After 9/11, it depended on your origins. The backlash against the Muslim community had shocked her. If someone from Luscano had been found planning or executing a terrorist act, she would have been vulnerable by association.

"When did you leave?"

"January 1991."

"An ugly time." He seemed to want to say more and Alma waited as he drank some wine to fortify himself. "My brother... Roberto...was kidnapped by two guys who came to the house he shared with other students. He'd spoken out against the junta and participated in some demonstrations. You couldn't call him an activist, not like Flaco, but he was courageous. I'm sure now that he was in La Cuarenta." And he repeated his brother's name, Roberto Seil.

Alma had stopped eating. She couldn't bring herself to tell Gabriel of the trucks leaving La Cuarenta at dawn full of prisoners, how they'd returned empty except for the guards and drivers.

Gabriel lit a cigarette. "A few years ago...Roberto's remains, his skull actually, was identified in a mass grave...upriver from the prison in a field. Imagine, Alma, he disappeared twelve years ago... and we still don't know how he died."

Maybe Roma was right. Maybe there were deeper reasons Gabriel worked in a cemetery. "So what happened?"

"The human rights group that organized the forensic work, they moved on to the Balkans. They're probably in Iraq now or Afghanistan. Crisis of the month."

"But this prosecutor, Lalo Martín —"

"Every government elected since the dictatorship promises a full investigation while they're campaigning. Once in office, they secretly agree to amnesty deals with military. Sometimes they'll revoke the immunity of certain officials to secure international aid. They might even go so far as to name a prosecutor, find a judge. Some charges are laid, media reports start circulating. As soon as they move to arrest anyone, the judge is discredited, removed or assassinated, a journalist's mutilated body is found in a car somewhere. Nothing's resolved and the more time passes, the more people want to move on and forget about what happened." He crushed his cigarette in the ashtray.

Alma played with the fork on her plate, contemplating Carlos Cruz and his ordinary existence. Gabriel poured the last of the wine into their glasses. Unlike Flaco who'd adopted a language from repetition so that when he spoke of Luscano's junta, the words spewed out effortlessly, Gabriel was struggling. Instead of diverting the conversation elsewhere, Alma stayed with him. "What about the generals who've been indicted in Chile and Argentina?"

Gabriel rocked on his chair. "If you look deeply...it was justice by public relations...basically to cleanse an incoming regime's image." He claimed the impetus for serious investigations into military dictatorships had usually come from foreign sources. The Germans who consistently sought justice for disappeared nationals in Uruguay during the seventies or the judge in Spain who pushed for Pinochet's arrest in London. "Last month was the thirtieth anniversary of the coup in Chile and Allende's death...and they still haven't nailed Pinochet."

September 11th, a day that had come to represent another horror, overshadowing Pinochet's coup in 1973. Alma was seven when her father left for his concert in Santiago. Hannelore had been frantic when she'd heard the news over Radio Luscano. "Your father is so naive," she said. "What if he doesn't even notice there's been a coup?" Of course he had and the orchestra had managed to board a plane for Buenos Aires before flying home.

Gabriel referred to the colonels and generals who'd retired with generous pensions and the protection of the oligarchy to which most of them belonged. They were slowly dying off and all they had to do was stall for time with the help of their lawyers and connections. Gabriel went on about the burden of proof. "There's no one left to testify. Like Roberto, they all disappeared.

"General Galtí, the one who masterminded the crackdown, he shot himself five years ago...one of my first burials, a nightmare. Despite their promises, the government can't antagonize the military. They've got the arms and tanks to do it all again, oust the president and take over the country. All that's stopping them is their neighbours, Lula in Brazil and Kirchner in Argentina. Did you know that both men were imprisoned during the juntas there? They've taken a stronger position on persecuting the military even though they haven't done much yet."

None of this was new to Alma. She'd simply relegated the injustice to a far corner of her mind where it wouldn't fester. She had nothing to add, leaving Gabriel to talk and talk, get the venom out. But it crossed her mind that both of them were too young to be this bitter.

Gabriel rose to pay the bill inside the shack. Alma watched a sparrow pecking an empanada crust on a nearby table. Clinging to the rim of a plate with tiny claws, the bird crumbled the crust with its beak. Another sparrow whizzed out from the bougainvillea so close to her she felt the flutter of wings on her face. It swooped to attack the crust. Then another one and another until at least a dozen sparrows were pecking at crumbs. From one fragile bird, the swarm became a menace.

Alma walked downtown as daylight faded with the setting sun. Carlos Cruz would be arriving home from work at this time. She'd mapped out his workdays and weekends but his evenings remained a mystery. Did he eat dinner, play with the children, watch television every night? She rounded the corner of Calle Libertad. Lights were on inside most of the houses and the smells of grilled meat and fried potatoes drifted in the warm air. With practised nonchalance she proceeded to the house, strolled past the window. Shadows moved behind the curtains.

By a neighbouring gate, a boy appeared holding a soccer ball. "What are you looking for?" He was twelve at most, skinny legs in high-tops, shoelaces untied. "I've seen you here before."

Alma walked past him to the corner and turned. The boy was still staring and beyond him, a figure left the house of Carlos Cruz, walking away from Alma and the boy. She hurried in the opposite direction, gambling that the man was heading towards Reconquista, perhaps the bar where he ate pizza, if that was him.

Alma cut through an alley. A streetlight up ahead illuminated the balding head and broad shoulders. She followed him down the busy avenue towards the old port. He entered the Plaza de los Marineros. A skateboarder crisscrossed the cobblestones in front of Alma. The rattling wheels had Carlos Cruz stop and turn. Alma ducked behind the statue until she saw him walk past El Barco towards a winding, narrow street. There were fewer pedestrians and Alma kept her distance.

A few blocks into the port, he entered a building with shuttered windows. Alma waited a few seconds, then approached the entrance. Through the glass doors, she made out a porter sitting behind a desk. A brass plaque on the wall indicated that the building housed the social club of Luscano's armed forces. Alma could imagine Carlos Cruz greeting his former *compañeros* with warm handshakes and *abrazos* before joining them at the table where they drank, played cards and traded war stories. "We fixed them, didn't we?" Smug satisfaction curling with the smoke from his cigar.

A ship's horn sounded from a wharf. There was shouting in the distance and a car drove by. Alma stood in the dark outside the stone building, built in the nineteenth century by the look of it, just another in a row of edifices housing brokers, shipping companies, marine suppliers. What could she do? If she stormed inside to confront him, his cronies would overpower her, throw her out of the building, call the police, have her arrested and she'd be back to where she'd once been, in a jail cell, helpless.

Inside the lobby, two men approached the porter and he picked up the phone, calling for a taxi perhaps. Alma scrambled into the doorway of an adjacent building. The men came outside and waited on the street. One of them glanced her way, elbowed the other, the two men leering. Alma hurried down the street. It curved into another and she reached a dead end. A huddle crouched by a wall, bottles on the pavement. Someone called out, "*¡Puta!* Show us what you've got." Alma backed away into an alley and soon she was lost in the labyrinth of streets purposely designed to disorient, the old *caudillo* strategy for protecting the port from attack.

She walked in circles, couldn't find the club again, didn't recognize a landmark, and the night deepened. To steady herself, she thought of Delmira Agustini and the next fragment she would type on her laptop. Blood on the mirror of the rented room, blood on the purse with the hand mirror, the death scene on the floor, a mirror held up to Montevideo. Nobody forced the poet to attend her own murder. With all her duplicity and secrecy, Agustini never gave up her free will.

Alma was limping from a blister that had formed on her heel. A group of sailors swaggered across the street ahead of her. She realized she was walking southward to the wharves and turned back until she found the slight incline that began the ascent into the city centre. She kept snaking uphill until she reached the river. The beacon on the cathedral spire flashed in the distant skyline.

Squatters' fires burned along the banks. Here was another barrio to be avoided. Alma took the unlit road running parallel to El Rio Pequeño. The blister on her heel burned but she didn't dare stop walking, not here. A pickup truck drove by. And for a moment, its headlights illuminated the prison. Alma could not distinguish the second floor, could not locate her lookout, six vertical bars on the opening in her cell. She wouldn't call it a window, not without a glass pane to protect from hot winds and mosquitoes. At that moment, Alma understood that she had access to something powerful neither Flaco nor Gabriel possessed: specificity.

Revenge could be hellish, but choosing the alternative, doing nothing, she'd wind up an aging academic with degenerate thoughts and negated memories, alone with her neatly arranged books. Or she'd end things the way Ernesto had. Giving up, the final manifestation of free will, then nothingness.

Alma approached the lights of cars crossing the bridge on Primero de Abríl and flagged a taxi home.

Part III

Today from the great path, under the bright and mighty sun,
Silent like a tear I have looked back,
And your voice from far away, with a scent of death,
Came to howl to my ear a sad "Never again!"

From "Sweet Elegies" by Delmira Agustini,
Cantos de la mañana (1910)

17

January 6

It's an intensely humid night. I'm at my desk studying, the pages of my books sticking to the sweat on my hands and arms, the pen sliding between my fingers. A horrendous racket shakes the house. Fists pound the front door, maybe boots as well. I rush out of my bedroom and down the hall. Two men are already inside. Our *muchacha* is striking them with a broom. The younger one restrains her. The other lunges towards me. I run towards the kitchen, to the phone, to get a knife, to hurry out the back door, I don't know. He grabs my arm and drags me down the hall. His arms lock around me. He carries me down the front stairs and shoves me into the back seat of a car. My face smacks the headrest. I'm screaming. He starts the car and the younger one gets in beside him, reaches back and pushes my head down.

On January 6, 1991, about 8:45 at night, I'm kidnapped from my parents' home, 24 Calle Buenos Aires in Barrio Norte. There are no witnesses to verify this account other than me and my abductors. My parents, not home at the time of my removal, are deceased and our *muchacha* now lives in Bolivia. Neighbours later questioned by my mother claim to have seen and heard nothing, not even my screaming.

At the time of my imprisonment, I'm twenty-four years old, a master's student at the University of Luscano. I've never committed a criminal act. My abductors do not verify my name nor do they provide a reason for my kidnapping. I never see any documents or a warrant, am never provided access to a lawyer.

The younger one plays with the radio dial. The corporal orders him to turn it off. *"Bueno, mi cabo."* I ask where they're taking me. *"¡Callate!"* The brakes squeal and the car swerves.

The car — American, black, dark green or navy — accelerates. Crouching on the floor, my face on my knees, I'm wearing sweatpants, sandals and a sleeveless top and remain in those clothes until my release. The corporal driving the car is aged forty to fifty, has brown eyes, a prominent nose and thick greying hair. He wears a blue shirt, jeans and a leather belt with a holster and a gun. The lieutenant has black eyes, short hair and a scar on his chin. He is wearing jeans, a blue polo shirt. Both men smell of cigarettes and beer.

We stop at a checkpoint. Light sweeps the car. I lift my head and see a uniformed guard in a booth. The car drives on to the entrance of the prison. The lieutenant pulls me out by the waistband of my pants. I stagger. The lieutenant grabs my arm. The floodlit yard is crowded with military vehicles, trucks and jeeps. The corporal takes my other arm and they march me into the building, through a series of doors and into an office with two uniformed men. My kidnappers leave. I never see them again.

One of the guards sits behind a desk. "Your name?" I consider lying, but decide not to. He asks me to spell out my name as he prints the letters in a book. The other guard demands that I remove my wristwatch and jewellery. I find out later that they sell these valuables for their own gain.

They're wearing navy blue uniforms, caps pulled low on their foreheads. I cannot recall distinguishing features. I remember asking, "Why am I here?"

"¡Callate!" The guard standing pats me down, searches the pockets of my sweatpants. "We should keep this one down here," he says, and they laugh. They walk me down a corridor of cells and stop in front of a metal door. They slide it open, shove me inside and lock the door behind me.

I stand there for a few minutes rubbing my cheek where it slammed the headrest in the car. A fluorescent light fixture in the cell gives off a faint bluish light. There are a number of men, six, I believe, sitting on the ground, leaning their backs against the walls.

One of them offers his jacket. "Sit on this." The cell is hot but I am shivering. I take the jacket and find a place near the door. A grille above the metal door does not provide adequate ventilation against the stench from a bucket in a corner of the cell.

The man who gave me his jacket introduces himself as Díaz. He is muscular, about my height and age. He has black hair, almost shoulder length, dark skin and high cheekbones. Later I find out he's a law student. Díaz introduces the others but I don't remember their names. Most are under thirty and students. Three are bleeding from cuts to their faces and arms. An older man vomits into the bucket. A medical student staunches a wound on this man's forearm.

At some point, Díaz speaks through the stunned disbelief. "We're being held in La Cuarenta." He's the only one who fully grasps that his detention is not some bureaucratic foul-up that will soon be straightened out. The rest of us are bewildered.

In what feels like an eternity but has probably been less than one hour, I've been kidnapped and brought to a prison across the river from the university. I've passed this building my entire life. I know that in the last year, people have been brought here without *habeas corpus* and that they are never seen again. Díaz says, "La Cuarenta's crowded. We're more than they can handle and that might work in our favour. If we're lucky, we'll be transferred to a prison in the countryside. Think clearly and stay calm. You'll be interrogated."

The medical student, the older man and I do not speak. Someone asks Díaz questions as if he's his lawyer. This person claims to have solid connections, uncles in the military, friends in government positions, contacts who have helped him obtain dispensations in the past — from military service, fines and speeding tickets. He is convinced they'll come to his rescue. First thing in the morning. A man next to Díaz promises we'll be released in a few hours and, as the night progresses, first thing in the morning. Others repeat the phrase like a mantra, first thing in the morning, although none of us has a watch. I have no sense of time passing.

"Of course we're all innocent," Díaz says. "And once that's established, we'll be released. The military doesn't make mistakes."

I understand then that one or more of my cellmates might be plants, put in the cell with us to extract information.

From time to time I discern noise from somewhere in the prison but can't pinpoint the source or the cause. I'm unable to prepare my mind for questioning. I breathe through my mouth to avoid the smell and contain my nausea, the impulse to urinate. I cannot use the bucket in the presence of six men.

January 7

A guard opens the door and calls out two names. The men leave as ordered and the door clangs shut. An hour or so later, the process is repeated. Díaz requests food and water. "You'll get that later," the guard says.

When Díaz and I are alone in the cell, he says, "Remember this: my name is Díaz Velásquez of 62 Calle San Martín. If you get out, contact my wife Mirabel and tell her I love her. I didn't have the chance." He repeats this several times, then asks, "And you? Any messages?" His words are terrifying. I cannot speak. The door opens and the guard waves me out. I hand Díaz his jacket and he whispers, "Be strong."

The guard slides a hood over my head and leads me down the hallway. We turn into a stairwell and I trip on the first steps. He pushes me up the stairway. I stumble down a corridor, hear voices, footsteps and a radio. The guard unlocks a door and shoves me into a cell. He takes the hood off my head. I ask for water. "Later," he says and leaves me in the cell. The door slides shut.

I am alone in the cell. It has a bunk bed with mattresses covered by thin blankets and an empty bucket. I walk to the small opening uncovered except for a grille of iron bars. I can't see the roads from this angle but I hear traffic, deduce it's early morning from the light and colour of the sky. I stand and breathe the cool air. The concrete walls are mottled. The floor slants towards the metal sliding door. It has two slots that open from the outside, one at eye level and the other near the floor.

An hour or so later, a hand slides a tray with tea and a package of biscuits through the bottom slot. I use the bucket and drink the tea. I save the biscuit for later when the sun appears, descending westward. Most of the day I stand by the window. I see the small figures of people by the river but they're too far away to call out to. I lie down on the bunk. The mattress stinks. Three or four times, a guard looks through the slot. I see his eyes. The slot slides shut. The heat of the direct sun has me sweating. I'm still thirsty. The next time the guard looks in, I request water. "*Callate.*" The silencing curse of my imprisonment.

After sunset, the lower slot opens. A hand in a rubber glove leaves a tray with soup and bread. I call out for water. Ten minutes later, the hand slides a bottle through the slot and a male voice demands the tray. The cell quickly cools off. I wrap myself in the two smelly blankets. I'm exhausted but cannot sleep. The cell is constantly lit by a fluorescent light. I pace the floor — eight steps wide, eleven steps long. Six bars over the window. Seventy-five indentations in the walls, as if someone hacked at the concrete with a penknife. At some point during the night I hear heavy vehicles on the road. It sounds like a convoy but I can't see the lights from my window.

January 8

I'm prone on the lower bunk bed when I hear the bells ringing from the cathedral. Tea and biscuits arrive on the tray. I'm left alone until late afternoon when the sun is blazing into the cell. The door slides open and a guard pushes a woman into the cell. She goes to the lower bunk and lies face down on the mattress.

After sunset, the slot opens to a tray with two bowls of soup, two spoons, two bottles of water and two hard rolls. I carry the tray to the bed. The woman pushes herself upright. We sit on the bed, crouching under the overhead bunk, the tray between us. She manages to eat slowly. Her hands shake. She stinks of vomit. I tell her my name and ask how long she's been here.

"What day is it?"

I tell her it's Tuesday.

"Four nights then. My name is Isabel and I've been here since Friday." She's older, thirty or so, has long black hair, deep-set eyes and a prominent nose. She tells me that she was abducted with her husband from the clinic where they both work as psychologists. They were separated as soon as they arrived in La Cuarenta. She too spent the first night in a holding cell on the ground floor. Then she was brought to a cell crowded with women on this floor. I ask her why I've been alone if the prison is so full.

Isabel gets up from the bed and walks to the window. "Two days ago, before dawn, they came to our cell and took everyone except me. They marched them down the stairs to the entrance. From my cell, I saw them being loaded onto the backs of trucks, each of them carrying a shovel, no hoods. There were at least fifty prisoners and ten soldiers with machine guns. They drove up the hill, disappeared down the other side of it. I stood by the window and watched light fill the sky. I swear I heard the shots. Ta-ta-ta. Ta-ta-ta. Black birds circled the sky beyond the hill."

Isabel holds the bars of the window, her long black hair rippling down to her waist. "The trucks returned, empty, just the drivers and guards."

I ask what happened to her today. At first she says nothing. I climb into the top bunk and lie down. Later, I listen to her voice telling how they tortured her husband in front of her. Interrogations, she says, occur during the day, three hours before lunch, three hours before sundown, always with a doctor in a white lab coat nearby. "They asked Federico questions about certain friends. He refused to answer. They burned him with a cattle prod, first on his chest. Then they asked me the same questions. When I refused, they burned him on his genitals. Federico fainted. They called the doctor. He entered the room and checked my husband's pulse, listened to his heart with a stethoscope. The doctor pronounced Federico fit for further questioning. They burned his feet and hands, his body convulsing with each electric shock. There was nothing I could do but vomit and weep. I told them what they wanted, names and addresses of our friends."

The bunk bed shakes with her sobbing. I cannot find words to console her. Isabel finally tells me Federico was carried out on a stretcher at the end of the day. She does not believe her husband will survive the night.

I doze off occasionally but Isabel wakes me up. "Please, I need to hear your voice. Tell me a story, a novel you once read or a film you saw." And so I tell her the stories of Todos Santos, a faraway village in Bolivia. Then I recite a monologue from a play. I talk until my voice is hoarse.

January 9

Two guards come for Isabel in the morning. I spend the day pacing and counting. My footsteps, holes in the walls, rocks in the river, birds in the willow trees. I sense new arrivals being locked into the cells on either side of me. I begin to work out the layout of the prison, partly from Isabel's description. The ground floor contains offices, holding cells, supply rooms and the kitchen. The second floor consists of rows of cells like mine flanking the exterior walls of the prison. The guards' room and the place where they torture the prisoners are located in the interior block. During the day and at night I hear boot-steps entering and leaving the guards' room, a radio or cards slapping a table when the door opens. I smell their food.

I am filthy. My head itches. A rash develops on my inner arms and shins. The trays continue to deliver two portions of food. I save Isabel's shares on top of my bed. Just before sundown, the cell door slides open and she stumbles in. Her lips are swollen and her arms are punctured with black sores. Her shirt sticks to her back. She slurs something I cannot understand. She sits on the lower bunk and peels her shirt off. I soak a corner of my blanket in tea and apply this to the wounds on her back. It is raw with welts, burns and strafing as if she's been rolling in barbed wire. I try to make her eat some bread but she refuses.

"Hunger strike," she slurs. "Federico's dead."

Her nose bleeds for a long time. She can't stand up so I hold her head back. She lies down on her stomach, unable to bear the blanket touching her skin.

I resort to poetry. Isabel says nothing, her eyes never close, and her forehead is hot. I recite the poet's verses through the night.

January 10

Just after the cathedral bells ring at dawn, they come for her with a hood. "She needs a doctor," I say.

"*Callate.*"

"Where is she going?"

The door slides shut. I'm left alone all day. Someone taps on the wall. I tap back. There's a pattern to the response tapped out on the wall but I never learned Morse code and can't decipher the message. When my tea arrives I ask for something to read. Later a hand slides a magazine through the slot. A battered *Hola*, six months old. I read about royal families and celebrities into the night. I hear the scratching of rats and scorpions. I feel them on my arms and legs. I recite poetry. The sound of my voice scares the creatures away for a while.

January 11

Two guards come for me in the afternoon.

"Where is Isabel?"

"We ask the questions around here."

They cover my head with a hood and walk me down the hall into an interior room. They bind my hands together and force me to sit on a chair. They remove the hood. The room is windowless. I'm sitting by a table. There's an opaque glass partition to my left. I sense someone watching me. I try to prepare myself. I want to fight back like Isabel did. By the time the officer enters the room, my body is shaking and my thoughts are incoherent.

He locks the door behind him and sits across from me, folding his hands on the table. He's wearing a grey uniform, has light brown skin, black hair and an oval mole on his forehead.

"Are you being treated adequately?"

I can't answer.

"I'm going to ask you some questions. I suggest you cooperate."

I might be nodding. I am out of control. I am suffocating.

"Who are you?"

It is not a question I anticipate. *¿Quién eres?* I state my name.
"Are you sure?"

I repeat my name. He asks for my date of birth, address, parents'
names. I deduce that they may not know who I am, that with all the
people being brought to La Cuarenta, they've lost track. He asks
about my studies, whether I've ever left Luscano, how I spend my
free time. The questions resemble a job interview. I try to look at his
wristwatch. I tell myself it will soon be over. Someone knocks on the
glass and he leaves the room.

I hear screaming, then the scuffle of boots and a drilling sound.
Men's voices, one pleading, "I don't know." My hands are still
bound. I can't cover my ears. I hear screaming, muffled sounds in
the distance, yelping. Then a voice shrieks, *"Me llamo Díaz."* He is
screaming his name so everyone will hear and know that he's the
one being tortured. "Díaz Velásquez! Díaz Velásquez!"

After a period of silence, the officer returns. He's carrying a
book and throws it down on the table. It is a copy of the university
quarterly published by my friends. I recognize the issue, fall 1990.
The officer sits down, opens the magazine and thrusts it into my
face.

"Did you write this poem?"

I nod.

"What gives you the right?"

I say nothing.

He lights a cigar. "This magazine is subversive. You criticize
the church. You incite and provoke."

I wonder whether my friends have been arrested and are being
held here, too. And why it took them so many months to arrest me.

"You are an enemy of the state." He blows cigar smoke into my
face. "You understand? You and your friends. Who are they?"

I'm confused. If he wants names all he has to do is to leaf
through the magazine on the table in front of him. I try to speak
loudly. *"Me llamo Alma Álvarez."*

I think he asks me again for the names of my friends. I hear his
watch beep, he glances at it and gets up. He stands behind me. I'm
choking from the stench of the cigar and fear. He accuses me of being

a subversive, an atheist, a traitor. I try to repeat my name. He puts the cigar on my shoulder and grinds it into my bare skin. I pass out.

Some time later, a doctor is feeling my pulse. My hands have been untied and I'm slumped over the table. The room reeks of cigar smoke. The officer returns and tells the doctor he's needed next door.

Two guards hood me and drag me back to the cell. I collapse on the lower bunk, praying for Isabel to return. The pain from the burn on my shoulder spreads down my arm and back. I hear a tray being slid through the slot in the cell door. I crawl towards it. One ration of tea and biscuits. Isabel is dead. I think I am next.

January 12

The cathedral bells are still ringing when the cell door slides open. A guard puts the hood on me. I stumble out of the cell, barely able to walk. The burn on my shoulder is hot. I am shaking and sweating. I wonder how I'll be able to carry a shovel, let alone dig my own grave. I trip on the stairs. The guard steadies me and leads me down a hallway. He hands me over to two men who push me through the doors to the entrance. They shove me into the back of a car. The car speeds. I retch from the motion, from fear. I think I am about to be executed. The minutes pass. The brakes squeal and the car stops. Someone opens the back door, yanks the hood off my head. The light is blinding. By the time I stumble onto the street, the man is back in the car. He's not wearing a uniform, has dark bushy hair and a moustache. I'm too dazed to take note of the car's make or colour. I realize I am standing on Calle Buenos Aires in front of the gate to my parents' home. It is just past seven in the morning.

The foregoing presents the facts of my kidnapping and imprisonment in La Cuarenta. I reserve the right to amend or expand this testimony should certain details or chronologies come to me later. It is written from memory of my own free will, without coercion or prompting.

Alma Álvarez
October 4, 2003

18

Lalo Martín wedged himself into the idling car, briefcase on his lap. Flaco drove through the late afternoon traffic. He glanced over at Lalo's profile, noting the stooped shoulders, the shadows beneath the deep-set eyes. Perhaps the sea air would refresh them both. Flaco wondered whether the sculptor's studio was far enough from the capital to be safe. What were the odds that Luis Corva was being bugged, that *they* possessed the technology to eavesdrop the studio on the seaside bluff, out of range for cell phones? It was naive to assume, based on *his* presumption, not theirs, that the artist's workplace should be sacred. Flaco silently raged against this enemy, even more obscure than during the junta, a pack of carnivores, rabid behind their respectability. He clung to the notion that Luis Corva was protected by international fame. The most vulnerable of them all was sitting next to him. He had to resist calling Lalo Martín every morning to make sure the man had made it through the night.

They reached the coastal road and the traffic thinned for a while. Around a bend, the road straightened to a line of vehicles inching forward. Flaco slammed on the brakes to avoid rear-ending a truck. Alongside a blood-red cliff, two PFL jeeps were parked on each of the narrow shoulders, forcibly stopping the cars and trucks. Four officers manned the improvised checkpoint. One of them approached La Vieja.

"Fucking police state." Flaco rolled down the window.

Lalo reached for his wallet in the pocket of his pants and pulled out his federal identity card, the *cédula* with the thumbprint, photo and personal data every Luscanan was obliged to have on hand at all times. Flaco reluctantly rummaged for his.

The officer leaned in, took the cards and scanned their faces.

"What are you stopping us for?" Flaco asked.

"We're looking for contraband. Car registration, please."

He reached into the glove compartment, dug through the jumble of cigarette packages and papers for the pale green document in a plastic case. "Do we look like smugglers?"

"Standard procedure, sir."

"You think they do this in other countries? You think this is standard?"

"Open the trunk."

Flaco got out of the car. He unlocked the trunk and watched the officer's hands. He knew their tricks, the planting of a little bag of white powder and the subsequent theatre of surprise and outrage. The officer lifted a crowbar, felt around the trunk and nodded. Flaco slammed the trunk.

"Turn on your headlights." The officer stood in front of La Vieja, arms crossed over his chest.

Flaco got in the car and complied. "How much do you think they want?"

"Ten pesos?" Lalo shrugged. "But wait." He removed a plasticized badge from his briefcase and reached across Flaco, flashing it at the officer. The policeman regarded the clip-on pass to the Ministry of Justice and smiled. "Sorry to trouble you." He waved them on.

Flaco started the car and drove off in a slow zigzag, hoping to spray the officers with gravel and exhaust fumes.

"I could denounce them, you know," Lalo said.

"Would you?" Flaco asked, knowing the answer. What was the point? This was a tradition, the end-of-month improvised checkpoints where the PFL stopped cars on some pretext to collect the bribes that would feed their families, pay rents, leverage a paltry wage into something sustainable.

Flaco flicked on the radio and tried to focus on the litany of world crises broadcast by Radio Luscano. Tight security greets Bush in Pakistan. A probe of espionage at Guantánamo prison widens. Then the regional news: the drought and mad cow embargo, a meeting of Luscanan and Paraguayan officials to resolve the border dispute. President Kirchner moves to revoke amnesty laws for military officers accused in Argentina's Dirty War. In Chile, President Lagos promises to redress the human rights abuses under the military regime but has yet, the announcer dryly states, to overturn the amnesty imposed by General Pinochet twenty-five years ago.

"Twenty-five years!" Flaco looked over at his passenger. "I'm not waiting that long." The sun's rays glanced sideways onto the Bay of Luscano. Shadows streaked the road like lances or swords, an abandoned arsenal of weaponry. Even his thoughts had become militarized and to bolster his resolve, Flaco resorted to crafting the news release in his mind. *Luscano, November 1, 2003. A new sculpture commemorating the disappeared is unveiled today on the grounds of La Cuarenta, the notorious prison where hundreds of Luscanans were detained without cause, tortured and executed in 1990 and 1991.* He thought of adding *during the nightmare of the junta,* then dismissed the idea. Just the facts, no adornment necessary. A car appeared, heading towards them on the narrow road, and Flaco managed to swerve just in time.

Lalo Martín turned the radio off. "Alma's agreed to see me."

"When?"

"Thursday morning at ten."

The same time Flaco gave his class on the *vanguardistas.* He tried to think of who could adequately teach Gabriela Mistral and Alfonsina Storni in his place but, oddly, only Alma came to mind. Worse, he wondered why Alma hadn't told him of her decision. He'd seen her at the university just the other day, playing piano with Emilio in a rehearsal room.

"She's bringing a written testimony."

Flaco envisaged Alma in the courtyard bent over her laptop. It would be painful but also purging, he hoped. It struck him that the absence of pressure had prompted Alma to act. A lesson for him — knowing when to be quiet as important as when to speak.

La Vieja jolted along the rocky trail leading up to the studio and he parked next to Corva's car. The door to the studio was open but there was no sign of the artist inside. They retraced their steps across the field. Flaco spotted tracks of damp earth leading towards a line of shrubs. Behind the shrubs lay a dense grove of carob trees. They followed the tracks into a clearing.

The sculpture was placed on a wheeled trolley that Corva must have pulled into the clearing. Sunlight reflected off the titanium sheet. It was shaped in tent-like angles over a mass of bodies in various stages of decomposition, some still fleshy and alive, others skeletal. In one corner, a limb protruded. In another, a hand reached out. The base, a platform of reddish-brown wood, stood as high as Flaco's knees. In a corner of the clearing, Luis Corva sat cross-legged on a cushion, his gaze focussed on his work, hands resting on his knees.

A *tero* screeched from the upper limb of a carob tree. The bird's cry seemed to ricochet off the titanium and pierce right into Flaco. His cursing alerted Luis Corva, who rose slowly and approached the two men. His normally pale face was flushed.

"Were you meditating?" Flaco asked.

"Repenting."

"There's nothing to repent. The sculpture is —"

"It's Yom Kippur. Day of fasting and repentance.

"We wouldn't have come today had we known."

Luis Corva waved off the apology.

"You want us to help you pull the sculpture back?" Flaco asked.

"It needs to be out in the elements for a while. I want to see how the piece weathers rain, dew, the salt air and sun." Luis Corva retrieved the cushion he'd been sitting on.

Inside the studio, the worktables were strewn with sketches. Wood shavings and particles of sand crunched underfoot. Luis Corva cleared the sofa of books and magazines. Lalo Martín sat down and opened his briefcase. "Here's the revised list." He handed over the stapled pages.

"How many?" Flaco craned for a glimpse of the names.

"Three hundred and eighty-seven."

Luis Corva leafed through the pages. "You've highlighted the additions. That will help. I'll get these to the students first thing tomorrow." He sat on a stool.

"Your students?" Flaco asked.

"I had to do it this way. It would have taken me too long." Corva explained that as part of their assignment this term, his students would be engraving the names on marble panels to be inlaid on three sides of the sculpture's base.

Flaco glanced at Lalo Martín. "Don't give anyone the full list, divide it up among them." All along Luis Corva had resisted the idea of adding names to the sculpture. For aesthetic reasons, Flaco presumed, but he'd argued for the importance of names to families who'd never had the opportunity of identifying and burying their dead. Names were the markers of human existence, transcending all other existential details, such as birth date, eye colour or even the thumbprints on identity cards.

Luis Corva lifted a sketch from a worktable. "This will be engraved on the fourth marble side of the base."

In memoriam   los desaparecidos
2003 a.d.

Flaco lit a cigarette to compose himself. The words, their simplicity, moved him. Sadness, but also gratitude to the sculptor. "Where did you get the marble?" It must have cost a fortune but Corva refused to discuss a commission.

"Gabriel Seil hooked me up with a local supplier. The marble is white with light grey flecks, works well with the sandstone and titanium." Luis Corva removed his glasses and rubbed his eyes. "I'm not convinced about having all those names engraved on the base. I'll go along with it, leave enough room for new names to be added should you discover more." He looked at Lalo Martín. "But understand, the precise figure doesn't matter to me. One person taken from their home, imprisoned, tortured, killed for no reason, is cause enough to grieve and remember. It's not a numbers game."

"Morally, I agree," Lalo said. "But we all know people need quantification for outrage and there's never been an official body count."

"At the end of the junta," Flaco said, "we knew hundreds had been abducted, but who cared? Luscano was a little blip in a forgotten corner of the globe."

Corva replaced his glasses. "In Argentina, some 30,000 people disappeared from '76 to '83 and I'm telling you, the rest of the world didn't pay much attention."

"When I go to Congress and the media with a report," Lalo said, "I need numbers and names. Some documents recently recovered were written by quasi-illiterate recruits. We've had to do a lot of checking, painstaking work neither perfect nor complete, to get the 387 names. When I file the interim report, it must be based on factual evidence. Let artists express the nuances of the suffering."

Flaco picked up the list and scanned the names. During the junta there had been many lists, some shorter, others longer than this one. Lists of banned books (to burn), lists of troublemakers (to eradicate), blacklists (to sabotage). With absolute control and stunning clarity, the lists had provided easy-to-follow directives down the chain of command. The list in his hand was the result of those lists, an unintended by-product of the military's compulsion and more than ironic. Here they were trying to account for those lists, producing a list of their own. Each name on this list, a stone dropped in a well, the ripples reaching into families, friends, lovers. And the deniers. A short list with exponential repercussions.

As he was leaving the studio, Flaco noticed a yellowed drawing tacked to the wall. A primitive depiction of a leafless tree. His four-year-old could do better. Looking closer, he saw roots traced from the trunk, long tentacles reaching into the earth, each with a label: Jews, Psychiatrists, Journalists, Communists, Artists, Franciscans. Corva said it came from an Argentine navy training manual on how to eliminate the tree of dissent: amputate its roots.

19

Days of pacing the courtyard, writing, then deleting and rewriting, reliving the shock and disorientation, the terror and the origins of her scar, the ugly mound of mottled skin where she'd been branded on her shoulder. Forgotten details retrieved from memory, activated by words. *I remember* repeated, until specificity emerged: the title of the book she'd been studying that night, the words of the poetry she'd recited in her cell. Then editing out the details that made no difference to her testimony. The name of the book or the poem that saved her didn't matter to anyone but herself and it mattered deeply. Alma struggled to bear down on the significant details, those that would give her testimony credibility. She slept sporadically and woke up thirsty and jumpy, too distraught to leave the house.

When she was finally done with the writing, she took a taxi to the university, cajoled a librarian into letting her print two copies of the document. Then she walked to the bookstore and handed Roma the envelope to hide in the basement in the safest of places where the banned books had been stored during the junta. She returned to the house knowing if she stopped to look for Carlos Cruz now, she'd risk giving herself away. Self-preservation kept her home until Thursday, when she rose, showered, and dressed, drinking a cup of warm milk instead of coffee so as not to disturb her imposed calm.

She entered the revolving doors of the Ministry of Justice. A brilliant chandelier dangled from the ceiling. Its bulbs illuminated the alabaster statues, goddesses of truth, liberty and victory, positioned on the marble floor. Surrounded by this lavish decadence, it struck Alma that there'd once been a vision to make justice a cornerstone of a newborn country named Luscano. As she strode through the foyer, clutching her bag with the envelope inside, she considered the irony of it all.

She entered an elevator with the men and women arriving for work, lawyers with briefcases and cell phones, busy purveyors of justice. She was relieved to escape their aftershave and perfume when she got out on the fifth floor. At the end of a desolate hallway, Alma found the Special Prosecutor's office and rang the buzzer.

A young man opened the door, introduced himself as César and directed her past the desks to a table by a windowsill. It was surprisingly noisy, with people talking on phones, typing on keyboards, making photocopies and sending faxes. Alma had expected to be alone in a small office with Lalo Martín. He came towards her now and leaned against the wall by the window. Unlike the expensive attire of the lawyers in the elevator, Lalo's suit was shabby, the jacket frayed at the sleeves. César brought a stack of binders. "These contain the photographs."

Alma withdrew the envelope from her bag. Once she'd handed it over, there was no going back. "The photos, are they recent?"

"We've tried to catalogue photographs from the time of the junta," César said, "for every member of the military whose name has come up or who we know was posted at La Cuarenta. Some are group shots taken in the barracks, others are graduation pictures from the military academy." He set the binders down on the table, and pulled a wooden chair up to it.

Alma held the envelope. "I might have to revise this once I've seen the photos."

"Of course," Lalo Martín said. "Memory is fickle. We understand that."

She glanced out the window. Below, in the Plaza Federal, office workers crisscrossed the cobblestones. A group of elderly women sat drinking coffee on the patio in front of La Loca. She knew Gabriel ate breakfast there every morning but she couldn't see him. The two men regarded her. It was too late to bolt. She handed Lalo Martín the envelope and they left her alone with the binders.

Alma sat down and reached for the top binder on the stack. She opened the cover. Within a plasticized sheath, three versions of a man's face stared back at her. She did not recognize him but she knew his type. A military man, short haircut, prominent ears and a stubborn jaw. She heard someone talking on the phone, arguing. It was hard to concentrate. She looked up and looked down again. Still no recognition. She turned the page to a sheath with one photo. She stared into the eyes. Nothing. She turned to the next one. After several pages, she flipped more quickly. How ordinary these men were. You could find them at a football game, in a grocery store, at the post office. Mostly young, some recently enlisted and proud in their new uniforms, probably from poor families in the countryside. She knew nothing about military rankings, could not distinguish the army from the air force. But if they were in the binder, they were suspected of evil.

An hour passed and she reached for the second binder. In the first few pages she recognized a face, or rather, the scar on the chin of one of her abductors. In the photo, he was sitting on a jeep, grinning ludicrously at the photographer. Black eyes and cropped black hair, the crooked row of teeth. He'd been snarling as he'd leaned back to shove her head down. Alma was somewhat certain. His face evoked the raunchy smells of beer and cigarettes. She noted the page number on a blank sheet César had given her and beside it, the word "lieutenant" to remind herself.

She continued turning the binder's pages and the faces began to blur so that they seemed to repeat themselves, although when she flipped back she saw they did not. She stretched her legs and looked out the window. A group of students loitered by some benches. They were carrying signs but she could not make out the lettering. In front of La Loca, the table where the elderly women had been sitting was now occupied by two men with short haircuts, white shirts and dark pants. They appeared to be photographing the students with their cell phones. Informers for the PFL, most likely.

In the last binder, the men were older, some with medals on their uniforms. Page after page of unsmiling but clean-shaven men, their chins lifted with pride. Alma stopped at a studio-quality portrait of a man in a grey uniform visible to the shoulders, no cap on the head, the prominent mole just below his hairline.

The face did not appear more or less cruel than the others. Just uninteresting, the eyes too close together, as trite as the books he read in the pizzeria on Saturdays. Detective stories with murders neatly solved and justice brought to bear on the criminals. Alma noted the page number and underlined it twice.

She continued, hoping to find the doctor who'd taken her pulse, one of the guards, or the man who'd driven her home. One face seemed familiar, that of a guard who'd come for Isabel. She noted the number, placed a question mark beside it.

When she'd gone through all the binders, she returned to the faces she'd recognized. Alma was sure of the first now, certain that this was the young man who'd pulled her out of the car by her sweatpants. Then she turned to Carlos Cruz again, trying to imagine him being arrested from his home on Calle Libertador in front of his family and neighbours. Would he resist or be cowed in humiliation? She suspected he'd put up a fight, at least cursing the men who'd come for him, calling them traitors and lackeys. Then she wondered if she'd be capable of taking a lit cigar and putting it out on his shoulder. Isabel, Díaz, and all the others would still have suffered for nothing. Bearing witness had only deepened the terror of her week in La Cuarenta, brought it back to memory's foreground. It did not provide closure, that North American word. Quite the reverse, unstoppable now.

"Would you like a coffee?" She jumped, surprised to find César standing by her chair. She asked for a glass of water. Lalo Martín came out of his office and sat across from her. He held her document in his hand. She drank the water as César brought another binder, thicker than the ones she'd been reviewing. He opened the binder and laid it down in front Alma. There was Isabel in a scarlet dress, her black hair to her waist, hand on her hip, the nose lifted in defiance.

"I thought she was a psychologist."

"It's her, then," Lalo Martín asked, "the one in your cell?"

"Definitely."

"Isabel Gómez. An amateur dancer apparently."

"She was never found?"

Lalo Martín shook his head.

"And her husband, Federico?"

He consulted the index. "Disappeared." Then he located another photo in the binder. "And him?"

Díaz posed smiling between two men who resembled him, brothers or cousins. His shoulders were lifted, his hands in the pockets of his jeans.

"I heard him being tortured." Alma handed over the sheet of paper with the three numbers. "I recognized these two for sure and the one with the question mark, possibly. The first is one of the men who kidnapped me from my house. The second is the man who… questioned me on my last day."

Lalo Martín opened the binder and studied the photograph. "We'll try to find him."

It will be easy, she wanted to say, given that he lives nearby on a cozy street. And hangs out at the officers' club in the old port. But she decided to wait and see what they came up with.

Alma's attention was drawn to a commotion outside. Lines of protesters, most of them young, were streaming into the plaza from a corner street. Those at the head of the line carried a banner, but she couldn't make out what it said. César mentioned that the government had announced the sale of a large parcel of land to a consortium. "They're going to build a casino, hotel and golf course. There's a march today to protest the development for its environmental impact. On the river and surrounding wetlands."

Lalo Martín suggested that they reconvene tomorrow. He and César would draw up a list of questions and draft a formal statement for her to sign. He took her hand. "It's an act of courage for you. We know that."

Alma did not feel a sense of relief when she left the Ministry of Justice. Instead, what came to her was familiar — the combination of anger and resolve that had motivated, no, enabled her to leave Luscano in the first place. And it would be so easy to flee again. All she had to do was book her flight back. It was too late. She had to see it through, see what would happen to Carlos Cruz.

Alma stepped through the revolving door into the stifling heat. She stood facing the backs of policemen lined up to guard the entrance to the Ministry of Justice. Beyond them, protesters jammed the plaza. They were cheering a young woman who stood on a bench shouting through a bullhorn. Drumbeats sounded in the distance. The boisterous noise was completely unlike the stunned silence in 1990. She and Roma, curious about the amassing crowds, had hurried to the plaza. They were in wordless shock as they watched the tanks roll over the cobblestones. Minutes later, General Galtí and his cohorts marched into Government House. Then nothing happened. Alma and Roma dispersed with the others. When she got home, Hannelore was glued to Radio Luscano. The newscast confirmed the coup had been successful. With the tacit approval of the oligarchy and most of the middle class for whom the economic shambles of the country justified the prospect of a dictatorship and order, the President had resigned immediately. Not a single shot was fired.

Alma wedged between two policemen and pushed through the crowd of chanting protesters. She squeezed through the chaos, a laborious wending left and right around the clusters of protestors. Then a surge carried her forward as the marchers proceeded to Avenida Primero de Abríl. Immobilized cars and trucks occupied all four lanes of the artery. Some drivers honked their horns, while others had left their vehicles to curse the protesters. Sirens blared in the distance. Alma spotted an opening on the other side of the avenue, a pathway leading to campus. Better to avoid a protest she barely understood. Alma made her way around the vehicles on the avenue, lunged past a column of students and approached the riverbank.

A group of bystanders, Flaco among them, clustered beneath a willow tree. He greeted her quickly and pointed across the river but she couldn't see over the trees. Flaco helped her onto a boulder and she rested her hand on his shoulder as she watched the students approach the prison yard. Riot police equipped with shields and batons stared them down. The policemen stiffened, legs planted apart, and began beating their shields with batons. It was a provocation, the nasty sound of rubber striking Plexiglas. The protesters crept forward, some shouted through bullhorns, others held out cell phones and cameras to photograph the lines of policemen protecting

La Cuarenta. Competing against the banging of the truncheons, a group of drummers advanced, Roma among them, a bandana over her nose and mouth, a large drum strapped to her shoulders. They were within metres of the riot police.

"Stop," Flaco said, his voice low like an offstage director. "Stop now."

A convoy of jeeps approached the rear entrance of the prison yard, followed by the cavalry on horseback. All they had to do was cut off the road between the bridge and La Cuarenta and the students would be trapped.

"Stay calm, deliver the message, show them your numbers, and leave." Miraculously, the students slowed to a stop. They did not grab stones and hurl them, did not lob bricks or bottles from their knapsacks. While a television crew filmed the protesters, two students managed to infiltrate the column of policemen on the far side of the prison. They shimmied to the second floor, rappelled up to the roof and moments later a red banner was unfurled across the wall of the prison. *¡No al casino! ¡Sí al medio ambiente!*

The crowd hooted and applauded as the perplexed policemen turned to look up. By the time they spotted the banner, the pair had slid down the prison wall and were running into the crowd. The protesters turned and proceeded back across the bridge, dispersing into the avenues. Flaco yelled, "They did it!"

Alma jumped off the boulder. "You were behind this?"

"My students came up with the plan."

"More effective than any of the protests during the junta." Alma didn't let on that the prospect of La Cuarenta's destruction appealed to her, a symbolic erasure even if it wouldn't negate what had happened inside.

"We didn't have the Internet." Flaco offered to walk her home. "You can tell me how it went with Lalo Martín."

"Does anything happen in Luscano without you knowing it?"

"Plenty. And none of it good."

Alma told him she'd identified one of her kidnappers and an officer who interrogated her. "From photos, of course."

"It must have been tough."

"Coming back was tough." All along, her return to Luscano had led to this reckoning engineered by Flaco. "You knew I'd end up doing this, didn't you?"

"I hoped you would...but how could I know you'd have the guts?"

A group of students approached them, one of them calling out, "Doctor Molino, did you see? They got the banner up." They told Flaco of the videos and photographs they'd be posting on social media. Flaco advised them to stick to the facts. "Nothing triumphant. Not yet."

He took Alma's arm and they navigated the mass of students and professors in the quadrant. Many stopped to speak to Flaco, but he didn't linger, sensing Alma's need to go home. He led her down the side streets to avoid the crowds, telling her of his plans for La Cuarenta. After the memorial for the disappeared was unveiled in the prison yard, he envisaged a renovation of the prison to convert it into a museum of modern history. "One with audio-visual installations documenting the last twenty-five years. Film clips of the junta, displays of the cattle prods, hoods and shovels, all the implements of evil." He hoped the university would help with the funding and the government as well. He spoke of all this, clomping along next to Alma, sweat coating his forehead.

On Calle Montevideo she stopped at a stand to buy water and they drank from the bottles. She looked at him. How could he be so sure of himself? "I don't know, Flaco. Tourists walking around in rooms where people were tortured. A memorial, maybe, but a museum?"

"Better than a casino, don't you think?"

They turned onto Reconquista where a man was stapling fliers onto a telephone pole. They were advertisements for a bullfight.

"Another issue my students are willing to take on."

"Good for them. I've never understood the fascination with —"

"It's our legacy, *chica*, left by the Spaniards. The blood and violence began with genocide, the slaughter of the Mapuche and Quechua, the Guaraní and the Querandí, and left us with the bullfight...the battle in the ring between man and the snorting energy with horns capable of goring to death." Flaco gestured like the boy who'd played Che in her courtyard. "Read your Lorca. The matador steps into the ring, beloved and courageous."

"But bravery dies and it's a brutal death." Flaco was wrong about her guts. If I was really brave, she thought, I'd have gone to see Díaz's wife to deliver the message he'd entrusted with me in the holding cell.

Flaco addressed the sky, his fists clenched, more despairing than macho. *"Because you have died forever, / like all the dead of the earth, / like all the dead who have been forgotten / on some heap of snuffed-out dogs."*

In Lorca's "Llanto por Ignacio Sánchez Mejías," Alma recalled, the matador is killed at five in the afternoon.

20

After her second session with Lalo Martín, she returned to the house and hesitated by the front gates. Across the street, a *muchacha* swept the neighbour's driveway. The leaves of the jacaranda rustled. It was usually a gentle, soothing sound, but today it felt menacing. Alma strained to hear banging or someone searching the rooms over the sound of the broom swishing the pavement. Finally she unlocked the front door, walked through the living room into the dining room, the kitchen, the bedrooms and bathroom. She pulled back the shower curtain and checked the tub. She opened closets. Outside, the courtyard seemed empty. Or was it? The noonday sun, almost directly overhead, shaded the corners.

Alma sat down and tried to assess the situation. Lalo Martín's words, "the situation," as he'd outlined the dangers of sabotage and expected revenge. "Before Christmas, I plan to table an interim report. I'll request an in camera session with a judge and present the affidavits and evidence collected to date. There could be a backlash." He described the tactics of intimidation that he, César and others working in his office were experiencing.

Alma made the mistake of asking, "What about Carlos Cruz?"

His name had not yet come up and Lalo Martín picked up on this, asking how she knew his identity. Alma explained that she'd caught sight of him recently.

"Did he recognize you?"

"No."

"Leave him to us."

"Will he be arrested?"

"You have to let us handle that." Lalo Martín emphasized safety, said the element of surprise was critical to finding witnesses willing to cooperate. Alma sensed he had little to go on, that he needed an insider who dared confess, who wanted to set things right even if his own life or his family's would be in peril. Carlos Cruz was not such a man. Not a cell of remorse in his body when he paid for his cigars and newspapers, the arrogant tossing of pesos on the counter. No, Alma thought, he'll resist them to his death.

And then to allay her fears, he'd added, "In your case, there's a deterrent to repercussions, your citizenship." He asked how long Alma planned to remain in Luscano. "I'll need you to testify at some point." Things would stagnate during the holidays but he expected his work to accelerate in the new year.

Alma made no promises, stating firmly that her sabbatical would end soon, that she'd have to go back to teach in January. Later in the meeting, César had asked about her release. Alma disclosed the little she knew. "My mother claimed she called Patrón Pindalo." César noted this down, glancing at his boss. "I can't do much with second-hand information," Lalo Martín had said. But it seemed crucial that the trail would lead outside the military into the tentacles of power.

Sitting in the courtyard, Alma felt divided between two versions of herself. There was the exile stifling her past in that other life in Montréal, writing and teaching, defining herself as she wished. It was a predictable existence, structured yet disconnected. All she had to do was to release the pause button held since her return. But now there was this version, her decision to testify rooting her in Luscano, a reckoning she had to pursue until she'd dealt with all the truths that were in her power to uncover. In either case, she had to manage her fears, could not afford to regress into paranoia, jumping at every sound, hiding out in the house alone.

Alma went to the kitchen and phoned the bookstore. Roma launched into a detailed retelling of the protest. Alma listened for a break. Patience plus the concession of privacy would be the cost of having her friend live here. She finally got to the point of her call.

"I'll get my stuff and come over tonight. By nine at the latest."

Alma had a rehearsal with Emilio in the evening. She promised to leave the key with a neighbour.

"Do you have any food?"

Alma opened the fridge, empty but for her staples of bread, yoghurt and fruit. "Not really."

"I'll stop at the market on my way."

Alma hung up and dialled the embassy in Montevideo, which, since the Canadian budget cuts of the nineties, also covered for Luscano. A receptionist answered and put on her on hold. As she waited, Alma contemplated Flaco's words yesterday, his recitation of Lorca's "Absent Soul." He'd been trying to warn her indirectly through the bullfight, its legacy of bloodshed. He could never tell her straight, "Bearing witness is a huge risk, beware." It was a repeat of that afternoon in 1990 when they'd gathered around the table in the student lounge, Flaco, Alma and their friends, to plan the next issue of *Voces acalladas*. Flaco had argued that it had to denounce the junta. Opening a file of manuscripts, he'd decreed, "Your poem, Alma, and Armando, your essay." What had they done to Armando? She'd seen his photo in César's binder among the disappeared. Flaco had never stopped to consider the risks, had never spoken directly of the dangers. And he himself had not written any of the words that had cost them all so much. Had it been worth it? Armando's essay, "These Darkest Nights," had become their short-lived manifesto before the crackdown. In the end he'd died for nothing. She had to have it out with Flaco, could not allow herself to be intimidated by his eloquence and passion.

A Canadian official came on the line. Alma booked a meeting for December, explaining that her mother had died and she required officially certified copies of the death certificate translated into English. And she asked that her presence in Luscano be noted, dictating her phone number and address.

Then she went about preparing the house for Roma's arrival. It seemed easier to empty her bedroom. She filled the suitcases on the floor, then ferried them into the room next door. Alma sat on her mother's bed. It bounced a little too easily. She'd have to get over it, the queasiness of sleeping on the deathbed. Despite Xenia's airing out, smells lingered — a sour milk odour of disinfectant, medication and residue of her mother's night sweats — conjuring the memory of Hannelore's face, her pallor of surrender, that dawn when Alma had returned from the beach. She'd never seen a dead body before, had never imagined her mother so deflated, her great spirit dissipated.

Alma opened the wardrobe and packed up the clothes that Xenia had not taken with her. Silks and linens, the dresses of past celebrations, slid into a box where they lay intermingled, a collage of happier times. She emptied the drawers of stockings and scarves, panties and bras, feeling voyeuristic, almost trashy.

In a bottom drawer, she unearthed a stack of files labelled with the names of Hannelore's students. Inside, her mother's notes on their progress, the texts covered, payments received. Near the bottom of the stack, one file stood out by its name. Alma opened it and read her mother's telegraphic notations. "A mess, can't concentrate, possibly anorexic." Beneath another date of tutoring, "French voc. poor, comprehension vague. English slightly better. Assigned her a Storni poem to translate. Brought me her poems instead, said I should keep them. Heartbreaking, her mother's murder, the poems all about death and she's only 16." In the same file, Alma found the poems written on looseleaf in a childish handwriting. A sonnet about an imaginary conversation with a horse, two poems on the sea and a third entitled "My Mother" describing the recurring visions of a female ghost. The poems were not all about death, that was Hannelore's typical exaggeration, but they provided the pretext.

Before leaving for the university, she found Hannelore's address book and dialled. A long pause followed her request to speak to Celeste Pindalo. "*No, Señora, vive en Miami.*"

"I have something of hers. Her father may want it."

The *muchacha*, her voice as young as a teenager's, explained Patrón Pindalo was away on business, due back tomorrow. "Come by at five. He's usually home by then." A stroke of luck, the maid's insouciance. She didn't ask for Alma's name.

Emilio and the singer were already rehearsing when Alma arrived. She sat down at the piano and watched them. Susana was striking, a tall woman with black hair as long as Isabel's, and dressed in layers of brightly woven fabrics. Her mezzo voice sounded like the sea, primordial and self-aware. Emilio put down his violin. "We better start. Susana has a gig tonight."

Alma ran though a quick scale, then she nodded. The violin began but Alma missed her opening and they started again. She got it right the third time and Susana's voice joined the instruments. Melancholy as a *fado* singer's, her voice suited the piece, balancing the frequencies of the piano and violin. Susana had a good ear and agility, quickly adapting the rhythm of the poem to the phrasing. Although Alma played as well as she could, she was clearly the weakest of the three. "Let me hear the two of you do the piece."

She listened, feeling an internal echo to the question, "Who are you?" posed in that needling voice. Some bars later, contemplating Roma's generosity and love, her willingness to drop everything to help her, Alma heard the answer, "*Soy yo.*" I, the one who survived.

"*Testigo de tanques en la Plaza, ¿por qué nos has fallado?*" Witness to tanks in the Plaza, why have you failed us?

"*En el humo de libros quemados tu silencio nos ha lastimado.*" In the smoke of burning books your silence has wounded.

Then a pause, tapped out on the piano by Emilio's bow, during which Alma had a vision of herself. It wasn't blurry or incomplete, like that of a victim. There was a wholeness to it that had her thinking she'd finish the book on Agustini. She'd finish speaking out. She'd confront Patrón Pindalo. Courage sourced from her father's music.

Emilio dropped her off in his car. Every room was lit in the house, usually the darkest and quietest on the block. Inside, the aroma of roasted tomatoes and peppers, cheese, onions and garlic filled the hallway. Roma greeted her in one of Xenia's aprons and gave her a massive hug.

Out in the courtyard, the long table had been dragged to the centre, rows of candles flickered among plates and cutlery. A group of women, sitting on chairs, was playing an assortment of drums, guitars and an accordion. Alma helped carry a pot of sauce from the kitchen and they sat at the table, breaking the fresh bread, eating

Roma's pasta, drinking wine. Roma's friends argued and lamented, they complimented the cooking, told anecdotes and described adventures. Some of them were artists, a few were shop owners and teachers, most of them were gay and none of them were strangers to suffering. That simply, the house was transformed, Alma's habitual sparse evening meal usurped by a feast.

After clearing the dishes, they sang, danced and played drums. Alma watched mostly, happy to witness Roma's exuberance. Past midnight, when everyone else had left, she helped Roma wash the dishes. She hung the damp dishrags on Xenia's clothesline by the back door and followed Roma into the courtyard for a last glass of wine.

"Look how clear it is." Roma traced the stars of the Southern Cross with the wine glass in her hand.

Alma thanked her for coming. "It's been a long time since this courtyard witnessed a party. Hannelore would so approve."

"My friends loved it!" Roma regarded her. "They're gay, you know."

"Are they open?"

"Most of them aren't. The Church...still too powerful. Gay marriage is going to be a long time coming to Luscano. But Chichi, she sat next to you at the table, she's a lawyer and active in the community."

Chichi had told Alma she'd learned about the Canadian Charter of Rights and Freedoms at a conference, and was working on getting a similar charter passed here. Alma repeated this to Roma.

"She's got a big fight ahead of her."

"*Everyone has the right not to be arbitrarily detained or imprisoned.*"

"Say that again, my English is rusty."

Alma repeated the line from section nine of the Charter which she'd learned in preparation for immigration proceedings. "That's it, the whole section, one line."

Roma's round glasses enlarged her dark eyes and lashes. "And they follow that rule to the letter?"

"No." Innocents resided in the prisons in Canada and they suffered unfairly. Injustice was not Luscano's invention. "But it's in the most important legal document in the country and that means something."

"All power to Chichi, then. Anything worthwhile requires a battle, doesn't it? Either you survive by muddling through and accepting things as they are or you risk a fight and learn to cope with fear."

"How?" Alma remembered the beatings in the eighties when gangs of skinheads went after the few gay bars in Luscano. She and Roma were teenagers then, and didn't have the money to go to bars much, but she'd still worried for her friend.

"You work on yourself to stay grounded. You get up and greet the day as if it's yours. 'Hey, thanks for showing up, I'm going to make the most out of you.' It sounds lame but that's what my younger self used to think in '91 on my way to work. Every so often, the owner of the bookstore gave us a list of books and told us to box them up. It was crazy, the titles they banned. One week the poets, then the Argentines, especially Sábato for his work on the truth commission, Chileans, Cubans and local writers. We were supposed to destroy the books but we stored them in the basement. A person would come in, ask for a banned book and I'd talk to them, get a sense of who they were. Then a decision. You look into the stranger's eyes. 'Will you betray me? Will I be tortured for selling you this book?' At the same time you're thinking 'do I want to be an accomplice to insanity?' So to hell with fear, you sell them the book they want. I guess if you're born gay in Luscano, being a dissident comes naturally."

Alma leaned towards Roma and described her sessions with Lalo Martín, explaining that the envelope Roma had agreed to hide in the bookstore contained her testimony of La Cuarenta. And then she spoke of the need for secrecy and the dangers Roma might face living here with her.

Roma did not flinch. "I'll stay as long as you want me to. We just have to establish some ground rules. There's one thing I wanna know. Did you think of asking Flaco to live here?"

"Actually, no. He might have misconstrued." And, Alma thought, I need to confront him and I can't if he's living with me.

"He'd have come, I'm sure of it. I always thought you'd end up lovers. So did your mother. The way you both quote poetry when you're stressed. He's crazy about you."

Alma braced herself. "Gabriel's been calling me. I'm going to an *asado* at his mother's house next weekend."

"You're kidding me." Roma laughed. "Remember, I've been his confessor. I know his baggage and he's another case of...never mind. You'll figure it out. Neither of you are kids." Then she laid out the rules. "I can't pay much in the way of rent but I'll cover the food and cook for you. Here's the deal: a closed bedroom door means out of bounds. If we stay out late, we let each other know or leave a note. Secret handshake?"

Roma spit on her right palm and held out her hand. Alma did the same. They shook and snapped their fingers, a high school ritual for sealing a promise. Then, before going to sleep, Roma double-checked the locks on the windows and doors.

21

It descended over the Bay of Luscano like a predator with a giant blade attacking the coastline. Patrón Pindalo breathed through his nausea as the helicopter dropped vertically onto the concrete pad. He stepped out first and ran towards the clubhouse, straining to lope with the same lightweight steps he imagined Javier Martinez taking behind him. Couldn't lumber like an old man with his youthful protégé gliding in his wake, not with the Saturday lunch crowd in the Barrio Norte Yacht Club watching from the windows.

A waiter accompanied him to his table in the alcove. Javier slid onto the banquette across from him and set his briefcase on the floor by his feet. The lawyer made a good impression, young and fit in his gabardine grey. Patrón Pindalo could feel the eyes of the diners boring into his back, imagining the whispered innuendo that, in less than six months, he'd already replaced his own son.

Patrón Pindalo ordered a salad and sparkling water. Javier hesitated for a split second, probably wanting a steak or something substantial. But he ordered the same. Good call. The lunch, a debriefing on the morning's meeting in Uruguay, would not be happy.

"What was learned today, Javier?"

"Looks like they might put up a fight."

"We knew that was coming. What did *you* learn today?"

Javier loosened his tie, then thought the better of it, and tightened the knot. "Patrón, I've spoken to those guys in the commission. They assured me —"

"During one phone call, maybe two? You should've met with them personally before dragging me to Punta del Este to be embarrassed by our lack of preparation. Jorge Centavo had no inkling, assumed we're opening a line of casinos here, in Uruguay, Brazil, God knows where. I wasted my time undoing his misconceptions and laying the groundwork you should have handled weeks ago."

"It's not my fault their internal communications are —"

"Had you actually gone there, you'd have seen what you're up against, entered their heads. My friend Jorge fears competition. But he's too full of himself to admit that a boutique hotel in this provincial outpost could pose a threat. Our one casino, small compared to his, emphasis on the hotel and golf club, that's what you capitalize on, Javier."

The waiter brought the bottle of sparkling water and a plate of lime slices. Patrón Pindalo made sure to continue berating the lawyer in front of the waiter. The flush in the young man's neck, his hands rubbing his pant legs, the anger was there under the surface when he ordered a Campari and soda.

Patrón Pindalo rose to make the rounds of tables, letting Javier seethe on his own. He shook hands and doled out *abrazos*, greeting the bridge crowd, the polo set, his tennis partners and the retirees. The Galtí widow placed her talons on the sleeve of his blazer. "How are you these days?" The nerve she had, after all he'd done to cover up her husband's suicide. He couldn't take the pity in her eyes.

Javier was tearing a slice of bread into pieces, his scarlet cocktail half empty. The salads were served and Patrón Pindalo, still queasy from the helicopter ride, half-heartedly speared a wedge of tomato.

"What about the environmentalists?" Javier asked. "The demonstration the other day —"

"Who was behind that?"

"A bunch of students, as far as I could tell from the news reports."

"So you weren't there."

"I was in my office working, Patrón."

"I heard it was a large crowd, not just a bunch, but hundreds of hooligans. These so-called green activists? You were probably in Yale at the time, but they took on a construction project a few years ago. I sold some land up the coast to a developer who planned to build some low-rise condos. When the activists got wind of it, they installed themselves in tents on the beach, tried to prevent the construction. After a week or two of media coverage, their numbers dwindled. When the builders arrived with bulldozers, a couple of activists tried to stop them. They were arrested, kept in prison a few days, enough to scare them off."

"So we wait them out. Postpone the prison's demolition."

"Why should we? Here's the thing, Javier. The protest last week was large. Luscano hasn't seen dissent on that scale in a long time. Even though the military bungled things, one of the junta's accomplishments was to remove the population's taste for protest. But I'm worried things have swung back."

"What can we do about it?"

"I'm supposed to ask you that question. You're in charge of this." Patrón Pindalo chewed a slice of cucumber. The thing was damn hard, or maybe his teeth were giving out, too.

"I can't stop the students. You want me to go find them and hand them envelopes as well?"

"That's your advice as lead counsel?" Patrón Pindalo dropped his fork on the plateful of salad greens, wilted and glistening with olive oil. He wanted nothing but to go home, check on his grandchildren, then lie down and rest his back.

"Listen, Javier. There's a professor at the university, a dean apparently. From an old Luscano family, but unlike the rest of them, he's a troublemaker. The name's Molino."

"Never heard of him."

"He's agitating to put up some kind of memorial on the grounds of La Cuarenta." Patrón Pindalo pointed a finger at Javier. "Go and see him."

"What kind of memorial?"

"For the so-called disappeared. This professor doesn't want the prison demolished. But he knows his students don't care about a few souls lost over a decade ago. So he agitates them, gets them going on an issue they care about, the environment. My sources tell me he's behind the protest."

"What am I supposed to say?"

"Talk some sense into him. Don't order him to shelve the memorial. Just find out what he's up to. Use some finesse for a change." Patrón Pindalo waved the waiter over and threw his napkin on the table. He signed the bill. "We'll continue this at the *asado* tomorrow. Come early, say eleven."

Patrón Pindalo strode through the yacht club dining room. His stomach was cramped and his lumbar ached, but he did not regret his treatment of Javier. The *asado* would heal the lawyer's pride. Nothing closed a man's wounds more quickly than barbecued meat, good wine and cigars.

A sailing instructor drove him home in one of the club's golf carts. Inside the house, he buzzed the *muchacha*. She came out of her quarters, hair a mess, half asleep.

"Where are the children?"

"At a movie, *Señor*."

He asked her to bring a glass of milk. He went into his study, lowered the blinds and lay down on the sofa. When the maid returned, he sat up and drank the milk. She found a pillow and blanket, placed them on the sofa by his side. "Patrón, there's a woman coming to see you this afternoon."

"Who?"

"I don't know her name. She said she had something of your daughter's."

"What?"

"I don't know."

"Your job is to know." Her chin dropped, long black strands of hair framed her small face. "You're too pretty for sadness. Wake me up when she comes." He shut his eyes but couldn't sleep. His stomach would not stop churning.

At exactly five in the afternoon, Alma approached the gates to the mansion. Her face burned from the sun and winds off the sea. She held the envelope with the poems over her head for shade as she waited by the intercom. A *muchacha* appeared from the house and activated a remote. The gates jerked open and Alma slipped through.

She crossed the driveway. By the three-storey house, a garden faced the sea, which shimmered behind a line of palm trees. A row of chaises-longues with white cushions was arranged around the swimming pool. The scene resembled an abandoned resort, swept clean and empty, not a towel or pool toy lying around.

The *muchacha* invited her to wait in an anteroom by the front door. On an oval table, silver-framed photographs were set in a row. Family portraits by the pool, in front of a Christmas tree, at a polo match, all dating from the sixties, by the look of the clothing and the hairstyles. One photo showed the couple alone, posing with the pope, an official photograph taken in the Vatican presumably. Alma registered the message these photos were meant to convey: here lives a well-connected and upright family. The oligarchy framed in hypocrisy but dated. Which begged the question, how much power did they still possess? Flaco would know, but she hadn't wanted to tell him of her visit here.

"*Señora, pase por favor.*"

The maid escorted her down a hallway and into a study, closing the door behind Alma. The study had a metallic feel, with its line of polo trophies, tiny statuettes of men on horseback. She shook the man's hand and introduced herself. He stood appraising her, his face as coppery as seaside cliffs. She couldn't tell if he knew who she was. "I am the daughter of Hannelore."

"I meant to convey our family's condolences but it was a bad time." Patrón Pindalo gestured for her to sit in a tubular chair. The air conditioning gave off a clammy breeze.

Alma remained standing, the envelope in her hand. "I heard about your son. You know they were buried on the same day at the Cementerio Real." Gabriel had told her of the double burial.

Patrón Pindalo moved towards the bar and offered her a drink. Alma asked for water. He stooped to retrieve a bottle from the small fridge in the corner. His movements were stiff but self-assured. He poured himself a finger of Scotch. An adjacent wall was decorated with framed maps of Luscano through the centuries, from the Guaraní settlements to the first official map following independence. República Oriental de Luscano looking out to the sea, sketched in ink on parchment, its coastline suggesting the craggy profile of a centurion.

He lifted his glass and touched hers gently with the rim. "What a woman, your mother. We called her 'the European.' I used to see her at concerts. She went for your father, I suppose, and was always elegant, an entourage around her. The *señoras* of Barrio Norte were jealous. They might have had the means, but your mother, she possessed the power...intelligence."

Alma sat down and put her glass on a coffee table. She was still holding the envelope, restrained the urge to use it to fan away his toxic politeness. He'd noticed the envelope, his eyes moving continuously, taking in her sandals, earrings and her breasts, like a horse-trader inspecting a mare.

He sat down on the sofa to her left. "Yes, she was cultivated and straight, a rare combination. You know she tutored Celeste, had the nerve to call me. 'Your daughter's a mess. You need to spend more time with her, Patrón.' It's rare in Luscano, someone I hardly know telling me what to do." His laughter was a bitter sound, escaping from the slit of his lips.

Alma sensed the exactitude of his memory. "I was going through Hannelore's things and found these poems by Celeste. I thought she might like to have them." She opened the envelope and held out the four pages of poems.

"Celeste lives in Miami now." He made no move to reach for the papers. Alma placed them on the coffee table. "She's coming tonight, as it turns out. Ernesto's children need her now. I'll give her the poems." He leaned back in the sofa and crossed his legs. "I've never cared much for poetry. Are they any good?"

"They are, considering Celeste was sixteen when she wrote them."

"She could've been a poet? That might mean something to her now." He swallowed a mouthful of Scotch and grimaced. "Although she'll find a way to blame me for the missed opportunity. What became of you, Alma?"

"I teach at a college in Canada, literature and Spanish to pre-university students, many of them from this continent."

"You've probably got a work ethic, the one thing I couldn't instill in my children. I thought they'd see their old man working and learn from me, just like my father's example influenced me. But they didn't have your mother, or any mother, for that matter. My wife died, you probably know that. I raised them and now I'm raising Ernesto's children."

He went on about his grandchildren. When he lifted his glass to his lips, she said, "In January 1991, I was brought to La Cuarenta. Unlike the other prisoners, I was released. Did you have a role in that?"

From the gleam in his eye and the curling of his lips, Alma knew he understood the real reason for her visit. "Just to be clear, I was never in the army. Of course, I fulfilled my military service at eighteen like everyone else, but after that I stayed away. I'm not a politician either, just a banker and businessman, pure and simple."

Alma waited through his digression as he tried to establish his credibility, perhaps out of respect for Hannelore or maybe just an ego-driven impulse to distance himself from the junta.

"They went overboard," he was saying, "And they were sloppy. When your mother called, I had to help."

"How?"

"I had some contacts."

"Who?"

"What difference does it make? You got out. And looking at you now, I can see you're fine." He had the nerve to pause, as if expecting gratitude. When Alma said nothing, he continued, "This wouldn't have anything to do with the prosecutor going around trying to dig up old resentments, would it?"

"I don't like not knowing," Alma said.

"Secrets and lies, they're not for me either. Your mother wasn't the type, she played straight. My son, Ernesto...that's another story...he was nothing but secrets and lies. He even..." He shrugged and regarded his glass.

"I'm not staying in Luscano long, but while I'm here, I want to clear things up."

"That's admirable, it really is, but I don't know anything more. I called someone I knew in the military, at the top. He's dead now, it makes no difference. But he arranged for your release."

"I'd like to know his name." This aging patriarch, for a moment, had held her fate in his hands. Alma stared him down.

He put his glass down on the table. "You should stay here. It's beautiful, there's no climate like it in the world. I'll help you find work, if you like. I know the rector at the university."

"Why would I stay in a place where a poem can put a person in prison and a phone call can get them out?"

"It could happen anywhere." It was chilling, his arrogance in the air-conditioned room under halogen lights.

"Everyone has the right not be subjected to any cruel and unusual treatment or punishment."

His lips tightened. Alma stared at him. He was embarrassed, couldn't admit his incomprehension of English. She translated the words for him and their source, the Canadian Charter of Rights and Freedoms, section twelve.

He laughed. "Are you that naive? I won't pretend to know anything about Canada, but I've seen enough of the gringos to know they may have a bigger arena and fancier names...special interest groups, lobbyists, ex-politicians...the ones behind the scenes with the clout to activate agendas, issue clemency, make sure their sons don't risk their lives in wars that line their pockets. Luscano's no different."

He started going on about George W. Bush. "I met him in Texas once...before he was president. A congenial type. He never served in the military but look at him now...all national security and military intervention. That's what the junta did, bring about national security and our economy's the stronger for it."

There was no point in debating him. Having confirmed his role in getting her out of prison, Patrón Pindalo wouldn't tell her more. Loyal to name and background, brutal in opposition, no doubt he'd gore anyone in his way.

22

Gabriel flung back the sheet and jumped out of bed, covering it with a duvet. He washed the pile of dishes in the sink, then swept the floor, sweat stinging his eyes. His efforts to clean up the apartment were interrupted by the ringing telephone. First his sister: "Yes, I'll bring the empanadas... No, Inés, I don't know her that well." Minutes later, his mother: "We'll be there by one... No, we're walking over... I don't know what she likes for dessert. Ice cream is fine." At forty-three, inviting a woman to a family *asado* should not stir up this anticipation and micro-planning. But he couldn't blame them. He too wanted it to be perfect for Alma.

Gabriel collected the accumulated newspapers and magazines on his desk. Blowing dust off the bookshelf, he found a photo of Aude and him in Buenos Aires and slid it between two books. Getting Alma here would require a massive detour after the *asado*, some pretext. He looked around. There was nothing to lure her with. Come back and look at my books? A glass of wine was all he could offer. Or coffee. Did he have any milk? He opened the fridge and found a carton, half full, that smelled reasonably fresh.

After showering he rummaged in the armoire for his last clean shirt, staring down his reflection in the mirror inside the door. Would you buy a used car from this man? A resounding no. But would he want to sell one in the first place? On the top shelf of the armoire lay the box with Roberto's notebooks. Perhaps he'd show them to Alma and she'd discover the entries on Aude and ask, "Whatever happened to this woman?" And he'd have to admit, "I looked for her and found her. She became my lover." He closed the armoire door, his reflection swinging away. Best to keep Roberto out of it. His brother had always been luckier with women.

Gabriel found a rag and sat on the bed, wiping the cemetery grime off his shoes. He still regretted never having brought Aude to his mother's home. She would have seen him in a context, loved by others, and absorbed their empathy. Of all the women he could have fallen for, he'd gone for Aude, first because she'd been Roberto's lover and second because she read only poetry, came from Estonia and, like him, lived a maladjusted existence that rendered her permanently exiled. Had her love been truly reciprocal, had the tenuous filament that held them together been stronger, she would have never followed her husband back to Ottawa. A few secret meetings later, she'd called it off. "I'm not suited for long-distance affairs, Gabi." Oh yes she was. Aude's real problem? She wasn't suited for love, too deeply immersed in herself. Best not to think of her either. He gave the apartment a last glance, decided it looked half decent and locked the door.

Outside, the warm breeze carried whiffs of coffee and fresh bread from a nearby café. Women in summer dresses were heading for Sunday mass, some pushing strollers or dragging their toddlers by the hand. These mothers struck him as beautiful this morning, the promise of summer in their bare arms and legs.

He walked to the corner of Primero de Abríl and waited until the bus chugged towards him. Once seated, he scanned the ads posted above the windows, their perky slogans originating from a different century than the bus spewing leaded exhaust fumes up the avenue. *Gracias*, the blonde *gringa* beamed, the cell phone in her hand wrapped in a red Christmas bow. She oozed happiness, that elusive state exploited by marketers and pop psychologists. Gabriel imagined an ad for the Cementerio Real. A woman wearing a tight black dress posed under a coral tree. *Gracias*, the caption would read, a grandmother floating blissfully in the sky above.

Did happiness even exist? Every emotion had its opposite. Working at the cemetery had exposed him to more than a lifetime of sadness. He occasionally witnessed a redemptive result from the personal tragedy incurred by death. There were some who mustered astonishing serenity in burying their dead. Even more powerful, a few mourners overcame past ruptures to reconcile with siblings or cousins with whom they hadn't spoken in years. He had seen them embracing by a grave.

Gabriel caught a glimpse of the cemetery's southeast corner by Castillo's house, and felt affection for the place, especially since he wasn't working today. Ever since Patrón Pindalo had come to his office and delivered the veiled threat to have him fired, Gabriel had been assessing his options. Supposing Bilmo dismissed him, where would he find work? Other cemeteries were smaller, run by families or affiliated with a church. He couldn't fathom going back to the bookstore and spending the afternoons gossiping with Roma. He needed a new Plan B. Aude had provided one, the fantasy that she'd call from Ottawa, begging Gabriel to come. That had been pure delusion.

He spotted the lineup wending out of the *empanadería*, pulled the cord and disembarked at the next stop. He'd placed his order in advance so Juanita would hand him the packets of warm empanadas, Castillo helping out beside her. Gabriel hoped that their happiness would rub off on him, and arriving at Alma's house, he'd be irresistibly gallant and cheerful.

It was the warmest Sunday so far this October spring. For many, it was the season's first *asado*, its rituals especially relished. All over Luscano, in backyards, on the beach and in the countryside, kindling was being ignited in barbecues made of blackened stones. Some tuned guitars in anticipation of singing after the meal. Others filled coolers with bottles of wines, sparkling water and soft drinks for the children. Empanadas were laid out on baking sheets and large cuts of meats and bulky sausages were extracted from refrigerators. By late afternoon, the scents of burning wood and sizzling meat mingled in the hazy sunlight.

At the Molino *finca* outside the city, Claudia and Ana set the table under the *palo cruz*, its outstretched branches offering yellow flowers to a cloudless sky. Isidro stood stoking the fire with a prong. The heat was intense and he removed his shirt, hanging it from a branch. Ana noticed the horse trainer's muscular back and elbowed Claudia. The women watched as he prodded the wood in the barbecue until they heard the sounds of Flaco shouting in the field beyond the garden where a football game was in progress.

"Over here!"

Fredo kicked the ball towards his father but Eduardo intercepted and dribbled it down the field. He kicked and scored another goal.

"Papa, why'd you tell me to pass? You weren't ready."

Flaco heaved, his hands on his knees, trying to catch his breath. It was killing him, this running. Thankfully, the bell clanged outside the kitchen and his kids, nephews, nieces, cousins and brothers ran off the field. Eduardo waited for him by the goalpost.

Flaco tried not to limp as he followed his brother towards a low stone wall encircling the garden. Eduardo pointed out the missing tiles on the roof of the house, the warped window frames and the sagging foundation. Flaco listened helplessly to the litany of defects. The plantation house, the stables and fields required more capital than he could save in a decade. "You've still got the polo ponies?"

"That's what's keeping us going. Pindalo pays well and on time."

Flaco rested on the wall, stretched his leg out and rubbed his sore knee. Eduardo sat beside him, drawing a butt from his shirt pocket. He smoked one cigarette a day, two puffs at a time, carefully saving the remnant in his pocket. Flaco handed him a king-size Parliament. "Have one of mine." They smoked, watching Ana distribute glasses of juice and wine beneath the *palo cruz*. Isidro prodded sausages on the barbecue. The man could have worn a shirt, Flaco thought. "Seems Ana's quite taken with Isidro. At my birthday party, she couldn't take her eyes off him." But that was back in July. Knowing his first wife, he'd given the affair no more than a month.

"He takes breakfast with the children every morning, rides with them after school."

"Is he good to them?"

"They love him."

Well, he thought, I get what I deserve. "How's business?"

"We've had to hire a few more security guards at the firm. The port's been busy lately. A few of the cruise ships have started stopping here. It's good for business."

"What do you know about this casino?"

"I'm hoping we'll get the contract. For the casino and the hotel eventually."

"Who's behind it?"

"A consortium, apparently." Eduardo stubbed the cigarette out on the wall, tamping the butt before sliding it into his pocket. "Word's out you were behind the protest last week. True?"

Flaco let his silence transmit the answer.

"They're going to demolish La Cuarenta any day now...you don't stand a chance."

"Ever heard of a lawyer called Javier Martinez?"

Eduardo shook his head.

"Phoned me for a meeting, claims he's working for Pindalo."

"You better see him, Flaco."

"I need a favour." He told his brother about Alma.

Eduardo listened. He'd inherited their father's poker face without the corresponding addiction to gambling. Flaco, more like his mother in temperament, tended to blurt things. But when he mentioned Lalo Martín, his brother reacted. "The guys hate him. They tacked his photo to the bulletin board at the social club. I know you're mixed up with him but watch out."

"I want you to assign a security detail to Alma, day and night."

"Who's paying?"

"I am...unless you agree to give your brother a break."

"We don't work for free and you can't afford it. Tell her to come live here for a while."

Flaco looked up at the solid house rising behind the garden. Nobody would harass Alma here, not with the security of the Molino name, Eduardo and his connections in the club where he found the ex-military guys to work for him. But it was no place for Alma and too far from the city. "She doesn't have a car."

"Let's eat, Flaco."

He hobbled behind Eduardo. "Please, *hermano*, just for a few months. She's going back to Canada after Christmas." He chipped away, begging like the little brother he'd once been.

The tantalizing smell of barbecued meat probably convinced Eduardo more than his pleas. "*Bueno*. A one-man operation in a car outside her house. She won't notice. But in return, Flaco, don't block the casino. That work will be our ticket. We'll renovate the house, pay the kids' school fees on time for a change and invest in this place."

Flaco whacked him on the back. "Anything you say, *hermano*."

"I'm thinking we'll get a herd of llamas. Their wool, I hear, is worth its weight —"

"Don't they belong in the cordillera? They spit, for God's sake."

"That's why I'll put you in charge of them."

"*Hijo de puta.*"

Armonía came running. "Hurry up, Papa. The sausages are ready."

Flaco felt a searing pain in his knee as he bent to lift her into his arms. He carried her to where the others sat and collapsed into the seat at the head of the table. "Ana, could you get me some ice?" He knew his proprietary tone was unkind and disgustingly macho, but it was a signal to Isidro: This is my family, not yours.

The trio tuned their instruments, testing the microphones and amplifiers set up by the pool. *Muchachas* were clearing the buffet, carrying platters and bowls back into the house. The guests, polo acquaintances and bank employees, sat drinking coffee under the umbrellas that shaded the tables. Behind them, the sea lay flat and intensely blue. At the first sounds of the Caribbean *merengue*, Magdalena and her friends were up dancing.

Patrón Pindalo was reclined on a chaise longue located as far away as possible from the speakers. He was glad to see his grandchildren having some semblance of fun. Less appealing was the sight of Javier Martinez leaning towards the décolleté of Ernesto's wife. Javier had come early as ordered, not remorseful but subdued, reporting that he'd set up a meeting at the university and prepared some new documents to placate the Uruguayans. Patrón Pindalo had sat him next to Celeste, hoping for some chemistry between the two. Celeste looked sad and dried out, her over-tanned skin like parchment. He couldn't blame Javier for hitting on the widow, but she ought to know better. The six months of mourning Ernesto were not even up.

Patrón Pindalo closed his eyes so he'd be left alone. He would have liked to slip into the house and look through his telescope again. Another shipment was due. Those Argentinean vigilantes couldn't get enough of the rifles. His stomach struggled with the excess meat he'd consumed, too heavy and greasy. Another downside of this aging business was that you couldn't eat anything good anymore. He rose to get a digestive from the bar.

Javier waved from the dance floor, shouting over the music. "You can't beat this, Patrón." In a broad gesture of his muscular arm, Javier took in the pool, the band, the sea gleaming beyond the terrace. "It's why I came back. No place on this earth is as civilized."

Patrón Pindalo poured cognac into a snifter. That's what he should have said to Alma yesterday. Civilized was the word that best described this life. Too bad she hadn't come to the *asado*. It had been spontaneous, the invitation before she'd left, an effort to placate. Truth was he needed some company. Alma had shown up, a trim and graceful apparition in his study, her stock desirable. And best, her aura of a well-travelled person yet familiar with the ways of Luscano. Alma would chase the pity away from people's eyes. So what if she'd been one of those almost lost by the army's inept handling of troublemakers? She owed him her existence. He'd called Galtí on her behalf, one of a few calls he'd placed after frantic friends had begged for help. Not always, of course. In some cases he'd done nothing. When Ernesto had told him that his friend, Roberto Seil, had disappeared, he'd opted not to intervene. The young man had been a bad influence, capable of drawing Ernesto into serious trouble. But Hannelore Álvarez, when she'd called, he'd been more than willing. What a woman! Strong, persuasive and beautiful.

Patrón Pindalo swirled the cognac in his glass, contemplating his meeting last month with Gabriel Seil. Like Ernesto, the man was

all obfuscation and weakness. His manoeuvring smelled of guilt.
Since then, he'd postponed trying to find out what Ernesto had done
with the documents stolen from his safe. He'd have to wait out the
consequences. His next move, throwing a wrench in this professor's
plans, might yield the truth.

He returned to his chaise longue and sipped the cognac. Javier
and the widow were dancing a tango. Who could blame her if she
remarried? Javier would be useful to have around. The children
might despise him at first, just as Ernesto and Celeste had despised
their stepmother. And they'd been right. Too late in life he'd learned
that children were often excellent judges of character. Magdalena
could sniff out a fake from across a polo field.

The cognac settled his indigestion but his chair vibrated to the
infernal beat of the pounding music. Closing his eyes, he tried for a
soothing image, came up with the opening of the casino, Alma on
his arm as they crossed the red carpet beneath a glittering marquee,
their entrance so grand everyone would forget the prison had
ever existed.

Manuel was midway through an anecdote Gabriel had heard at least
fifty times, his medical rescue of some politician he'd managed to
bring around after a heart attack. Like everyone else around the
table, Manuel had made it his mission to impress Alma. They'd served
her the choicest cuts of beef, kept her wineglass full, complimented
her dress, and placed the candles closest to her when sunlight faded
from the sky. Gabriel watched them warily. He couldn't blame his
sister or his mother for trying so hard, but Manuel was crossing the
line from welcoming a stranger into the fold to overt flirting. He
addressed Alma exclusively, his moustache gleaming with drippings
of his meal until even Gabriel's mother, polite to a fault, squirmed in
her chair. At the end of the anecdote, she delved in. "Tell me, Alma.
How do you find Luscano after a prolonged absence?"

Gabriel felt for Alma, but he couldn't come up with an elegant
interception. She handled the question well, mentioning the new
boardwalk along the coast, the charms of the architecture, streets
and plazas. "And of course, the trees and flowers." Alma gestured to

Emma's small garden, the white rosebuds creeping up the trellis, the blossoms on the lemon tree.

"And the people?" Inés asked. "Do we seem terribly Third World to you?"

It was painful, the loaded question. Gabriel mentally rehearsed their exit.

"There's poverty in Montréal. Homeless people sleep on the streets even in winter when it's dangerously cold." Alma paused to drink some wine. "What I notice most here are the delineations. The rich are very rich but small in numbers compared to the migrant workers from Bolivia and Brazil, the *muchachas*, gardeners and street vendors who are practically indentured, dependent on the goodwill of their employers."

"I couldn't survive without my *muchacha*," Inés declared.

"That's terrible," Gabriel said, "as if she's an appliance or —"

"You know," Emma intervened, "we're as attached to Milagro as we are to each other. She and I, our need for each other is mutual, especially now that we're both old."

Alma conceded that for women especially, *muchachas* represented another set of hands in the household. Working in Montréal, coming home late from teaching all day, she too would have liked someone to have cleaned, done the laundry, prepared dinner, and keep her company. "But I've noticed," she added, "that the shantytown by the river, once just a cluster of shacks, has taken over the area."

Manuel had to launch into a rambling diatribe on the illnesses, tuberculosis in particular, imported by migrant workers. Gabriel couldn't bear it and went into the kitchen, where Milagro stood drying glasses by the sink. "You should come outside and sit with us. It's beautifully warm tonight."

Milagro handed him a stack of plates, asking him to reach up and put them on the top shelf. "*Tu novia es muy simpática.*"

"She's not my girlfriend. Yet."

"I hope you find your happiness at last, Gabi."

When he returned to the garden, the conversation had turned melancholy, the trait of the Seils that regrettably, Gabriel knew he best represented. Aude had often chided him, "You're so pessimistic."

"Roberto," his mother was saying, "always played guitar at our *asados*. He's here with us, I can feel him." She gestured towards the sky above the ochre tiles of the house, where the new moon, a sliver of mother of pearl, was inlaid among the first stars.

Gabriel put his hand on Alma's shoulder, claiming he had to work early tomorrow. The good-byes and *abrazos* seemed interminable. Emma insisted on giving him the leftover empanadas and cutting some flowers for Alma, wrapping their stems in tissue paper.

They left on foot, Alma holding the bouquet and Gabriel carrying the parcels of leftovers. She laughed with him about Manuel's anecdotes but was careful not to criticize his brother-in-law directly. Not that he would have minded. A soft breeze picked up as they walked towards Barrio Norte and the sea. Alma seemed to be heading straight for her house and Gabriel couldn't find the words to suggest they walk to his apartment. They reached her front gate. He was surprised to see the house fully lit, to hear the sounds of drumming from somewhere inside.

Alma asked him in for a glass of wine. He followed her through the unusual layout. The courtyard, instead of being placed at the back, occupied the centre of the house, a rectangle beyond glass sliding doors. Within it, a group of women formed a circle, and there was Roma beating a drum between her knees.

In the kitchen, Alma found a vase for Emma's flowers and opened a bottle of wine. He was relieved she didn't suggest they join the others. Standing next to her, Gabriel detected the lingering residue of burning wood from the *asado*, a faint smokiness that enveloped them.

She didn't mind his presence next to her. Gabriel seemed intensely interested in watching the drummers through the small window in the kitchen. A few played Andean *bombos,* others, the small beaded drums of the Brazilian rainforest and timpani of Paraguay's jungle. The *asado* had been a reprieve for her, a nostalgic reminder of Luscano's charms set in the oasis of a family garden, and a distraction from the impulse to follow Carlo Cruz on his Sunday rituals.

Gabriel's mother represented the type she'd often wished for as a child, a gentle presence in contrast to Hannelore's cringe-inducing directness. And thinking of her mother just as Gabriel put his arm around her, she imagined the familiar voice uttering her opinion. "A cemetery administrator? Alma, please." She laughed and Gabriel, interpreting this in his own way, turned to kiss her. The drumming accelerated. This man, hesitant and, Roma was right, on the gloomy side, held her and Alma did not mind his taste of wine and cigarettes. They kissed until the drumbeats slowed to a measured rhythm, the cha-doom cha-doom cha-doom of a living heart.

23

Sara tapped on the open door. "Doctor Molino? A man's here to see you." A pale grey suit shimmered into the office. Flaco pushed aside the term papers and pointed at the chair across from his desk. The man sat down, snapped open his briefcase and slid a business card towards Flaco. Embossed with gold lettering, "Javier Martinez" followed by his degrees, BA *cum laude* from Dartmouth College, MBA from Yale, doctorate of law from the University of Luscano. Flaco looked up from the card. "So, Doctor Martinez — "

"Javier, please."

"What can I do for you?" Flaco went for irony with the American turn of phrase. It would have been more typical to comment on the card, mention some long-lost cousin who'd also studied at Yale, seek out a connection, however tenuous, Luscano-style and establish his own credentials in the process.

Javier laid a laptop on the desk between them. A few keystrokes and the screen displayed a PowerPoint, the images timed to change every few seconds. The first slide was the casino itself, a structure of glazed glass and asymmetrical juttings, set against a bright green background. The ivied buildings of the campus were reduced to pink shadows. More Miami than Luscano, the casino's design lacked any correlation to the nearby architecture of the university. Trees had been moved, shrubs added, colours enhanced, the river's murky water transformed into a sparkling blue. The slides flashed promises of job creation and tourist income among graphics of the hotel and golf course to be constructed on the fields where they'd executed the prisoners.

What was he supposed to say? Sara glanced at him when she placed the coffee cups on the desk. He couldn't meet the eyes of this student who'd marched with the others to demonstrate against the development. Like most of her friends, Sara had assumed one protest would bring victory. And maybe he had too, for a naive moment. But then he'd been summoned to the rector's office for a curt meeting. The rector explained that the demolition of the prison would proceed as scheduled and ordered Flaco to cease all activity aimed at sabotaging the construction of the casino. Waving aside Flaco's arguments, the rector told him Patrón Pindalo had offered a generous donation to the faculty with the understanding that the expanse of lawn behind Humanities would be designated a sculpture garden. "Your memorial for the disappeared will inaugurate the sculpture garden. It's a concession, Dr. Molino. If you don't take it, you're fired." Flaco stormed out of the office, leaving the rector waiting for gratitude.

Flaco swallowed his coffee in one shot while Javier enunciated the project's benefits. It was tempting to point out that legalized gambling in a country prone to corruption did not correspond to recent government affirmations on transparency and accountability. He let the lawyer's words pollute the office as he stood and walked to the window.

A bulldozer hunkered in front of the prison. Flaco looked down at the yellow machine. Would it be capable of breaking down the old walls or did they plan to use explosives? When Javier finished his pitch, he turned to face the lawyer. "Tell me, Javier, where were you in the early nineties?"

"Dartmouth, New Hampshire."

"So you didn't witness what happened here?"

"You mean the —"

"Do you have any siblings?"

"Two older sisters."

"Imagine this. You're in Dartmouth studying in your dorm and you get a call from Luscano. One of your sisters has vanished. Nobody knows where she is. Your parents have gone to the police, checked the hospitals and morgue, spoken to your sister's friends. They meet others on a frantic search. It turns out people are disappearing. The government denies this. You hear your mother's distress over the phone. What would you do?"

"Hypothetical. It didn't happen."

"It could have and did, repeatedly."

"Not to my family. The point is —"

"What if you later find out your sister was brought to that prison, over there across the river? Where she was last seen or heard screaming as they tortured her for no reason other than someone didn't like her, put her on some list, picked her up and —"

"I see what you're getting at, but —"

"As a lawyer, you know it's illegal, detaining people without cause, without *habeas corpus*. The years pass, your sister's gone, you wait for some explanation or maybe you give up. Your parents cannot. Their daughter was last seen in that prison. For them it's a sacred reminder...in lieu of a grave."

"Isn't that what your memorial is supposed to represent?"

"To tear down La Cuarenta would be the final negation that she existed." Flaco turned from the window to face the lawyer. "You work for Pindalo. Your job is to promote the project. But you're paying with your soul, understand? I can't stop the bulldozer. Pindalo's taken care of that. So what the hell are you doing here?"

Javier Martinez left in a hurry and Flaco took a sedative. He called Sara into his office, explained his focus was on preparing for the unveiling of the sculpture and asked her to convene his grad students for a meeting. Then he walked over to the studio in the faculty of fine arts. Inside, the apprentices were bent over marble panels. Luis Corva moved between them, verifying the chiselling of names. Flaco caught his attention and they stepped into the hallway. "How's it going?"

"It's difficult to keep them consistent."

"On time?" Flaco had been pressing to finish the work by the Day of the Dead.

"Should be."

Flaco told him about the rector's orders.

Corva cursed. "My works are in sculpture gardens all over the place. New York, Frankfurt, Buenos Aires and Lima...this was supposed to be different." He pointed out that the piece was specifically designed for the space in front of the prison.

Flaco suggested they walk to the proposed site behind the Humanities building.

Corva refused. "You should have worked this out before I even started the piece." The blame hit Flaco squarely on the chin. He let the sculptor spew venom at him, didn't mention that if they defied the rector and tried to unveil the piece across the river, it would be torn down within the hour. Then he convinced him, "Just take a look at the space, man."

They reached the expanse of lawn bordered by trees. Across the river, men with pickaxes hacked at the prison walls. Flaco tried to invent the merits of the site, that it would be visible from the casino's windows, that generations of students would appreciate the work. "And for now, yours will be the only sculpture out here."

After another sedative he met with the students, telling them straight. "The casino's on. Nothing can stop it." They were furious, arguing that Flaco had capitulated too easily, accusing him of never really supporting opposition to the land development in the first place. They asked to continue the meeting without him. Before he left, he spoke of his plans for the unveiling of the sculpture. He had to beg for their help, extracting commitments from each of them. Even Sara balked. In the end, the only reason they agreed to help, he figured, had to do with the upcoming end of semester exams and term papers. They wanted good marks.

In the evening, Flaco left the campus for Barrio Norte. He should have called first but he seemed to have lost control over time, was acting only on impulse now. His anger at the rector, compounded by the stinging fury of Corva and his students, festered into self-recrimination. He drove La Vieja over to Alma's, hoping for consolation. As he parked the car he noticed Eduardo's man in a black Renault, well positioned to observe the comings and goings at Alma's house. He felt the security guard's eyes on his back as he entered the gates. Eduardo had delivered and so had he. His brother was probably the only person in Luscano not disappointed in him today.

Alma opened the door, wearing a sleeveless top and shorts, and led him to the courtyard where Gabriel sat on a chair smoking. Alma left for the kitchen. Newspapers and books were scattered on the tiles. Flaco had expected to find Roma here, resented the comfort with which Gabriel lounged in his wicker chair. He sat down and reached for one of the books on the coffee table, a collection of poems by Delmira Agustini. "She's working?"

"Yes, I am." Alma returned with three demitasses on a tray.

Flaco picked up the porcelain cup. It reminded him of Hannelore, delicate but strong enough to contain the steaming liquid. Alma described her plans to visit the archives in Montevideo, apparently with Gabriel. This unsettled Flaco but what could he do? He spoke of the unveiling and asked them both to attend. "Saturday, November first. We've worked out everything except the music." He looked at Alma. "Emilio mentioned you've been working on a piece."

"My father's composition. He set my poem to music. But I don't —"

"You don't have to read it. Emilio says he found a singer."

Out of nowhere, she pointed at Flaco, raising her voice. "Remember, Flaco?" She clenched her hand into a fist as if she wanted to punch him. "Remember what happened the last time I let you talk me into something my gut was telling me not to do?"

"You're going to kick a guy when he's down?" he asked, slumping into his chair. "*Hijo de mil putas.*"

Gabriel pointed to the scar on Alma's shoulder. "It's the ones that did this to her. They're the sons of whores."

Palms on his forehead, Flaco rocked, the wicker chair creaking under his weight.

It was clear to Alma that Flaco was having some kind of meltdown. He looked terrible, like he hadn't slept or eaten properly for days. But she had to make him understand. Night was falling. She should turn on the lights but she preferred this shadowy scene, with Gabriel nearby for moral support.

Alma conveyed the cost of writing her testimony. Instead of working on the Delmira Agustini book, she'd lost weeks, her mental energy focussed on six days in January 1991. "And for what? Do you think it's going to bring back the disappeared?" She didn't wait for answers, kept talking, telling about her encounter with Patrón Pindalo. She was glad when Flaco responded with alarm, was aware that Gabriel seemed stricken. Too bad. She described the guilt she felt that others had died while she had survived. The residual fear of facing the man who'd tortured her and the dirty feeling of being an informer, even as she understood the importance of bearing witness. "Those responsible, dispensing the orders, they'll never be brought to justice. They're too powerful, Pindalo and his cronies." The old man's words had stayed with her. "It could happen anywhere." It could and did and what made Flaco think Luscano was special?

Alma hurled the blame and anger at Flaco until, exhausted by it all, she simply said, "I have to return to Montréal with *something* to show for my sabbatical."

Flaco nodded, his face grim. "I promise you if Lalo Martín fails, and I have never before admitted this possibility even to myself, I'll find a way. We could publish your testimony, shame Luscano and —"

"You don't give up." Alma stood up. "Flaco, it's my writing, my words. You don't decide. You've got the Molino name behind you. You're as untouchable as Pindalo, yet you have the nerve to pressure me."

Alma left the courtyard. She didn't know what Gabriel and Flaco were thinking, didn't really care. She rummaged around the kitchen, found a glass, a bottle of water left by Roma in the fridge.

The two were still frozen in their chairs when she returned with a glass of water.

Alma held the glass out. "Should I throw it in your face?"

It was that teasing voice that brought him out of it. "Just try, *chica*."

They heard a commotion in the hallway, the rattling of tins and bottles, and Roma came barrelling out. "Flaco, you're here too? Jesus, Alma, you don't rest. *Merluza* tonight, fresh from the docks."

24

Alma sat on the bed, typing on her laptop. A few rays of sunshine dappled the duvet cover. Through the open window she heard the gate creak and footsteps. It was just before eleven. Roma had left for work an hour ago. She listened, heard a soft tap-tapping on the door. Alma slid off the bed, crawled along the floor towards the window. This was the time the mailman usually came. Maybe he was bringing a postcard from Todos Santos. Nobody, not Roma, her drummers or Gabriel, could fill the space in the house left by Xenia. No sound of letters being dropping into the mailbox. The person knocked again, loudly. Nothing like the sound of pounding fists. Flaco had said someone from his brother's security firm was guarding the house, but still. Kneeling by the window, she looked out and caught a glimpse of a blue shirt, short hair over the collar. Alma stood up, brushing the dust off her knees, annoyed at herself for her paranoia.

She opened the door. "I was just in the area and thought I'd drop by." César stood on the front step. On the street, a man got out of a black car and sauntered to the gate. "Everything all right?" he asked. Alma nodded and he retreated.

César handed Alma a business card belonging to Lalo Martín. Scrawled on the back with his signature, "Please accompany César immediately."

The PFL occupied a misshapen edifice, once a colonial building to which several distinct wings had been added over the decades. Inside the entrance, a metal detector was manned by two armed guards in blue jackets. César showed them a laminated card, then led Alma past the throng milling by the wicket, where people waited to pick up their *cédulas* with an aura of hopelessness, as if they'd been there for days. The shabby corridors and the elevator smelled of La Cuarenta, a sour, institutional blend of bleach, sweat and something scorched, gun powder or the static of electrical currents.

Alma followed César down a long hallway. In the distance, a group stood quietly conversing, Flaco and Lalo Martín among them. Flaco's face was flushed. When he saw Alma approaching he crossed his arms over his chest as if to contain himself, leaving Lalo Martín to speak. The Special Prosecutor explained that an interrogation was in process, that he wanted Alma to witness it, that he'd asked Flaco to come for moral support.

Why then did Flaco refuse to look at her?

Lalo Martín turned to César. "His lawyer showed up an hour ago. They had a private meeting. We're just getting started." He opened the door to a narrow room with metal folding chairs facing a one-way window. On the other side of the glass was a larger room, where Carlos Cruz, in his striped polo shirt and trousers, sat hunched at a table. His lawyer, in a dark suit and tightly knotted tie, sat next to him, relaxed yet focussed.

Across the table, a woman asked questions. "Why did you leave the military?"

"I had my fifteen years so I retired."

"When was that?"

"In 2001, end of May."

"What was your last assignment?"

"An office job at the base in Campo Gitano."

The interrogator asked him to describe his duties. She was surprisingly young, her demeanour courteous. She did not take notes, relying on the recording device set on the table between her and Carlos Cruz. He gave bland descriptions of administration, paperwork, submissions.

Hearing his voice transmitted over the speakers into the room where Alma sat between Flaco and Lalo Martín was more than jarring. Her body stiffened, and she couldn't settle into her chair. Following him around all these weeks, she'd never heard him speak. That nasal voice brought back the moment of her interrogation in La

Cuarenta. Now it was his turn to answer questions. He had a lawyer to support him. She'd had nobody.

The interrogator asked about his previous job and the one previous to that, getting him to describe the months overseeing a remote border crossing into Paraguay, then a year at a munitions storage facility up the coast. His answers, although precise on dates and chronology, provided few details on his actual duties. Alma waited impatiently for the years of service to pass. She understood the reverse chronology, go for the most recent memory and work backwards, but wondered why the interrogator remained so passive, why she didn't call him out when he skated over his precise roles, titles and promotions. It was tedious listening to his monologues between the questions, his voice precisely as she remembered. When they reached 1995, the last year of the junta, the interrogator asked where he'd been stationed.

"Here in the capital."

"Your duties?"

"Transportation."

"To and from La Cuarenta?"

He shook his head as if puzzled by the question. "Vehicles and logistics. In 1993, the army purchased a new fleet of tanks and jeeps. I was trained to operate them and then responsible for delivering them to various bases and training others."

"And before that?"

"I was stationed in Government House, a staff job reporting to General Galtí. He travelled a lot. I accompanied him."

"When did you start?"

"1992...early in the year."

"And before that?"

"I was in Paraguay on assignment for most of 1991."

"For?"

"Training."

"What kind of training?"

The lawyer responded. "Luscano's armed forces had a long-standing contract to train their personnel with the Paraguayan corps. Señor Cruz attended a program in the base near Asunción."

The answer defied logic. Hadn't Flaco said relations between Luscano and Paraguay weren't exactly congenial? A good actor, Cruz let his lawyer answer the difficult questions. He never once glanced at the opaque window. He was careful. He knew he was being watched.

"What kind of training?" the woman repeated.

"Weapons, light vehicles, logistics." Carlos Cruz shifted in his chair.

"Who else was with you? From Luscano."

"My detachment."

"Their names?"

The lawyer smiled. "You're asking Señor Cruz to remember details from over a decade ago."

The woman persisted. "You don't remember a single colleague?"

"I was moved around so much. The army does this. It —"

"You're unable to name anyone from Luscano who attended the training in Paraguay with you?"

"No. I mean, yes, I am unable."

"And the names of the Paraguayans?"

"Don't remember."

"When did you return?"

"December, just before the holidays."

"Señor Cruz," the lawyer said, "was reassigned to the General's office."

"Yes, I know," the woman said. "It's the preceding months we are discussing. Where was he in January 1991?"

"In Paraguay. Look, this is a waste of —"

"And yet he can't name a single colleague."

"Evidently not."

He lied so convincingly, Alma's anxiety deepened into alarm. She turned to Lalo Martín. "You know he's not telling the truth."

"I do and so does she."

The interrogator changed tack and went back through the officer's career, his training, when and where he'd enlisted in 1986, at the age of twenty. He was just one year older than Alma and this realization came as a shock, that someone roughly her age had assaulted her, was capable of torture. The interrogator went back to the period of the junta, repeating her questions. Carlos Cruz answered with almost the same words as the first time. He was masterful. The obfuscation continued until the lawyer called for a lunch break. A guard escorted Carlos Cruz back to a cell.

Alma turned to Lalo Martín. "He'll never admit that he was in La Cuarenta."

"We'll catch him in some lie sooner or later." He explained that the woman posing the questions was the best of his staff trained in the psychological tactics of interrogation. "She's gauging his suggestibility, how willing he is to accept and act on suggestion, and his weaknesses, so that she can exploit them later. Deception," he said, "is essential. Allow him to tell his lies so that we can use the improbable statements later. Then scare him into talking by disclosing the consequences of his lies. Fear makes people talk. But he's not afraid yet by the look of it."

César opened a notebook. "You're sure that's him?"

"The man who interrogated me at La Cuarenta is the same person being interrogated." Alma paused. "He asked me a series of questions about my identity, then proceeded to extinguish his cigar on my shoulder. I recognize his face, the mole on his forehead, his voice and height. Carlos Cruz was in La Cuarenta on January 11th, 1991, the day before my release."

César nodded, writing quickly, then handed her the notebook. Alma verified that he'd recorded her words verbatim.

Lalo Martín and César decided to return to their offices and research ways to discredit the alibi. Alma asked if they'd be continuing the interrogation after lunch. "We have to question him quickly," Lalo Martín said, "until we have the legal grounds to detain him. But you don't need to be here." All they'd wanted from her was confirmation of the identity of Carlos Cruz. She tried to argue, but he refused. "It's best if you leave now." He asked Flaco to wait with Alma in the room to ensure she wouldn't encounter Carlos Cruz in the hallway. Inside the interrogation room, the lawyer was working his cell phone. He glanced at the woman writing notes. "You'll have to release him, you know that."

"How many are you representing?" she asked.

"I imagine we'll be seeing a lot of each other."

The institutional stench stayed with Alma long after they left PFL headquarters. Flaco convinced her to join him for lunch at a nearby café. They both ordered pasta but Alma managed only a few forkfuls. The grease on her plate resembled the sheen on Carlos Cruz's balding head. Flaco chewed quickly. She'd never seen him so tense.

"The part about him being in Paraguay," she asked. "How will they discredit that?"

"I don't know. Would he have had a passport? Would it have been recorded if he'd crossed the border? Are there faked papers created to show that the commanders were ostensibly in Asunción?"

"The military…they protect their own. They've covered his tracks." She saw in his eyes that he agreed.

"My guess is he was a fixer. Not a mastermind but a purveyor. They wanted to wipe out dissent and he was one of their foot soldiers."

Flaco insisted on walking her home. The sun bore down as they crossed the plaza. The Cathedral's shadows lay tightly by the structure's walls. Its spire pointed heavenwards, a finger accusing the gods. If she were to rewrite the poem, she'd render the structure hollow and meaningless, a metaphor for justice.

25

Alma turned to lie on her back, relinquishing the sheet to Gabriel. The midnight air cooled her limbs. She watched the curtain sway in tempo to the distant drumbeats carried through the open window from the courtyard. Gabriel breathed evenly and loudly. He'd come tonight with empanadas and a bottle of wine. Alma had needed the quiet, and so they'd eaten in the bedroom. She told him of witnessing the denials of Carlos Cruz. Gabriel had been horrified. He did not try to placate her with false encouragement, let her rage and pace the room and then he'd held her.

Alma struggled to relax on the soft mattress, the one on which her mother had died and her parents had lain together. Against her will, she conjured the image of her parents making love and then tried to dismiss it, overlaying it with Agustini's gothic symbolism. *Magnificent beds spread with sadness / Sculpted with a dagger and canopied / By insomnia....*

Her work on the poet crept in on a regular basis now. Alma was deep into her writing, the counterpoint to testifying and bearing witness. Her mother would approve. "Immerse yourself, Alma. But face up to things, stop trying to escape your fate." What would she say about the interrogation of Carlos Cruz? For the first time, she missed her mother, the strength of her intelligence and intuitive moral compass. "Let him sit and suffer in his cell, Alma." Is that what Hannelore would say? She wouldn't obsess, wouldn't linger on the ethical crevice over which Alma found herself suspended. Let Carlos Cruz suffer in a PFL cell. To hell with his rights. Stall the process until he breaks down and confesses. Alma wondered whether his wife and children would be allowed to visit, bring him clothing,

books and food. Lalo Martín was obliged to respect *habeas corpus*
to indict those who had not. She understood that. In the absence of
evidence, he'd be released, leaving Alma with a profound negation
of self, her words and credibility as a witness discounted, valueless.
The build-up to her testimony, the adrenalin of anticipated revenge
as she'd imagined Carlos Cruz punished for his brutality on behalf of
her cellmates, Díaz, then Isabel, who'd paid with their lives, would
be deflated, leaving her dangling in midair.

To overcome the vertigo she thought of Montréal, how the
fall leaves crunched underfoot on Mount Royal this time of year,
while in Luscano, the approaching summer delivered its hammer of
humid heat. She'd called a friend in Montréal last week. Stephanie
was organizing a Halloween party. She'd spoken of their friends and
costumes. How quickly that life, Alma's other world, had receded.

Gabriel stirred and turned towards her. His hand stroked her
leg. He cleared his throat. "What's the matter?"

She told him she couldn't sleep, blamed the drumming, the
humidity, the grease of the empanadas.

A car pulled up on the street outside. There were voices,
too faint to overhear. A door slammed, the car drove off leaving
night sounds, a clanging gate somewhere on Calle Buenos Aires,
jacaranda leaves shuffling in the breeze and the drumming, always
the drumming. Gabriel's hand moved from her leg to her upper arm,
his fingertips brushing the welt of mottled skin, too uneven for a
vaccination scar.

"What was it like, Alma?"

She shook her head and he seemed to understand. Not now.

Alma reached out and traced his scar. A pale hyphen connected
his eyebrows, caused by a childhood accident. As kids Gabriel and his
brother had been locked out of the house once and he'd tried to be
the big brother hero. But halfway up the ladder to the open window,
nervous with vertigo, he'd slipped and fallen, gashing his face on the
way down. Gabriel saw himself as a failure and struggled to shed this
defeatism as if working off a layer of skin. This effort moved her. His
eyes, a watery grey like the colour of the water in the river on its way
to the sea, regarded hers and she knew he was thinking of his brother.

"Gabriel," she said, "I often feel ashamed. A week, not even, six days at La Cuarenta. I allowed that time in prison to occupy so much inner space. It's nothing compared to what others endured."

Propping himself up against a pillow, Gabriel asked if she'd heard of Roberto Bolaño, the Latin American writer born in the fifties in Chile. "He died this year in Spain. But back in 1973, he returned to Chile from Mexico and was detained for eight days after the coup. Friends from high school helped him escape. He joked that it helped sell his books, called it the 'Latin American tango.' If his book didn't sell well, his publisher would exaggerate the eight days to a month, then three."

Alma remembered Bolaño's famous acceptance speech when he'd received the Rómulo Gallegos prize. "Didn't he say that everything he wrote was a letter of love or goodbye to the young people who died in the Dirty Wars of Latin America?"

Gabriel thought for a while. "Everyone thought that after the eighties, it would never happen again. Remember *Nunca más*, the Sábato commission's report in Argentina, the cleansing it seemed to promise? The disappeared, acknowledged and accounted for... the promise of never again. I was in university, you were in high school. Latin America was supposed to have been purged, cleaned up, democratic and free, remember? But we had the misfortune of being here in Luscano, the last holdout, slow learner and copier of everyone else. Luscano had to do it, too, have its dictatorship, have its war on terror, pave the route towards an unregulated capitalism. All the armies in the region were more than happy to help...share the dirty tricks they'd picked up during their juntas. Luscano, once it got going, did a very good job."

"What kind of place is this?"

There was no answer. Gabriel held her as if to absorb her distress. She leaned into him, heard his pounding heartbeat. There was a difference between being an outsider like Gabriel and being an exile. This difference involved shadings of identity, confidence and clarity. Hannelore had been an outsider with complete self-possession. Like Gabriel, she'd observed Luscano from a distance.

Flaco and Roma, who were of and about and by Luscano, remained tangled inside their roots, couldn't view the place dispassionately, but lived the gift of never doubting their identities. The exile's doubt was constant. The human mind, trained to compare, shifted between geographies, never satisfied. Living elsewhere gave a point of comparison, a second home with its own weaknesses.

Coming back, a form of reverse exile, exacerbated the doubt. There was nothing to ground her but Gabriel's beating heart.

26

He stood in his office, waiting for Sara, and contemplated the destruction down below. Two backhoes loaded prison rubble into dump trucks. The wreckage exposed the interior cells of the second floor. Clouds of pulverized concrete carried by the wind coated the university's walkways and windows with toxic dust.

All along, Flaco had wanted to be able to see the sculpture from his office but now it would be invisible from this vantage point. His reasons were selfish. He'd wanted to be able to look down and see redemption, the gravestone as work of art marking the wretched site that had consumed his friends. Creativity and art, literature and music fed the healing process necessary for the country to able to move forward. But the artists were mostly gone, leaving a fissure in the national psyche. What kind of country could emerge without its artists? A fascist, totalitarian prison without walls, a conglomerate of hotels and casinos and banks elevating money over humanity, guarded by drug lords and arms traders.

The words themselves, "sculpture garden," represented a whitewash of his intent, a total capitulation, more tourist attraction than solemn remembrance. If anything, his meeting with Pindalo's lawyer had redirected his energies and fuelled his outrage that a guy so apparently well educated, young and smart could be completely indifferent to the symbolism of this demolition and the dusty mirage of shame.

He was disgusted with his country and himself. Nervous exhaustion, the false confidence he'd been presenting to his students and Alma and everyone else, sustained by the pills in his pocket. The doctor had refused to renew the prescription, ordering

Flaco to wean himself from chemical dependency. And so he'd
come up with the plan. Immediately after tomorrow's ceremony
he'd jump in La Vieja and drive north to Porto Alegre. Stay for
a week, sit on the beach, eat seafood in cheap restaurants, read
novels and enjoy the Brazilian beauties. He needed the time out to
overcome the sense he'd let everyone down — Alma, his students,
and his children. This single-minded focus on the sculpture and its
unveiling had been necessary, he didn't regret any of it, but it had
cost him and he needed to regroup.

Sara arrived and spread *El Día* on his desk to show him the
article that his students were upset about. There was a photograph of
a PFL officer standing in front of a table of so-called evidence: rocks,
tin cans and glass bottles that "hooligans demonstrating on the site
of the planned casino had hurled at policemen trying to keep the
peace and protect the citizens of Luscano." The article, an in-depth
investigation occupying two full pages in the newspaper, concluded
that left-wing professors and anarchists with violent intentions were
agitating the students.

"It's a total fabrication, Dr. Molino. We have to respond."

"How?"

"We're going to write a rebuttal with our own photos. Showing
them it was peaceful. You were there. Nobody hurled anything. We've
got tons of witnesses." Sara asked him if he could provide a direct
quote and review the article before they sent it to the journalist. He
agreed, doubting the rebuttal would ever be published.

Flaco looked into her face framed by the curtain of dark
hair. Sara's serious resolve conjured Alma in that crucial meeting
thirteen years ago, when they'd decided to publish their dissent.
He'd replayed the meeting many times in his mind. Not one of
them, himself included, had paused to assess the consequences of
their words. He'd been propelled by the same enthusiasm he now
saw in Sara. The blame from Alma, expressed in her outburst, was
not misplaced. His whole life, the consequences of his actions and
gestures, had always been cushioned by the Molino name.

Sara said the students were planning further protests. "We may
have lost on the casino, but we're going to fight the golf course."

Not because the green turf would carpet the killing fields and burial grounds of the disappeared but because of its environmental consequences in a country facing a water disaster.

Flaco brought her around to his immediate concern, tomorrow's ceremony. They reviewed the schedule, who'd be attending, when to set up the stage and sound system. The news release had been emailed, the dignitaries invited, the families of the disappeared contacted. What if the PFL stopped them from coming? Eduardo had warned him that the recent arrests of former officers, including Carlos Cruz, had set things in motion. There would be repercussions. And, he'd reminded Flaco, most of Luscano opposed a ceremony acknowledging its ugly past.

Memorials were controversial, he knew that. Who cared about Luscano anyway? In the context of a century's suffering on this continent, in Africa and the Middle East, in Europe and Asia, what was the significance of a small sculpture on the campus lawn of a country that had contributed so little to history, culture and mankind? There were no heroes here, no great inventors or Nobel laureates. Just the brutal legacy of the genocide of indigenous peoples, then the *caudillos* pushing back the Spaniards and, centuries later, a few hundred young people made to disappear in the name of national security.

For the last few weeks, Sara and others had been agitating for a more lasting and, to them, relevant version of a memorial, an online tribute to the disappeared. Now she insisted on showing him the websites created to remember the executed, the disappeared and detainees.

Flaco sat next to her by the computer as she scrolled through the concrete memorials in Chile; the remembrance shrine in Chillán; a carved wooden cross for agricultural workers executed in Liquiñe; a stone commemorating seventeen woodworkers killed in Chihuio in October 1973; the Park for Peace in Santiago erected by Villa Grimaldi — the torture centre set up after the Pinochet coup in Santiago.

Moving on to Argentina, Sara showed him ESMA, the Navy Mechanics School in Buenos Aires, the largest of 400 detention and torture camps operated by the military in Argentina, and the online wall of memory, photos of the disappeared created to capture the immensity of suffering inflicted by Argentina's military. Sara clicked on an Andean city called Salta, in the north, and he saw the list of the disappeared, their names, numerous Álvarezes among them. It was powerful, reading those strangers' names, here in Luscano hundreds of kilometres away.

Sara left him on the Polynational Memorial, a virtual record of the disappeared in armed conflicts, "We have to get Luscano added to this database, Dr. Molino." Then she left, with the promise she'd be there early tomorrow morning.

For the rest of the afternoon, Flaco sat at his desk reading through the website's record of human suffering. He scrolled in reverse chronology until the parameters of his life closed and he felt himself alone in a small cell, his petty anxieties superseded by this massive and infinite toll…Somalia Civil War, Darfur, Eritrea versus Ethiopia, Hutus versus Tutsis, Western Sahara war, Namibia versus South Africa, Sri Lankan Civil War, India versus Pakistan in Kashmir, the Santa Cruz Massacre in East Timor, Memorial to the victims of the attack in Bali, Russia versus Chechnya, Bosnia against the Serbs, the Troubles in Northern Ireland, El Salvador and the FMLN guerrillas, Colombia versus FARC, Peru versus the Sendero Luminoso, Argentina's Dirty War, the Dos Erres Massacre in Guatemala, the Disappeared in Chile, the Cambodian Holocaust, the Vietnam War Memorials, the Yom Kippur War, the Sino-Indian War, the Oran Massacre in Algeria, the South Korea National War Memorial, the Katyn war cemetery, the museum in Auschwitz-Birkenau, the Peace Memorial in Genbaku Dome, Hiroshima, the Sino-Japanese War, the Memorial to International Brigadiers in the Spanish Civil War, the monument to the Mexican Revolution, the Armenian Genocide Memorial in Yerevan….

Flaco understood. Evil never dies, it simply relocates.

27

"Hang on, *Señor*." Castillo steered the truck onto the sidewalk into a column of thick black smoke. Gabriel ducked to avoid the palm fronds whipping into the window. The pickup jolted past cars and panicked pedestrians. The stench of burning rubber infiltrated the open windows. Gabriel coughed, tightening his grip on the vases of flowers in his arms.

At an intersection, a dozen protesters stood behind flames shooting from a pile of tires. Policemen leaned against the hoods of their PFL jeeps. Castillo veered onto Calle Florida. Gabriel turned back to look at the milling protesters covering their mouths with handkerchiefs. They appeared ordinary enough, pensioners protesting cutbacks perhaps, or worse, *agents provocateurs*. He'd expected trouble, wouldn't put it past the military to blockade the university or incite a riot. Castillo narrowly missed an oncoming fire truck as he pulled into a narrow lane between the faculties of law and fine arts. He slowed over the cobblestones and stopped the truck by the Humanities building to the receding wail of sirens.

Gabriel stepped down with the vases. Castillo unlatched the tailgate and removed the stands and cordons. They carried their armloads across the sloping lawn. The setting struck Gabriel as perfect, a natural amphitheatre with willow trees and shrubbery as backdrop. In front of a raised stage, a team of students was assembling rows of folding chairs. Next to it, the sculpture gleamed in the sunlight.

Flaco waved them over. From his imploring gestures, Gabriel deduced that he was arguing with Luis Corva. The sculptor's face was flushed, his arms crossed over the bib of his overalls. Between the two men, a beige tarp lay folded on the ground. "We're at an impasse," Flaco said. "I want to lay this sheet over the sculpture and when everybody's here, have it removed. Create some drama."

"Why lay a sheet over a sheet?" Luis Corva shook his head of white hair.

The two men regarded Gabriel. For days, Flaco had been calling him for logistical advice, assuming that all the burials he'd orchestrated endowed him with the necessary insights as to how this ceremony should unfold. Castillo whistled softly. "*Qué trabajo*," he said, gazing at the tented mass of limbs and writhing figures. Gabriel couldn't bring himself to read the names etched on the base. Not yet. "What do you think, Castillo?"

From the intensity of the man's gaze, Gabriel guessed he'd soon be carving a replica of the statue in the workshop where he reproduced Luscano in miniature. Castillo discerned details in a single glance that Gabriel missed in years of staring. "Let people see it like this. You don't need to cover it."

Satisfied with the verdict, Luis Corva left for his office to change his clothes. Smoke drifted through the buildings down the lawn. Gabriel mentioned the protest and burning tires.

"Anyone armed?" Flaco asked.

"The PFL is there, fully loaded and doing nothing."

Flaco muttered something about it being the rector's problem. Gabriel could barely hear him over the feedback and clamour of the sound crew testing microphones. Shouting over the din, Flaco introduced Gabriel to Sara, the point person in charge of the ceremony, and left for the stage. Sara was twenty at most, with round brown eyes and a walkie-talkie in her hand. She'd been just a child during the junta, yet here she was organizing the only event ever held in Luscano to honour the disappeared. Sara directed him to arrange the vases on the front corners of the stage.

Gabriel stooped to rearrange the camellias, ferns and flowery branches gathered by Castillo early this morning, removing a few stems whose blooms had been decapitated during the truck ride. He kept an eye out for his mother and sister and mostly for Alma. She should have arrived with Roma by now.

Once he'd finished with the vases, he helped Castillo set up the stands and cordons to ensure the first-row seats would be reserved for the rector's guests and Flaco's, the two groups separated by an aisle down the centre of the audience. The chairs formed at least twenty rows from the stage back towards the ivied building. But would anyone show up? The news release had been published verbatim in *El Día* yesterday morning. Radio Luscano had broadcast news of the event several times. In the last days, Flaco's students worked their social media and some had even dropped flyers at bookstores and cafés and posted them on telephone poles throughout the city.

Flaco instructed Sara to wait for his signal for the 387 seconds of silence. "Family members or friends may come up to…" His voice was drowned out by a ferocious racket from across the river, where a crew was jackhammering the concrete remains of the prison. Flaco clenched his hands. He could wade through the water onto the other side and attack them. The students stopped their preparations, stunned by the deafening noise. After an excruciating interval, the crew put down the jackhammers to separate the stones with pickaxes.

Flaco took one of his remaining sedatives, discreetly he hoped. A school bus pulled up across the lawn and a dozen children were shepherded towards the stage by the Franciscan choirmaster. Rubén hurried over to shake his hand. "This is something, Flaco."

"We'll see."

"I overheard some women after mass speaking of the event. They were afraid to attend, never having set foot on the university grounds. I told them to come. When they asked me why, I said, 'one word: remorse.'"

"Is that the official position?"

"Sadly, no." The Franciscan turned to settle the choir down.

Later, when Flaco was standing by the lighting booth, he saw the priest lead the children to the statue. They kneeled on the grass to study the names, touching the marble and peering at the bodies. There were fewer of them than at the dress rehearsal. Flaco was certain some parents had prevented their children from performing. He observed the priest crouching alongside the children, explaining and pointing to the ruined prison. Flaco would also have to find words to explain to Armonía and Fredo, who were coming with Ana, and to Beno, who was coming with Aurora. How would he convey to his children the meaning of the implicit violence of the sculpture without causing nightmares and trauma? He'd have to ask the Franciscan.

Flaco felt a hand on his shoulder and turned to find Alma standing in a black dress, her hair pulled back under a narrow-brimmed straw hat. He embraced her. "Are you all right?" She nodded. The jackhammers started up again.

Alma covered her ears. "They work on Saturdays?" she asked, mouthing the words. Flaco couldn't hear her above the assault. She left him to look for Gabriel in the crowd around the stage. He found her first and when the racket subsided, she asked where Castillo was. Gabriel explained he'd gone to the gates to wait for Juanita. They sat down on two of the folding chairs in the front row. Fifteen minutes to go, according to Alma's watch. The ceremony was scheduled to begin at twelve o'clock sharp, the exact moment the cathedral bells tolled for noonday mass. She silently questioned the wisdom of timing the event so precisely. Luscanans were notoriously late. The noxious odour of burning rubber hovered over the lawn. Another bout of jackhammering started up. The deafening noise, like the protest by the gates, was surely intended to sabotage the ceremony.

Alma regarded the sculpture and tried to invoke the faces of Díaz and Isabel. It was for them that she'd attended. But in the glow of an eye peering out from beneath the metallic covering, in the hand extended, she saw herself. She felt a sudden burning pain and began to hyperventilate. She fanned her face with her hat.

Gabriel took her hand. "What is it?"

She shook her head. Luis Corva, wearing a scarlet jacket of frayed velvet, took his place a few seats over. Absorbed in his thoughts, he seemed unaware of Alma and Gabriel to his right. A man sat down next to Gabriel. He was the son of Pedro Malú, the musician whose songs had carried them through the junta. Flaco's colleagues took their seats. Alma recognized them from his birthday party. Across the aisle, a group arrived in suits and dresses, led by the rector and a woman with a helmet of white hair. "That's General

Galtí's widow," Gabriel said. She was followed by politicians, the mayor, Patrón Pindalo and an emaciated woman with large sunglasses and bleached hair. The jackhammers resumed and Patrón Pindalo broke off from the group and strode away, cell phone pressed against his ear. His voice carried as he shouted, "Tell them to stop immediately...the rest of the day...go to the site, Javier, if you have to." He snapped the phone shut and returned to the seats. Spotting Alma, he crossed the aisle. "That's Celeste sitting over there next to my place. I gave her the poems. Did she call to thank you?"

Alma shook her head.

"I'll have to remind her." Patrón Pindalo took his seat among the rector's entourage. Alma imagined him saying, "That's the Álvarez daughter, the one I helped get out of La Cuarenta." Taking credit for her existence. Patrón Pindalo craved respectability, sought to wear it like his blazer and grey trousers.

Alma leaned across the seats to tell Flaco that Pindalo had ordered the hammering to stop. Flaco tilted his head towards a group of seats occupied by photographers and cameramen. "The media, quite a turnout." Swivelling, Alma noticed the rows of seats had filled. Many stood at the back and others sat in the grass.

At twelve o'clock the bells began to toll in a solemn two-note beat. Spotlights crisscrossed the titanium before settling on the stage. Led by Rubén, the children's choir sang a melody that caused a flutter of recognition. "*La rana cuchichea 'tranquilo' al sol bajando del cielo....*"

Virtually everyone present had the song stored among their earliest memories. "*Duerme, duerme, duerme...*" The children's voices transcended the viciousness embodied in the sculpture. "*Cierra tus ojos y sueña con la brisa serena del río...*" Xenia had sung the lullaby to Alma, her father had played it by her bedside on his violin. "*Precioso inocente mío....*" as if the children were singing the dead to sleep.

Patrón Pindalo averted his gaze from the sculpture, which struck him as a contorted piece of metal and less than appealing for a sculpture garden. Still, it had been a stroke of genius to endorse this cultural event, so well attended by the friends and colleagues he'd implored to come, his influence visibly manifested. His thoughts careened from the casino to the latest shipment of arms as he tried to resist the memories evoked by the choir's lullaby. He rarely allowed himself to reflect on his childhood, a regimen of work and study imposed by his father. Against his will, the moment emerged, seventy years ago, in a dark bedroom of the house, a *muchacha*'s hand on his feverish head, the image superimposed by his wife cradling Ernesto in the clinic as she sang to her newborn. All the inhabitants of those memories were dead. What was the point? The past is the past. Even his daughter, seated next to him, was half-dead herself.

This morning, as Damian drove them to the university, Celeste had accused him of killing Ernesto. "And now, you've brought me back to die, too. Are you happy?" He'd begged on behalf of Magdalena and Patroncito, they needed her, an aunt of their own flesh, a Pindalo, for God's sake. And his frail daughter had summoned a ferocious strength. "Need me for what? I'm cursed, they're cursed, and let's face it, you're cursed too." She spat the word at him, "*¡Sinvergüenza!*" In front of Damian and the grandchildren she'd called her father shameless.

Roma and Chichi began to drum the ancient rhythms of the Guaraní who'd once lived alongside the river, who'd witnessed the arrival of the Spaniards and were killed in the ensuing carnage. A troupe of dancers surrounded the sculpture. Among them, a woman in a white shift with long dark hair moved across the grass, dipping and writhing to the drumbeats as if fending off invisible attackers. Alma thought of Isabel. Even in her cell, after her body had been beaten and burned, Isabel had been as resolute as this woman dancing on the grass, embarking on a hunger strike to protest the conditions in La Cuarenta.

The drumbeats receded. Flaco walked to the podium and gestured across the river to the demolition site. "We are at the scene of a crime and the evidence is being destroyed. With this sculpture we acknowledge the hundreds of people taken from us, brought to La Cuarenta, tortured and made to disappear. The ones you loved, sat next to in school, argued with, danced with or passed on our streets. Remembering them today, we reclaim our past."

Gabriel scanned the audience for an armed maniac. A few candidates stood out, stereotypical burly types with short haircuts, their hands never far from concealed weapons. But with the cameramen and oligarchs present, they couldn't act. Cowards preferred the clandestine protection of night for their abductions in unmarked cars and executions in anonymous fields.

To his far left, green moss dangled from a willow trees, and the vision of Ernesto lying there in the grass resurfaced. Without Ernesto's one act of courage, many of the names carved in the marble would not have been known.

He reached for Alma's hand, grateful that her name was not among them. Wherever she went, Montevideo or Montréal, he'd follow, his destiny not tied to place but to this woman beside him. That possibility overcame the paranoia incited by the likes of Patrón Pindalo. And Carlos Cruz, despite his claims of an alibi, remained in prison. Lalo Martín had convinced a judge that releasing Cruz would jeopardize the investigation. In the meantime, Gabriel had developed a knot of worries around Alma. He worried for her safety, that she'd leave Luscano, that she'd wake up and decide Gabriel was not for her. He worried about the unveiling today and how others would react. The ceremony's success depended on the participation of the families of the disappeared, but there was no single organization that linked them. Flaco said he was counting on those who'd lost loved ones to come together, find solace after years of denial and disregard. Emma would be coming, Inés with her children. How many others? The mentality of a typical Luscanan was to see how everyone else reacts before choosing a course of action, often nothing, just silence. That had been his position during the junta and his shame weighed on his heart like a stone.

The mayor, a man facing corruption allegations, delivered a speech praising the university for its commitment to social justice. A congressman stood up and, making it clear he'd been studying abroad during the junta, promised a new chapter for Luscano, what with the casino and hotel project planned across the river and the world-class sculpture garden being inaugurated today.

Luis Corva vaguely heard his name mentioned by the man on the podium, but was more preoccupied with the dust raised by La Cuarenta's destruction streaking the titanium. Yesterday, when the piece had been towed from the studio on the flatbed truck, slow going on the winding coastal road, he'd sat in front with the driver and watched the onlookers. He'd seen people glance towards the back of the truck, observed their double-takes as they crossed themselves or bowed their heads. These spontaneous reactions meant more to him than any politician's or critic's assessment.

From his seat on the lawn, the sculptor zeroed in on the flaws. The hand under the titanium should be angled as if reaching from the deepest hell. There were inconsistencies in the names etched on the marble. Corva would make the adjustments, seasoned enough to know that artists endured an infinite reassessing of their work, the desire to seek an elusive perfection. He accepted this self-criticism, recognized it in his friends — the musicians agonizing over compositions, the poets crafting lyrics, and novelists moving characters through narratives. The more authentic the impulse to create, the greater the self-doubt.

Luis Corva could not forgive those who felt compelled to explain, overloading their creation with irrelevant meaning. Flaco had asked him to speak today and, for a few seconds, he'd been tempted to tell of his personal stake in history. His father's assassination in Estonia, the escape through Europe with his mother, the family members lost to the camps. How eventually, after the Holocaust and in the revolution of the sixties, he'd actually believed that mankind would never repeat such a horror. But then in 1976, when his friends began disappearing from Buenos Aires, hauled off at night, dumped live from military jets in death flights, he'd had to face the truth. Horror upon horror was the trajectory of civilization.

He'd stayed in Argentina through the Dirty War, until the bombing of the Jewish centre, when he'd witnessed the shattered windows, the dead and bleeding victims. A perpetual refugee, he accepted that his light-filled studio on the cliffs abutting the Bay of Luscano was a temporary stop. There was no escaping the cruel repetition, the arbitrary killing of those who found themselves in the wrong country at the wrong time. Nobody knew he'd strewn the dust he'd collected that September day in New York over the base of the sculpture. Ashes to ashes.

Emilio and the singer took the stage. A few bars of the violin and Susana's smoky voice rose like humid vapours feathering heavenward. *"Luscano sufre tanto, asaltado al anochecer, / las estrellas caen, gotas de sangre sobre el mar."*

The final refrain rose to the trees, gliding over the crumbling prison, down the riverbed, across the sea that ebbed and flowed along the craggy coast. *"Los sacerdotes no dicen nada. / Hace frío, siempre llueve / muchos desaparecen este otoño del año noventa."*

Then it began, the six and a half minutes of silence, one second for each of the disappeared.

A woman rose and laid a stem of white lilies by the base of the sculpture.

Two elderly men, brothers by their resemblance, came forward with a framed photograph and leaned it against the marble.

Families approached with flowers, a cross, statues of the Virgin and photographs. Someone left a book. Some touched the names and lingered by the statue.

Gabriel accompanied Emma, Inés and her children up the aisle. Emma carried a bundle of white camellias from her garden and placed it by her son's name. Alma watched them, trying to fathom what they had endured all these years. Roberto's existence negated by the state. The only evidence, his name in the prison ledger, pages before hers. Gabriel had shown her the photocopy he kept in his safety deposit box at the bank.

Her parents and Xenia had lived through their own hells the week she'd been in La Cuarenta. She felt their presence here with her, as the minutes passed, a condensed history of unspoken eulogies. Artists and journalists, musicians and lawyers, psychologists and students disappeared, leaving Luscano to progress in fits and starts, prodded on by Flaco, Lalo Martín, Luis Corva, women like Roma and Chichi, whose integrity held the place together, gave Luscano its spirit, fragile, but despite everything, enduring.

At the end of the ceremony, the rector rose to deliver concluding remarks, in which he expressed the university's gratitude for the generous contribution from the Pindalo family for the sculpture garden envisaged on this very lawn. At the mention of his name, the benefactor rose from his seat, placed his hand on his heart to acknowledge the applause. Photographers rushed to kneel on the lawn before him, snapping shots to ensure the old warrior's photograph would make the front page of *El Día*'s late edition.

28

They are, for the most part, well-meaning. The few who ask "What was it like?" To be imprisoned, they sometimes mean. Or to be in exile. Even worse, to be in exile in your own country. "Read your poetry," comes to mind as a response. But that's not sufficient for most. Prose is needed to spell things out. So you take her words and make them yours. Breathe your life into them, aware that it's easier to write of her suffering than your own. Often, it's the best you can do.

Para ver cosas bellas

One night you're snatched from your life and brought to a prison a few kilometres from your home. People you've lived among push, shout and threaten, they starve and torture you. You squat in a cell with a barred opening that looks onto a river. It is the summer of January, sweltering by day, dank at night. In the company of rats and scorpions, you hear the screams of others.

You contemplate your life as a series of disjointed scenes and wonder what you've done to cause this violence. You pace the cell and count your steps. Fear makes you jumpy. You lose threads of thought, you cannot formulate conclusions. You're always thirsty. You don't remember when you last ate or washed. In this hell, you search for sustenance. What lies inside that you can reach for? You breathe in the smelly air, you breathe out.

Turn out the lights... words emerge fragile as sprigs...*and behold things beautiful.* You exhale. *Close all doors and enter illusion...*the words pull you elsewhere. To a desk, clean hands holding a book, your former self, safe and sane. Briefly you remember who you are.

After an interminable time that in reality amounts to a few days, you're dropped back into your life. But you find you're no longer that person, you have absorbed a hell. Symptom one: you can't look at yourself in a mirror. Symptom two: you obliterate sensual memory, the screams, the smell of your burning flesh, the taste of fear in your unwashed mouth. Symptom three: you cringe from touch. Symptom four: you condemn your survival. Guilt festers, you can't shake off the awareness that others suffered much worse. Memory closes with your wounds. Among the confused details of your imprisonment, you remember one truth. A dead poet saved you.

Calzada de silencio

With so much vested in her work, you obsess about the poet, forming hypotheses and theories, wondering what would have become of her had she survived as well. After three collections published in her lifetime, how many more poems were inside her? She might have extended to fiction or essays. She might have achieved eminence, been invited to lecture in North America or Europe. How would she have continued her artistic revolution, the expression of a woman's heart? Gabriela Mistral and Alfonsina Storni were inspired by her. Juana de Ibarbourou considered Delmira her older sister. Had she lived, who else might she have inspired?

She would have participated in the emancipation of Uruguay from provincial outpost to cultural centre, beginning with the Perón years, when intellectuals fled Buenos Aires for Montevideo. Delmira Agustini would have witnessed the prosperity as Uruguay became known as the Switzerland of South America and the rich flocked to the beaches in Punta del Este, before it became today's celebrity haven with its Conrad Hilton casino, its yachts and beachfront estates belonging to Hollywood and Russian expats.

Her politics would have taken shape. She died too young to have her convictions truly tested, but the open spirit of her poetry makes it impossible to imagine she'd have lived the years of military dictatorships in silence. When the Tupamaros were formed in 1963 by middle-class students agitating for change, Delmira would have understood their frustrations. After they were killed in peaceful demonstrations, she would have spoken out. And when they resorted to kidnappings and guerrilla tactics, she might have tried to intervene, convince them that their violence against the urban conservatism of Montevideo was a deadly mistake. In the junta of 1973, Delmira would have been three years shy of ninety. Would she have denounced the generals and alerted her people to beware the tactics inspired by Pinochet? The rounding up, the torture and disappearances executed by a military trained in the U.S. and abetted by Washington at a distance.

We can only imagine how far her courage would have gone. How far does anyone's courage go when a branding iron is held to their flesh?

Your theories are hypothetical. Despite the submerging in poetry, music and painting, the reaching towards things beautiful, she dies in a rented room shot in the head by two bullets. All the masks she invented for herself couldn't save her. Final silencing of the exile who never left.

La senda más negra

Another century, another continent, and you stand facing rows of desks. You ask the class to turn off iPods, phones and laptops, wait as they rummage in knapsacks, whisper and pass notes, settle down from their treks through the snow. The students, seventeen to twenty years old, are the sons and daughters of people who have journeyed from El Salvador and Mexico, Honduras and Nicaragua, Colombia, Peru and Argentina. When they speak, you hear the variegated *castellano* of the Andes, pampas, coasts and islands. You are doing the *modernistas* with them and by now you can predict their responses to the poets. They like Rubén Darío for his anti-Americanism, César Vallejo for his heroic populism and the love sonnets of Pablo Neruda.

Today you're teaching Agustini. Most will not have read the textbook in advance and you provide the context. They half listen until you mention murder, suicide, *sangre*. The rummaging and yawning cease. They like their details gory. You ask them to open their texts to a verse. Then you call on the loner in the class to read it out loud because the poet was a loner too.

At first he recites without absorbing the words. Surreal images of *caranchos*, intruders and demons, angels and statues, stars and serpents. Then vampires, lips that kiss and curse, poison, daggers and swords. The young man's face reddens, the others are silent. They recognize the singular violence of a southern spirit, the passion of a voice their age.

The words and cadences come back at you from the concrete walls. The mute winter light outside the windows makes you hurt for the bluest of skies you left behind. You look beyond your reflection, momentarily visualizing her blue silk slip, hair curling over her shoulders, her frank gaze on the back of the student bent over her poem.

And then you tell them of her legacy. Her body rots in the *tierra* of Uruguay. Her real remains are her poems. Delmira Agustini believed the poet is a seer who brings light to suffering. She considered the labour of creating poetry divine, and her works stand for liberty of the highest order, liberty of spirit. Her poems lead like a trail of polished pebbles, words that made her contemporaries so uncomfortable. The track gleams in the moonlight, transforms in time into an open highway: follow me to freedom. In the Americas, you say, her anthem still resonates.

When you tell them of her last hour, there are questions and discussions. Who was he, Miss? Did she plan to die in that room? Even the loner expresses an opinion. Her anguish was real, he says, it must have been a suicide pact. Another student argues, no, she wanted to live. Her husband was crazy!

Two hours pass and when they scramble to leave, you remind the students that the next class falls on Valentine's Day. For this gringo invention, they are to bring one dish of food from their country, *algo muy típico*, and one page of their writing, poetry or prose. It will be a fiesta, you promise, you'll bring *humitas*, typical of the Andean region where Ernesto Guevara was assassinated in 1967. And in that moment you think of your loved ones back home with a longing you've tried to shed. It clings like a second skin.

Mi alma

Exile. It's an exhausting masquerade. You recreate yourself, fake happiness and a sense of belonging and hope that by trying hard enough, the pretense will become real. You're drawn to other travellers and sometimes, you'll find connection with a national excited by the exotic. Together, as friends or lovers, you attempt to cross cultures. The most direct path to assimilation is to fall in love, integrate through sex. You try to dismantle your roadblock to intimacy, the vault in your mind where you store your horrors, shed the second skin. You might succeed at metamorphosis. You're isolated at times, but you endure.

One day you find the courage to return, walk the streets memorized in your internal map. In a state of hyper-awareness, you encounter the smells and tastes you'd missed so much. Nostalgia fades. You are no longer who you were. You've become someone else and you discover you're an exile in your own country now. You try to recreate your sense of belonging in the arms of another damaged soul.

Someone asks you to speak out. Tell what happened, how you became an exile. You find yourself entrapped, your deepest self too exposed. The fight resumes, you're a mayfly caught in a mesh of arguments. Break the silence. Speak out so that your country can move forward, so that this never happens again. And yet you know it keeps recurring. Here and there on the globe, the powerful decide a certain person, a certain segment is inconvenient, has written subversive words, must be eradicated.

Para entrar la Ilusión

You owe her this. Not a eulogy but a final snapshot of the effect she had on strangers. A photographer perhaps, whose camera, much like a poem, compacts reality into an image of hidden truths and ambiguities.

The scene unfolds on Calle Sarandí, a fashionable street in Montevideo. A carriage pulls up to a studio and Señora

Agustini steps out first, followed by the poet. "Hurry, Nena. The photographer's waiting."

Let's say he's Corsican, French-speaking and, like many of the immigrants here, well adapted to his new country. He's setting up the Graflex and lights in the studio although he much prefers shooting outside to capture the subtropical flowers and vines, the *plátano* trees in the city's resplendent light. He's obliged to take portraits to earn his livelihood. At least this one will be credited in a book of poems. Laying out the unexposed plates, he hopes the session will be short. The name Agustini means nothing to him and he foresees a pale, gaunt youth with eyeglasses.

Imagine the photographer's surprise when a woman of notable girth enters the studio followed by a girl who looks to be no more than eighteen. Only later, he learns she's actually twenty-three. The photographer, Domingo let's say, greets the mother and before he can address the poet, Señora Agustini establishes the ground rules. The portrait must be taken in profile, emphasizing the best features, the little earring, the flower in the hair, the pearls around her neck. It must convey the poet as chaste, for that is what she is!

Domingo's only thought is how to get rid of the mother. This requires tricky manoeuvring. Women are restricted in Montevideo, they can't go out alone, walk the streets, be seen unaccompanied by a man. They're obliged to swim on segregated beaches, covering themselves from neck to ankle. Domingo affably plays the artistic card, asks the mother to leave the studio for just an hour. He must concentrate, he cannot speak. The lights heat the studio. The mother's upper lip is coated with sweat and because he's the best photographer in Montevideo, she capitulates and leaves.

Delmira sits on the banquette facing the lights. He looks through the lens at her. She's turned her face for a profile shot. Such an obedient daughter. The mother's paying, so he'll comply, then take the shots he thinks best capture the poet. She says nothing as he steps from the tripod and approaches her. He moves her hair, tilts her chin. She doesn't flinch. Domingo shoots. Then he comes to take her by the shoulders. She faces the camera. He tells her to look over his left shoulder. He shoots again. Back and forth he walks between his subject and the camera. She doesn't recoil when he touches her, but she doesn't respond.

Domingo can't know how monumental it is to be touched by a man in a manner she's explored in her poems, experienced in her fantasies and rarely in reality. When the mother returns, the poet says, *Vous êtes un artiste et je vous admire.* He replies, *Au revoir. S*he shakes her head. *Désolée.*

When he reads of her murder in *El Día,* the photographer recalls the small gloved hand taking his before she left the studio, the honesty in her blue eyes as she rebuffed him. Ten years later her last collection is published. In a bookstore on Calle Sarandí he discovers how it is that she's haunted him all this time.

> *In your chamber covered with reverie, make waste*
> *Of flowers and of spiritual lights; my soul,*
> *Shod in silence and dressed in calm,*
> *Will go after you down the darkest path of this night.*
>
> *Turn out the lights and behold things beautiful;*
> *Close all doors and enter illusion;*
> *Uproot from mystery a handful of stars*
> *And cover with flowers, like a triumphal vase, your heart...*

—Delmira Agustini
from "The Encounter"
Los Astros del abismo (1924)

A Concise History of Luscano

by Dr. Federico Molino

Translated from the Spanish by Hannelore Stern Álvarez

In the beginning a peaceful community of villages lies nestled along
the coast and riverbanks. Until the clear summer day, some say in
December, others January, when a flotilla appears on the horizon.
Two children are playing on the sandy beaches of what's now known
as the Bay of Luscano. Nearby their parents are hauling in fishing
nets when they hear the cries. "Look! Look!" The children point to
the horizon. Word travels and eventually most of the villagers gather
to watch the approaching ships. When they drop anchor only the
wisest of Guaraní sense danger. In a month, following sign language
offers to trade and help orient the newcomers, the community will
be wiped out.

Battlefields transform the land. Spanish ships are followed by
Portuguese and later British fleets. Survivors learn the significance
of waving white flags. The bloodshed seeps upriver into the forests
and low mountainsides. Indigenous communities are massacred and
those that survive retreat further inland only to encounter the Spanish
conquerors bushwhacking down the Andes in search of precious
metals and jewels. Missionaries arrive, sent by the King of Spain, to
build churches and convert those who have not fled. On the site of
today's cathedral, a chapel named San Luscano after a minor saint
is constructed for the forced weddings of Guaraní women to Spanish
men. Thus begins so-called integration. Generations of mixed blood
or mestizo offspring establish plantations to grow food, markets to
sell their wares and inns offering rooms and meals to travellers. The
port flourishes with trade, shipbuilding and fisheries. Franciscans
open schools and teach their Catholic doctrine. Resistance merits
hanging and torture. In the plaza, one of the remaining Guaraní
leaders is bound by ropes, his arms tied to one horse, his legs to
another. The horses are whipped to gallop in opposite directions.
The man is torn apart.

Caudillos emerge as new leaders in the nineteenth century. One, Hector Molino, owns a prosperous plantation of corn, sugar and livestock. Inspired by Bolívar's exploits in Venezuela and Bolivia as well as San Martín's victories in Argentina, Chile and Peru, he plots to expel the Spaniards from one of their last strongholds. He and his vigilante friends and neighbours, sworn to secrecy, meet for months planning their battle. Trading sugar and tobacco for arms, they amass a ragtag army equipped with rifles, slingshots and deadly poison-darts while waiting for the opportune moment. It comes in March 1895, when a fleet of Spanish ships is destined to stop over from Cuba. Lookouts are posted on the cliffs, and a messaging system, delivered by horseback and mule, is devised to alert the cavalry. Molino prepares a shadow government of councillors to seize power once the attack is underway. On the night of March 15, the ships drop anchor and as Spanish naval forces come to shore, they are attacked by a band of caudillos waiting on the wharves. Most of the Spaniards retreat to the ships. Those who try to enter the port are scalded to death by cauldrons of boiling water or oil dropped by boys from the second floor windows of the buildings along the winding alleys. The Spanish oligarchy, occupying the mansions on the shores of Barrio Norte, is given two days to leave then summarily executed. On April 1, 1895, a provisional government declares the newly formed country of Luscano an independent republic.

Peace is, and will remain, elusive. The caudillos do not have the luxury of celebrating freedom. Every border, south to Uruguay, west to Paraguay and north to Brazil, is subject to ongoing battles with the new republics and the last holdouts of Spanish and Portuguese mercenaries severely weakened by the independence wars fought throughout Latin America. The flag of Luscano, red and navy blue for blood and sacrifice, flies at the port and on government buildings. New laws, most favouring the landowners, are enacted, a Luscanan currency is introduced with one peso featuring the portrait of Hector Molino and trade routes are established. The council of Luscano is renamed a congress consisting of ten members designated from the thriving port city and countryside plus five senators appointed for life. Senator Molino dispatches an envoy of plantation owners to New York, a foreign policy initiative that paves the way for future ties with the Americans and significant borrowings from the US treasury backed by Luscanan commodities. The leader of the delegation, Patrón Ernesto Pindalo, returns with promissory notes in hand enabling him to establish Luscano's first bank.

Power structures inherited from the Spanish colonialists persist. Landowners alone may vote, then business owners and eventually, educators and clergy. The early caudillos build an army, drafting poor villagers as foot soldiers. With continued skirmishes to establish Luscano's borders, most of the country's income is designated for military purposes. Gradually, with the expansion of voting rights, democracy begins to take hold, resulting in increased access to education and medical care. But after the Great Depression and temporary decline in American trade, elections in the early thirties are largely rigged until a left-leaning coalition incites Luscanans to demand fair voting systems and increased citizen rights. Protests and blockades escalate. The port is essentially shut down for six months. But in 1940, just as Hitler is bombing Britain, General Augusto Fernandez engineers Luscano's first post-independence military coup. Under his leadership, the junta endures for ten long years, aided and abetted by General Perón in Argentina, who aligns himself with the Germans until the end of World War II when, smelling impending defeat, he declares himself on the side of the Allies. General Fernandez does not follow suit. The Americans retaliate, weakening Luscano's military government. In 1950, the first democratic elections are held in a decade.

Luscanans are often described as fiercely independent and somewhat insular, more intent on upholding the traditions of family and community than on what transpires outside their borders. The country accepts a certain quota of immigrants particularly from Italy and Eastern Europe, as well as neighbours fleeing hostile environments, all of whom assimilate relatively quickly. This tradition continues throughout the twentieth century. For a long period, the country's democracy endures even while military regimes and dictatorships decimate the region. Exiles from Argentina, Uruguay, Chile, Brazil, Bolivia and Paraguay arrive in Luscano throughout the seventies and eighties, most just passing through. They tell of abductions and torture, of state surveillance and terrorism targeting artists, activists, Jews, psychologists, journalists and intellectuals. Few listen to their stories; those that do naively cannot fathom how such tactics would ever work in Luscano. In the late 1980s, at an American-led conference in Bogotá, delegates from Luscano align themselves with one of the region's last dictatorships, Chile's Pinochet regime, and are dismissed by US Department of State officials as a "bunch of loose cannons."

The bloodless coup – as it's first called – presages another terrible chapter in the country's history. In 1990, a handful of senior armed forces' officers led by General Adolfo Galtí storm Luscano's Government House to seize power. For five years, the military inflicts state-sanctioned violence, abducting and imprisoning without cause hundreds of citizens in La Cuarenta and other prisons in the countryside. When the prisons overflow, the incarcerated are taken to fields, given shovels to dig graves and trenches, and executed. Many leave Luscano, seeking exile in neighbouring countries and abroad. Morally and financially bankrupt, the military concedes power to Congress on the condition that a full amnesty is declared for all members of the armed forces. In 1995, Ferdinand Stroppo is elected President, gaining a second term five years later. At the time of writing, Congress is considering amending Luscano's constitution to allow Stroppo to run for a third term in 2005.

Discover Luscano posters, reflecting the government's efforts to attract tourists, depict the country's landscapes, beaches and inland waterfalls, subtropical vegetation and wildlife, and the colonial architecture of the capital. Vestiges of the Spanish conquest can be seen in the baroque design of the Cathedral of Luscano, the intricate marble carvings at the Royal Cemetery, the ironwork of the balconies in the old port, and the ivied buildings of the University of Luscano established by Franciscans in 1825. But the innocence of two children playing on the beach and waving at seafaring newcomers five centuries ago has long been lost. If there's music to be heard in the plazas and cafés, murals to be seen on the walls by the stairs to the old port, and poetry to be read in the bookstores, it is because some element of the human spirit – involving a deep connection to the land and sea and sense of community – passed on by generations of indigenous peoples has miraculously transcended a violent history. At dusk, if you stand on the beach by the Bay of Luscano and listen carefully, you might hear a faint drumming underlying the creeping tide, the trilling songbirds in the palmettos, and the guffawing of swamp-bound frogs. Some say it is the heartbeat of doom, others the murmur of hope.

Selected Bibliography

Among the many books I consulted in writing the novel, the following were particularly important to my research.

Delmira Agustini & Latin American Poets

Selected Poetry of Delmira Agustini — Poetics of Eros edited and translated by Alejandro Cáceres, Southern Illinois University Press, 2003.
Delmira Agustini — Poesías completas, edición Magdalena García Pinto, Cátedra, Madrid, 2000.
Pasión y gloria de Delmira Agustini — Su vida y su obra by Clara Silva, Editorial Losada, S.A., Buenos Aires, 1972.
The FSG Book of Twentieth-Century Latin American Poetry edited by Ilan Stavans, Farrar, Straus and Giroux, New York, 2011.
The Oxford Book of Latin American Poetry — A Bilingual Anthology edited by Cecilia Vicuña and Ernesto Livon-Grosman, Oxford University Press, New York, 2009.

Argentina & The Dirty War

The Flight — Confessions of an Argentine Dirty Warrior by Horacio Verbitsky, translated by Esther Allen, The New Press, New York, 1996.
The Argentina Reader edited by Gabriela Nouzeilles & Graciela Montaldo, Duke University Press, 2002.

Prisoner Without a Name, Cell Without a Number by Jacobo
    Timerman, translated by Toby Talbot, Alfred A. Knopf, New
    York, 1981.
*The Real Odessa — How Perón Brought the Nazi War Criminals to
    Argentina* by Uki Goñi, Granta Books, London, 2002.
I Remember Julia — Voices of the Disappeared by Eric Stener Carlson,
    Temple University Press, Philadelphia, 1996.
A Lexicon of Terror — Argentina and the Legacies of Torture by
    Marguerite Feitlowitz, Oxford University Press, New
    York, 1999.
*Nunca más — Informe de la Comisión Nacional sobre la Desaparición
    de Personas*, Editorial Universitaria de Buenos Aires, 1984.
The Story of the Night by Colm Tóibín, McClelland & Stewart,
    Toronto, 1997.

Chile & Pinochet

Roberto Bolaño: The Last Interview & Other Conversations, with an
    introduction by Marcela Valdes, translated by Sybil Perez,
    Melville House Publishing, New York, 2009.
Desert Memories — Journeys Through the Chilean North by Ariel
    Dorfman, National Geographic, Washington, D.C., 2004.
Diary of a Chilean Concentration Camp by Hernán Valdés, translated
    by Jo Labanyi, Victor Gallancz, London, 1975.
*The Condor Years — How Pinochet and His Allies Brought Terrorism
    to Three Continents* by John Dinges, The New Press, New
    York, 2004.

Additional Sources

God's Spies — Stories in Defiance of Oppression edited by Alberto
    Manguel, Macfarlane Walter & Ross, Toronto, 1999.
La fiesta del chivo by Mario Vargas Llosa, Taller, República
    Dominicana, 2000.
*Surviving the Long Night — An Autobiographical Account of a Political
    Kidnapping* by Sir Geoffrey Jackson, Vanguard Press, New
    York, 1973.

Other Authors & Works Cited

Jorge Luis Borges from "The Guardian of the Books," *Jorge Luis Borges — Selected Poems* edited by Alexander Coleman, Penguin Books, New York, 2000; page 283.

Jean-Paul Sarte from *Huis Clos*, Meredith Publishing Company, New York, 1962; pages 91 & 45.

Pablo Neruda from "Maybe We Have Time," *Pablo Neruda — Isla Negra — A Notebook,* translated by Alastair Reid, Farrar, Straus and Giroux, New York, 1981; page 337.

Paul Valéry from "Le Cimetière marin" (The Seaside Cemetery, 1920), *A Survey of French Literature — Volume II: The Nineteenth and Twentieth Centuries* by Morris Bishop, Harcourt, Brace and World Inc., New York, 1965; pages 266–268.

César Vallejo from "Los heraldos negros," *The FSG Book of Twentieth-Century Latin American Poetry*, edited by Ilan Stavans, Farrar, Straus and Giroux, New York, 2011; page 102.

Shabistari from "The Secret Rose Garden — The Written Faith," *The Essence of Sufism* by John Baldock, Eagle Editions, London, 2004; page 204.

Federico García Lorca from "Lament for Ignacio Sánchez Mejías," *Federico García Lorca — Collected Poems,* edited by Christopher Maurer, Farrar, Straus and Giroux, New York, 2002; pages 825–826.

Canadian Charter of Rights & Freedoms, www.laws-lois.justice.gc.ca/eng/charter, Sections 9 & 12.

Polynational War Memorial, www.war-memorial.net.

Acknowledgements

My journey into the works and life of Delmira Agustini (1886–1914) began over a decade ago when I was invited by Dr. Lady Rojas Benavente to a recital in Concordia University on International Poetry Day. A student recited "The Intruder" (the alexandrine sonnet introducing Part II of the novel). Who was this poet who, in 1907, dared express such eroticism? My research led me to many books, notably the following bilingual collection and source for the Agustini poems cited in the novel: *Selected Poetry of Delmira Agustini — Poetics of Eros,* edited and translated by Alejandro Cáceres, Southern Illinois University Press, 2003.

Since then it's been an adventure, creating an imaginary country, sketching maps, inventing streets and landmarks, and spending years with my cast of characters. Drawn from my encounters in the region, Luscano is an amalgam of Uruguay, Argentina and Chile in miniature. Creating its history afforded temporal liberties justified, I believe, by worrisome trends such as the rise of state surveillance and the silencing of dissent witnessed today, not only in Latin America.

The novel is dedicated to my late parents, with gratitude for the books my mother championed, the violin music my father brought to our house and their indefatigable joie de vivre. Displacement and suffering never extinguished my parents' compassion and capacity to love.

Heartfelt thanks go to my publisher, the extraordinary Karen Haughian and her team at Signature Editions, for their dedication in editing the novel and bringing it to life.

I also wish to acknowledge the support of the Canada Council for the Arts which was instrumental in allowing me to complete the novel.

I'm grateful to many family members and friends for their insights and inspiration.

And to my beloved Otokar Pogacnik, infinite gratitude for his unwavering devotion to our motto: *amor & cachondeo.*

About the Author

Cora Siré is the author of a novella, *The Other Oscar* (Quattro Books, 2016), and a collection of poetry, *Signs of Subversive Innocents* (Signature Editions, 2014). Her fiction, essays and poetry have appeared in magazines such as *Geist, The Puritan, Montreal Serai, Arc Poetry* and the *Literary Review of Canada* as well as in numerous anthologies. She lives in Montreal.

Eco-Audit
Printing this book using Enviro 114 SchoolBook Smooth Blue White instead of virgin fibres paper saved the following resources:

Trees	Solid Waste	Water	Air Emissions
4	190 kg	15,489 L	623 kg